WITH VIOLETS

WITH VIOLETS

ELIZABETH ROBARDS

AVON

An Imprint of HarperCollins*Publishers*

This book is a work of fiction. Names, characters, places, and incidents are products of the author's imagination or are used ficticiously and are not to be construed as real. Any resemblance to actual events, locales, organizations, or persons, living or dead, is entirely coincidental.

HarperCollins books may be purchased for educational, business, or sales promotional use. For information please write: Special Markets Department, HarperCollins Publishers, 10 East 53rd Street, New York, NY 10022.

FIRST EDITION

Designed by Rhea Braunstein

Library of Congress Cataloging-in-Publication Data

Robards, Elizabeth, 1964–
With violets / Elizabeth Robards. — 1st ed.
p. cm.
ISBN 978-0-06-157912-7
1. Morisot, Berthe, 1841–1895—Fiction. 2. Triangles (Interpersonal relations)—Fiction. 3. Manet, Édouard, 1832–1883—Fiction. 4. Women painters—Fiction. 5. Brothers—Fiction. 6. France—Fiction. I. Title.
PS3620.H684W57 2008
813'.6—dc22 2008017644

13 14 15 OV/RRD 10 9 8 7 6 5 4 3 2

They will become painters.
Are you fully aware of what this means?
It will be revolutionary—I would almost say
catastrophic—to your bourgeois society.
Are you sure you won't curse art,
because once it is allowed into such a
respectable and serene household,
it will surely end by dictating
the destinies of your children.

—Joseph Guichard

Chapter One

PARIS—1868

WHEN I awoke, I did not know I would make his acquaintance that afternoon. As I opened my eyes and set my bare feet on the cold floor, I had no idea a simple meeting would shatter my existence and refashion it into a world I would scarcely recognize.

If I had known, I might have chosen differently. Alas, it is effortless to retrace one's steps and spot the turn you should have taken.

What is not quite so simple is to opt for the safe route and spend a lifetime out of harm's way pondering what might have been.

I have seen him in the Louvre. We have exchanged glances. Polite nods. Single words. No more. It isn't proper because we have not been formally introduced.

I cannot help but notice him. His fine clothes and fair hair set him apart from any man I have ever laid eyes upon. He commands attention and compels the beholder to drink in his being. A masterpiece who speaks to the soul.

It happens weeks later, as I study the Italian painters,

copying Rubens with my friend Rosalie. I hear men's voices echoing behind us. Indiscernible, only tones and inflections, patterns of speech reverberating like a symphony of color in the nearly empty *musée* gallery. One timbre dark and rich as umber shadows. The other, vibrant as vermilion.

I do not have to turn around to know. I had memorized his voice, his gestures, as he copied the Italians and the Spanish.

The manner in which he attacked his brushwork—painting. Stopping. Retreating. Studying. Stepping forward to begin again. Then, as if he sensed me watching, he would momentarily abandon his dance and glance up, his gaze snaring mine like a mesh net. He would smile, nod. Before I could summon the grace to look away, he was lost again in Tintoretto.

I should have felt ashamed for staring so brazenly, but I did not. Odd that Propriety would drop her weighty baggage now, prohibiting a look at him.

The murmur of voices stops, all is quiet save the rhythmic *tap, tap, tap* of shoes and walking stick on the parquet floor.

The conversation resumes, not ten feet behind us, muted by veiled whispers.

Rosalie paints in oblivion. How I envy her calm.

Chewing the wooden end of my brush, I fix my gaze upon the bare breast of Rubens's water nymph, determined not to falter in the face of this contingency.

I'm glad I wore my green dress, although it is covered by the frightful gray painting smock. Of course, I shall not remove the cover-up. Nor will I preen and primp like an idiot. I will act natural, as if his footfalls are not sounding directly behind me.

Rosalie murmurs. The sound washes over me in cobalt waves. I plunge the tip of my brush into the vermilion, swirling it around so the lovely brashness coats the bristles. I dab at the water nymph's nipple.

"Bonjour, Mesdemoiselles."

I tighten my grip on my palette.

In my peripheral vision, I see Rosalie whirl around. Too anxious. *"Bonjour, Monsieur Fantin."*

Moistening my lips, I kept my gaze upon my canvas, wait five beats, then turn, as if I have just realized we are no longer alone.

"Bonjour." My voice sounds cold and thin, an icicle melting under the brilliance of spring sunshine.

"Mesdemoiselles, may I present Monsieur Édouard Manet."

I press my thumb into the edge of my palette until my hand begins to tingle.

"Monsieur Manet, I give you Mesdemoiselles Rosalie Riesener et Berthe Morisot."

"Bonjour." He bows, quick and proper, over his silver-tipped walking stick. "I am quite familiar with Mademoiselle Morisot's work. I have often enjoyed it at the Salon. I am a great admirer."

His words resonate in the *musée's* great gilded hall. Admirer? *Of moi?* I had no idea he even knew my name.

Is he teasing me?

His smile appears genuine, but if I ponder his words too long, I sense a hint of mockery in the upturned corners of his mouth.

"Merci." I fight the urge to retreat. I am not good at conversing with men. Words never come easily. Maman berates this fault. She says people will think my silence proud or sullen. Still, I would rather remain mute than spew nonsense.

Oh yes. It is best the meeting came as a surprise, that Monsieur Fantin gave me no notice of the introduction. You see, I am of a mind to create monsters in my head. Not that I think Monsieur Manet a monster.

Au contraire.

Although, the sheer magnitude of his persona frightens me as much as it thrills me. I admire his freedom, his sincerity, his willingness to explore and express what is real, what is true. He is at once terrifying and glorious. And breathtaking.

A true master.

He steps closer, walking around to the working side of my easel. "What have we here?"

My throat tightens, and I believe I understand how Eve felt in the garden when she realized the full magnitude of her nakedness.

It is just a painting, Rubens's *Queen's Arrival at Marseilles.* I tilt my chin to meet his gaze.

His eyes search my face, and his lips, curve into a pleasing smile. "Beautiful."

Mon Dieu, he is bold. I have heard tales of his exploits, but who was to know how much had been embellished. He is not a bohemian. For all appearances, he is a proper gentleman, if not a dandy.

My gaze shoots back to the water nymph's lush form. I feel Monsieur Manet watching me, a casual assessment. Yet, I sense the man is fully capable of consuming all in his possession.

If I were prone to blush, it would happen now. Thank heavens my body does not make a habit of betraying my emotions. Of all my strengths, I am grateful for containment.

I take a deep breath. The smell of linseed oil calms my rattled nerves. I touch the tip of my brush to the ocher paint intending to deepen the shadow under the nymph's breast, but as the brush strokes the flesh-colored curve, the vermilion bleeds through. The resulting orange-tinged streak resembles a gruesome, bleeding gash.

Monsieur Manet's mouth is pressed into a straight, measuring line. "Why do you mix those colors?"

A claustrophobic tingle courses through my limbs. "Monsieur Manet, I beg your pardon, but I cannot work with you peering over my shoulder."

"Excuse me, Mademoiselle. I, too, could not work under such conditions."

If I have offended him, he is too much of a gentleman to make an issue of my faux pas. Surely, he will bid me adieu and take his leave. I feel sick at the thought of confessing to Maman that I had finally made the acquaintance of the great Édouard Manet and succeeded in affronting him in less than a quarter hour.

Yet he lingers. "Perhaps I might offer one suggestion?"

I say nothing, which he must mistake for acquiescence. He steps closer, our bodies a breath apart. As bold as you please, he plucks my brush from the palette. Long, clean fingers sweep my thumb. A tingling glow spreads across my breasts and throat, and I step back to create space between us.

Unaffected by the familiar contact, he simply loads paint onto the brush. I am relieved he does not look at me. For if he had, I fear he might have seen a gaping idiot staring back; a girl rendered stupid by the touch of a man.

Rosalie and Fantin abandon their conversation and observe Manet at work. Awestruck, I watch him heal the wound I have inflicted. Even Rubens could scarcely have done better.

I have been studying this painting for weeks. Yet as I watch him transform my ugly blunder into perfection, it is as if I am seeing it for the first time.

Rosalie sends me a quizzical glance.

But I do not stop him. How can I make her understand when even I do not?

In the presence of the old masters, with the gaze of the water nymphs raised to the heavens, and a disapproving Maria de'Medici staring down upon us, I must resemble a servant, obediently holding the palette for her master. A girl thoroughly consumed by the power of genius.

He finishes. Thrusts the brush toward me, looking quite pleased with himself.

I reached out to reclaim it, but he does not let go. To my horror, he gives it a little tug, pulling my hand, brush and all, toward him. His eyes sparkle like two shiny gray pools.

"Yes, beautiful, indeed," he mutters.

My mouth is dry. "Monsieur, you are bold to take such liberties. I am not your student."

"Mademoiselle, I do not take students under my wing. I am far too busy with my own work to accept the responsibility of fostering another's creative whims. Even if I did, you are much too accomplished and your reputation far too superior for me to make such base assumptions. Please forgive me if I have offended you."

Still holding the brush, he takes my hand in his and bows. This time there is no playful tug. Just my small hand consumed by his, rugged and large.

His skin, touching my skin.

Purely.

Honestly.

A strange sensation winds its way down my spine and blossoms in my belly. I draw my hand from his and placed it on my middle, trying hard to breathe. It is as if someone has cinched my corset so tightly it has stunted my breathing. A fever brews and spreads to my face and extremities, pooling in delicate places of which proper ladies should not take notice.

"Mademoiselle? You do not look well. Sit down, please. Let me help."

His hand is at my elbow now. I let him escort me to a wooden bench in the center of the gallery, where I sit.

"Berthe?" Rosalie kneels in front of me, the cool backs of her fingers pressed to my cheek. Her touch helps me focus and reminds me of all I have heard about the purported effect the illustrious Monsieur Manet wreaks on the fairer gender. How his quick mind and clever wit captivate both men and women.

I am furious with myself for acting like such an *imbécile. Je ne suis pas une femme légère.* I am not a silly woman. I should be immune to such base nonsense, especially concerning a man who surely has as many mistresses as he has controversies swirling around him.

"I must have caught a chill." Yes, that's it. "Rosalie, we should call it a day. I have exhausted myself."

"Certainly. I will gather our belongings."

I sit for another moment.

"Please allow Monsieur Fantin and myself to see you home safely."

"That will not be necessary." I stand, feeling stronger.

"Mademoiselle, it is our duty," says Fantin.

I shake my head and silence him with a wave. The last thing I need is to arrive home with two men in tow. That would make it impossible to salvage a shred of dignity.

"As you wish, Mademoiselle," says Monsieur Manet.

He and Fantin exchange a glance. I walk to my easel to relieve dear Rosalie of packing my paints.

Manet lingers as I wipe the wet paint from my palette, taking care not to get the remnants on my hands. I wrap the wooden board in a cotton cloth.

"I fear I am leaving you with a most unfavorable impression," he says.

"*Non.* I am simply exhausted. For that, you cannot blame yourself."

"Then you will give me another chance to improve my standing?"

"I am afraid I do not understand, Monsieur."

"I would like the opportunity to present myself in a better manner."

"As you wish, Monsieur."

I drop the brush into my bag, then slip out of the gray smock and smooth the bodice of my dress.

His gaze traces my motions. "Very well, then."

"Very well."

He motions to Fantin. *"Au revoir, Mesdemoiselles."*

"Au revoir, Messieurs," calls Rosalie.

The two men walked away. But as they reach the gallery door, Manet turns back to me and tips his cane. "To second chances, Mademoiselle."

Chapter Two

There are certain people whom one loves immediately and forever.

—Unknown

"I CANNOT believe you met him," my sister Edma laments as we paint side by side in our studio. "The one day I do not go to copy and Fantin brings Manet around for introduction. I shall never forgive him."

If she has expressed her displeasure over missing the introduction once, she has bemoaned it a million times since I met Manet not even twenty-four hours prior. Edma and Maman hang on every word, begging for details until they are satisfied they have drained me of all I might offer.

Usually, Maman accompanies my sister and me to our copying sessions, but yesterday Edma chose to forgo the Louvre in favor of receiving Adolphe Pontillon, who has been calling on her these days more often than I care to acknowledge.

Given a choice between art and romance—well, to Maman there is no choice when romance is concerned. She and Edma stayed home to entertain Adolphe, and I went with Rosalie for the morning.

I do not know who is more distraught over missing the excitement. But at least my mother has dismissed her disappointment with a simple, "To think of all the hours I have sat in that wretched musée. I turn my head for a moment and *voilà!*"

Maman and Papa are good sports. While most parents insist daughters of marriageable age not approach a hobby such as painting, as more than a fleeting fancy, mine indulge.

"The talent you and your sister possess brings your father and me great joy. Not as great as the day you shall marry, but in the meantime, it shall suffice."

I know there would come a day when she and Papa expect me to lay down my brush and give my hand in marriage. For the time being, Edma's blossoming relationship with Adolphe seems to deflect attention away from my utter lack of interest in the men who come courting.

In the studio, Edma lets loose yet another misery-laden sigh. I blend emerald into the leaf of the still life I'm painting. "I cannot help it if you had better things to do yesterday than attend to your copy studies."

She rolls her eyes. For a moment we paint in silence.

"How is Adolphe?" I ask.

"Fine. Is Manet very tall? You did not mention his height."

"Edma, this is becoming tiresome. You have spoken of nothing else this morning. Tell me about your visit with Adolphe."

"There is nothing to speak of where Adolphe is concerned," Edma says. "It is all so very dull. My whole life is dull. You could at least humor me. When you tell me of the meeting, it makes me feel as if I shared the experience. I should think you would realize that, but *non,* you choose to hoard him all to yourself."

I *am* hoarding a few details. One in particular: that despite

Rosalie's presence, it seems he saw only me. And I am happy for it.

I cannot tell this to Edma or Maman. It would sound foolish. So I hold back this delicious detail. Something to savor. Like a child with a stolen sweet, I shall enjoy the private thought as I lie awake retracing the meeting in my head.

Second-guessing every gesture. Every smile. Every word.

His hand on mine.

In my mind, I move toward him without hesitation. We stand so close I feel his breath on my cheek, my ear, my neck—

"Are you listening to me?" Edma huffs and scoots her chair away from her easel. The legs sound the impatient growl of wood raking over wood. But she does not stand up. Instead, she leans into the portrait and works with staccato jabs.

"Perhaps now you shall be more interested in your copy work at the musée?" I arch a brow at her in a way that usually makes her smile. She frowns, but then her scowl gives way to a wicked smirk.

"Oui," she says. "Perhaps we have gained a great eagerness for what the masters might teach us."

We laughed together. I am happy to see her spirits rise.

"In fact," she says, her eyes bright with a fresh scheme, "let's visit the masters now. Come, Berthe, let's go."

This suggestion, or possibly her exuberance, makes me feel as if I am walking down a steep staircase unsure of my footing. I inhale deeply—the scent of paint and oil and hydrangeas. My stomach pitches.

"Lunch is almost ready. We shall go Friday."

"But today is Wednesday. That is two days away. Why not today?"

"Edma, think. Do you believe he lives at the Louvre day

and night? We have no guarantee he shall be there. Besides, I do not wish to appear overly anxious. A few days absence shall suit us."

"It shall not suit *us*. You are only thinking of yourself, and that is not fair."

"*Non*, my dear, dear Edma, what is not fair is that you are having a tantrum over something so minuscule."

She stamped her slippered foot, the thud punctuating her temper. Her dark, upswept hair emphasizes her flushed cheeks. She looks so childlike with her pink dress peeking out from her open painting smock. Paintbrush in hand, her arms dangle along the sides her chair, and she pouts.

I chuckle. I cannot help myself.

Edma glares at me and flings her brush onto the paint-splattered table that stands between our easels. It sounds like a carillon as it strikes the grouping of glass jars—some holding pigment and brushes, others half full of linseed oil—finally resting among the mélange of sullied palettes and stray paint tubes.

She stands.

I turn back to my still life and blend a perfect highlight on the flower petal. She plops down onto the brown divan along the wall behind me. The old piece of furniture *poofs* and creaks under the stress.

"Hmmph."

I see the action so clearly in my mind's eye, a most unrefined expression of displeasure reserved strictly for the rare occasion when my sister and I disagree. Three hundred and sixty days of the year we get on famously.

When we do not, even the smallest issue seems catastrophic.

It hurts me to know she is angry. But it nearly paralyzes me to think of facing *him* again today.

Too soon.

Too eager to see how he plans to paint himself in a better light.

The odd swirling sensation returns to my belly. It curls my toes inside my slippers. I squeeze them hard to counteract the wooziness. At least this time the feeling does not take me by surprise. I can best just about anything that does not surprise me.

I turn in my chair to my face my sister, sitting on the divan with her elbows resting on her knees, her chin on her palms, a scowl firmly fixed on her pretty face.

"Do not pout, Edma. If you must go to the Louvre, see if Maman will accompany you. If he is there, you may *hoard* him all to yourself."

"Qu'est-ce que c'est?" Maman's voice, as crisp as a primed white canvas, calls from the doorway. She breezes into the room, clutching a letter. Her rosy cheeks and the pale blue of her dress in harmony with her silver hair. She looks from Edma to me. "Is everything alright?"

Edma snares me with her eyes. Her glance is a warning. Her eyes are two poison darts.

I say to Maman, "We were just discussing technique."

"Oui," murmurs Edma, still glowering. "I was telling Berthe her *perspective* is all wrong. The flower—" she frowns at me, "it is *much* too big for its vase."

Maman walks over to my painting. She studies it for a moment, then turns back to my sister.

"I think it is charming. I see nothing wrong." She frowns. "Sit like a lady, Edma. I have brought you up better than this. You are peevish today."

Edma scoots to the edge of the divan and sits rod-straight, but she does not try to hide her displeasure.

"Perhaps this will cheer you up." Maman waves a crème-colored note. "Madame Auguste Manet has invited us to supper tomorrow evening."

The name *Manet* crashes like cymbals in my head. I feel a light-headedness that seems to lift me up and render my body numb. I watch Edma spring to life and hurry to Maman's side.

It takes a moment for the implication to register: The note may have been sent by *Madame* Auguste Manet, his mother, but the invitation has *Monsieur* Édouard Manet written all over it. So this is how he plans to impress me. On his own terms, his own turf.

I should have guessed as much.

"One day's notice?" Maman looks pointedly at me, and I feel myself settle back into my body. "Does he think we are so unpopular we have no other engagements?"

I open my mouth to speak, but Edma cut me off.

"We do not have plans. If we did, I should think we would cancel them. It is not every day we receive such an invitation."

Maman holds out the letter to me. A briar rose. If I do not handle it carefully it will prick me. With my forefinger and thumb, I take it from her outstretched hand. Edma appears at my side, grinning, a sheepish gesture of reconciliation. Her shoulder presses against mine as she leans in for a better look. I hold it so we may both read.

The note, dainty black script on steadfast crème card stock, simply says, "Please come for dinner, forty-nine rue de Saint-Pétersbourg, Thursday evening, seven o'clock. Regrets only."

Regrets.

Is that what I fear? Regret that I will discover him a mere mortal? That the champion of all that is shocking and real will be a fraud? Proven to be just a man?

"We will go?" I ask Maman.

"I suppose. Since your father is away, it shall give us something to tell him when he returns. And I shall have the chance to judge for myself if your Édouard Manet is as charming as you claim."

My stomach feels like a rock dropped into deep water.

Edma grabs my hands and pulls me up from my chair. She turns us about in circles, crushing the note in her grasp. The corner of the stiff paper cuts into my palm.

Why should I worry?

I have always been immune to the wiles of courting men, why should this be different? Most men are all charm and very little substance. Each with expectations for me to favor him above my painting. Each one demanding a compromise. Sadly, I have never met a man who outshone the promise of the next image that would court me. Tease me. Seduce me. Until I lay it down on my canvas and have my way with it.

Edma and I stop spinning, but my mind continues to whirl. The paintings, hung one upon the other on the studio walls, dance around me as I try to regain my equilibrium. I glance down at the crumpled paper in my hand, and I have the very unsettling sensation of the world shifting under my feet.

In a boudoir perfumed with Violettes de Parma, Edma and I chatter and share confidences. Giddy worries. Sudden panics. Trepidation born from silly designs.

"When Fantin called yesterday, he told me Emmanuel Chabrier played Saint-Saëns' *Danse Macabre* last week at the Manet's *soirée,*" Edma says, breathless. Her eyes sparkle as she brushes my hair. She pauses and studies me in the glass. "What shall be your first words to Manet?"

In my mind, I have rehearsed the scene a million times, but put to the test, I cannot recall a single syllable.

"I suppose I shall say, *'Bonsoir.'*"

"That shall certainly set his heart aflame."

"If so, I would say he is too easily impressed."

Edma sets down the brush. I know she can see right through my act. I pick up the silver hand mirror with trembling fingers and study my reflection.

I close my eyes, draw in a shallow breath, and set down the mirror. There is the crash of crystal. My eyes fly open, and I catch a perfume bottle just before it rolls off the dressing table. The stopper comes lose and liquid splashes on my hands. The sweet scent of violets floods my senses and calms my rattled nerves.

Edma giggles.

I cannot help but laugh with her. Dear, sweet Edma, the one who knows me so well, sometimes better than I know myself.

As we tie laces, cinch corsets, smooth folds, and straighten bonnets, the mood is lighter than it has been in days. Hiding my desire like a gold ring tucked away inside a delicate ivory box, I perfume my dreams with what remains of the spilled violet water and still my unsteady hands with the sweep of satin gloves.

Finally, when there is nothing left to do save leave for the soirée, I check my reflection in the hand mirror one last time. The pretty trinkets on my dressing table shimmer in the half light. One careless gesture will send the bibelots smashing to the floor.

But this time, as I return the mirror to the table, a slow, deliberate gesture, my hand does not shake.

Chapter Three

Entering the hall, she meets the wife . . .
Words stick; does not manage to say anything.
Presses hands together; stands hesitating.
Agitates moon-like fan, sheds pearl-like tears.
Realizes she loves him as much as ever,
Present pain never comes to an end.

—Anonymous, China

WE travel in the cold rain from our home on rue Franklin to the soirée on rue de Saint Pétersbourg. The foul weather does not dampen my spirits. Yet it takes but three hateful words to ruin my evening:

Madame Édouard Manet.

He is married.

It does not make sense. *Elle est une vache.* She is a cow.

Inside the lavish drawing room, the distant rumble of thunder sounds as I gape at the profile of the fat, dowdy woman playing Chopin on the piano. Her hair, parted in the middle, is pulled back in a severe chignon. The style emphasizes a round face that seems to have swallowed up her chin and redistributed it in three tiers of gelatinous flesh that dance as she pounds on the keys. Her upturned nose is too small for her masculine face, and in conjunction with her pursed, thin-lipped mouth, she looked as if she smells a fetid odor. All broad shoulders, bosom and tree-trunk waist, she is a sausage stuffed uncomfortably into her gray silk dress.

This is Madame Édouard Manet?

I wonder if I have heard Madame Manet, *mère*, correctly.

Edma leans in and pinches my arm. I want to scream, but I do not.

Madame Manet, *la mère*.

Madame Manet, *la vache*.

Unfathomable. Obviously, there has to be something more to this relationship than beauty. I do not know why it throws me. I guess I thought a man whose very existence was built on aesthetics, a dandy in his own right, would surround himself with beauty in every facet of his life.

"Suzanne is a very gifted pianist." Our hostess pauses as if to let us appreciate the melody drifting from the instrument. Madame Manet, *mère,* is petite with dark auburn hair and large, worried blue eyes, which swim like twin oceans across her angular face. Her narrow shoulders slope under her black mourning dress, and her mouth turns down at the corners giving an air of downtrodden displeasure even when she speaks of the positive.

As she talks, my gaze drifts across the line of gilded crown molding to a large portrait suspended by a maroon cord. The canvas hangs in front of the mirror above the fireplace's intricately carved mantelpiece. The painting is of Madame Manet and a handsome gentleman, who must have been her late husband as I can see a marked resemblance to Édouard.

My gaze falls to the lush deep red Turkish rug stretching the length of the parquet floor. Reflected in the mirrored walls, the lavishly furnished room seems aflame in tones of gold and red.

The tempo of the song increases, and I glance back at Suzanne. Her pudgy hands flying over the keys.

Je ne comprends pas. I do not understand how a man with such an eye can find anything beautiful in this woman, and it irritates me.

It must be a joke. But common sense dictates the high improbability of our hostess making a joke of her son's matrimonial status. Never in my life have I so desperately craved inappropriate behavior in an elder.

Suzanne pronounces the final weighty chord, and two men standing near the piano applaud. She smiles demurely and immediately begins another song.

"The great composer Franz Liszt encouraged Suzanne to come to Paris from Holland to pursue her music," says Madame Manet. "She and Édouard moved in with me after they were married."

The comment buzzes like a gnat I wanted to swat.

"Was she the success Monsieur Liszt predicted?" I surprise myself with my irreverent tone. I cannot look at Maman.

Madame Manet lifts her lorgnette as if peering through my veiled words to the heart of the insult.

She tilts her head to the right. "But of course she was successful, Mademoiselle. She married my son."

Thunder erupts, closer this time. Edma giggles a nervous little laugh. I am sure she intended to cover my rudeness by treating the exchange as folly.

I suppose I deserve the verbal slap, but I do not need my sister making excuses for me, spoken or implied. The stuffy room is closing in on me. I want to leave. I do not belong here.

It is on the tip of my tongue to ask for the return of my

mantelet so I might bid the good Madame Manet *adieu*, when I spy *him* across the room, standing just outside the far interior doorway; an apparition under the chandelier's flickering, yellow candlelight.

From the tip of the knotted tie, peeking out from his tweed vest and buttoned-up waistcoat, to the smart line of his trousers, he is a startling sight.

Suzanne shifts into Beethoven's *Moonlight Sonata.*

Not as difficult as the Chopin, but even I must admit its beauty. She plays it flawlessly. No doubt showing off her range.

I wonder how long *he* has been watching us, and whether he read the affront in his mother's body language after my gauche comment.

The pull of his gaze promises to monopolize my attention, but I resist. After all, he is a married man. I do not care to flirt or be flirted with by someone who is otherwise attached. What is the point?

I focus on an arrangement of six landscapes hung on the wall between him and the piano.

Again, thunder roars outside, a clap loud enough to command attention away from Suzanne's droning music. Everyone starts, but she does not break her rhythm. She does not even glance up at the commotion of newly arrived guests in the entryway.

Édouard moves toward us. I fold my hands into the pleats of my skirt so not to fidget. It is a foolish notion to think I could travel home alone in such weather. If I mention it, Maman and Edma shall not hear of it. And I cannot bear to spoil their evening.

"*Madame et Mesdemoiselles,* welcome." He takes my mother's hand and bows.

"Ah, Édouard," says Madame Manet. "Please entertain the Morisots. I must greet our new guests."

Manet straightens. "With pleasure."

His mother ambles off toward three men, two of whom I know; Alfred Stevens, who has recently painted my portrait, and a waterlogged Fantin, who looks as if he has blown in with the storm. He spies Edma and turns the brightest shade of red I believe I have ever seen.

The third man looks rather sour. In fact, he emits all the joy of a wet cat. He seems quite disgusted as he roughs rain from his beard.

"I am so very happy you would brave such weather to join us," Édouard says to Maman.

She titters and purrs an appreciative greeting, but by that time his eyes are already fixed on Edma.

"Who is this lovely young woman?"

Edma swoons. Like clay waiting for his warm hands.

I have the urge to pinch her like she pinched me earlier. Luckily, Maman takes charge. "Monsieur Manet, this is my daughter, Mademoiselle Edma Morisot."

"Enchanté." He bows, but does not take her hand.

I am glad. And even happier when his attention shifts to me, his gray eyes like a stormy afternoon sky.

"You have already made the acquaintance of my youngest daughter, Berthe."

"Of course." He neither bows nor takes my hand, but his words are a warm embrace. "I have been anticipating this evening, Mademoiselle."

Maman stiffens, and I can feel the air tense around her. From the corner of my eye I see movement. Madame Manet ushers the new arrivals to our huddle.

It is good to see Fantin and Stevens, who shifts a brown paper package from under his arm to his hands. The familiar faces take the edge off the evening. Buoyed by their company, I relax.

The third gentleman is named Edgar Degas. Another artist. I know of him. I have even admired his delicate pastels, but before this evening I had never had the good fortune to make his acquaintance.

"Mademoiselle, your portrait came out beautifully, if I may boast." Stevens hesitates an instant, then hands Édouard the package. "Here, this is for you."

Manet tears away the paper, revealing a small gilded frame. Probably something Stevens has painted as a gift for the occasion. Édouard's mouth tightens and his jaw twitches.

Madame Manet glanced at it. Her eyes widen and she seemed startled, even slightly taken aback. Then she blinks and snaps into action.

"Allons. Allons." Come on. Come on. She motions Maman, Edma, and me to follow. "You eligible ladies must make the acquaintance of my younger, unmarried sons, Eugène and Gustave."

As we exchange formalities, I feel Édouard's gaze fastened to me the way eyes in a portrait seem to follow one around a room. Suzanne plays on without looking up, and Madame Manet points out a young man lurking on the far side of the piano. I had not noticed him until now.

"Léon is Édouard's godchild. Suzanne's brother." She spat the words as if they left a bad taste in her mouth, but I was beginning to wonder if that was not just her manner.

The boy stood quietly leaning on the piano. He seemed to be reading music over her shoulder, but then I noticed him turning the pages for her. The two appeared content in their musical world, side by side in companionable silence, undaunted by the milling, chatting guests, who have made themselves quite at home by the time the dinner bell sounds.

Our hostess claps her hands. Everyone quiets and Suzanne stops in the middle of a stanza.

"Dinner is served. Please, let us go into the dining room."

Degas and Madame Manet lead the procession. I think it sweet when Édouard offers his arm to Maman.

He is not at all living up to the image of the rebellious rogue who brazenly paints naked women purely for the shock value. I am not sure if the discrepancy in character—or the enhancement thereof, depending on one's viewpoint—disappoints or makes me happy.

Édouard Manet is proving to be a gentleman through and through.

Mannered.

Sophisticated.

Attentive.

Although, not so dutiful to his wife. I have not seen them exchange so much as a glance all evening. She may as well be a hired musician for all the attention he pays her. He may as well have been a single man. But he is not. He is married and far be it for me to question the strange ways of man and wife.

"May I have the pleasure?" Eugène extends an arm. I slip my hand through it, and we fall in line behind Edma and Gustave. I glance back and smile at Fantin, who trails alone behind us.

He clasps his hands behind his back and whistles.

"Oh, come here." I offer my free arm to him, then cast a questioning smile to Eugène, who does not seem the least bit put out by my gesture.

Ahead, Stevens escorts Suzanne, and it dawns on me that we have met everyone except the one I am most curious about: Suzanne. I find it quite peculiar Madame Manet would make such an effort to sing her daughter-in-law's praises and not present her once she had finished her musical performance. It seems incongruent.

Suzanne dutifully takes her seat at the extreme opposite

end of the table from where Eugène has deposited me. Madame Manet graces the place of honor at the head of the table.

Degas, to Madame Manet's left and Suzanne's right, sits angled away from the younger woman with his full attention trained on our hostess.

As we await the first course, Stevens, Gustave, and Fantin engage Edma in conversation. Poor Fantin, it is evident that he is quite smitten with my sister, but he seems to not know quite how to express himself.

I dare say, Eugène vies with Édouard in monopolizing Maman's attention.

And there sits Suzanne.

All alone in the midst of the crowd, as if mute without the voice of her music. There is no doubt which Madame Manet is the lady of the household.

As a manservant ladles the soup, Suzanne rises and whispers something in her mother-in-law's ear. Madame Manet nods. Suzanne takes leave. No one stands.

The room is so alive with merriment no one seems to notice her departure. I suffer a pang for her. I know how it feels to be alone in a crowd. My gaze drifts to Édouard, who is nodding intently at something Maman says. His eyes snap to mine as if I have called his name, and my breath catches. In that instant, I realize perhaps somewhere deep down, on some base level, Suzanne and I are not so dissimilar.

We dine on the sumptuous feast under the champagne glow of candlelight. Potage Saint-Germain; grilled red mullet; lamb chops on a bed of asparagus; roasted woodcock; truffle salad; glace aux fraises; cheese; fruits; and nuts.

The delicious aromas and diffused colors—all contrasts and shadows—swirl around the room, weighing heavy and intense on the night, bathing it in the smoldering warmth of a humid summer sunset. The food is superb, yes. But just as the heat of summer steals my appetite, tonight I have no enthusiasm for food. What I crave is the delicious company, the energy of the evening.

Maman is in prime form, entertaining Édouard and Eugène, reveling in the attention they lavish upon her. I rather enjoy sitting back amidst the hum of conversation, drinking in the festive energy.

Eyeing Édouard, Maman dabs coyly at the corners of her mouth with her napkin. She touched his arm. "Tell me about your work."

"What would you like to know beyond that I paint pictures that enrage the critics? Have you not read the vile things they publish about me in *Le Soir*?"

Maman's hand flutters to the brooch at her neckline. "Indeed, I have seen your name in the news." She sips her Bordeaux. "Not always in a favorable context, I must admit."

Édouard shrugs. "I am in the fortunate position to live well without the necessity of selling my paintings. The critics and their tiny minds are of little consequence to me."

"Ah, to be in such an enviable position." Stevens empties his glass. "You can afford to paint your brazen naked women because you do not have to kowtow to the establishment with the rest of us peasants."

"If you do not like the way the Academy runs things," says Degas, "do something to change it. Do not just sit and whine."

"Wine? Yes, please, I would love more wine." Stevens holds out his glass to Degas and laughs. "Oh, I see, you do not mean *wine.* You mean do not *whine.*"

Degas frowns, and I wonder if the dour little man has a sense of humor. Really, I find Stevens's antics quite funny.

"Rather than playing the buffoon, it would serve you well to take a stand against the stodgy academicians who dictate the direction of art. Their views are criminal."

Édouard leans back in his chair, looking amused.

The manservant fills Stevens's glass. He sips it. "Unfortunately, I am not of the means to paint a nude shopping the Champs Elysées for the shock value."

"I am not merely painting to shock," says Édouard. "We must be of our time and paint what we see."

"Even Napoleon the third has not had influence in changing the minds of the old Academy stodgers, and he has tried," counters Stevens. "I depend on the Salon, and it would be the end of me if I alienated the establishment."

"And we all know how Napoleon handled the Maximilian Affair. Pulled out of Mexico and left the emperor to the gun." Degas sneers. "He only runs with a cause until it no longer suits his purpose. If you are content to do nothing to change the Salon, then you are worse than he."

Madame Manet taps her wineglass with her fork.

"That is enough. I will not have gory political talk at my dinner table. If you must argue such matters, save it for your cognac and cigars."

I can appreciate both Stevens's and Degas' points. The Academy has a firm grasp, dictating the direction of modern art. Many, myself included, believe they need to move forward, away from the staid mode of history painting. We are more than halfway through the nineteenth century, yet art does not reflect the times. But who is so bold as to slap the hands of those who hold an artist's fate in their fat fists?

I watch Édouard as Maman speaks to him. I revel in being able to gaze at him freely, unself-consciously, and it dawns on me that it is his unpretentious freedom that draws me to him. His ability to just *be.*

He is taking a stand against the status quo by painting what he must. In turn, he suffered a brutal beating when the Salon shut him out. It is that rebel quality coming from someone who, for all appearances, resembles the perfect gentleman that I find rare and endearing.

And I must admit very, very seductive.

Yes. *Très seduisant.* Extremely seductive. *Ahhh,* to be so liberated to even utter such a forbidden word as *seduisant.*

"You are awfully quiet, Mademoiselle." His eyes are a soft caress. "I hope tonight's conversation has not offended you."

"Monsieur Manet, I am not easily shocked. I should think art a most inappropriate profession for someone with a delicate sensibility."

"Très bon." He leans closer, resting his chin on his palm. His elbow touches my dessertspoon, sending it askew. I want to straighten it, set it back in its place, but I do not.

He reaches over and teases the silver handle with a manicured finger, leaving it out of line. Then starts to say something, but stops.

"Comment?" I sip my wine, watching him over the rim.

He hesitates. I can see the great wheels turning in his mind as his gaze drops to my lips. What I imagine him thinking frightens me. I drop my gaze and it lands where his shirtsleeve pulls from his wrist. I glimpse the hair on his forearm, curly and golden downy in the candlelight; the subtle masculine line where the hair stops and the skin grows pale and smooth. I want to touch him there. To judge for myself if, as promised, the texture of hair and skin hold the very essence of all things male.

I should not notice such things, in his wife's home, at his wife's table.

But it is not his wife's home.

Nor her table.

Even so, he remains a married man.

Unattainable.

Forbidden.

The trill of Maman's laughter slices the air. She is captivated by Eugène's conversation, and I glance back to Édouard and find him still watching me.

"Do tell me what thoughts go through your mind to provoke such a look." His voice is honey, tempting me to taste that for which I should not hunger.

I toy with the idea of actually speaking my thoughts. Right there with everyone around us, I want to offer a coy smile and stroke his naked wrist and tell him *that* was what brings such a look to my face.

I lean in a bit.

"Perhaps . . ." I bite my lip. "Perhaps I shall tell you sometime. Once we know each other better."

Warmed by the wine and soothed by the faint sound of the falling rain outside, a breathless sense of pleasure spreads through me.

"Then I hope we shall know each other better," he says. "Very soon."

He smiles, and I am moved by the same force that coaxes the earth around the sun. Although, I do not know who is rotating around whom. We seem to float up and out of the room, away from the party and pointless polite conversation. Again, I am gripped by the overwhelming need to touch him, to press my hands to his cheeks, to let his warmth course through me.

He refills my wine goblet with Bordeaux from the decanter on the table, then raises his glass to mine in a toast. The crisp *ping* of crystal sounds a personal symphony. For an instant I feel unsteady, as if I am gazing through the cheval glass at the male image of myself. It is nonsense, but somehow in that instant, I know him intimately. Deeper than the cutting rubbish published by critics. Beyond the surface glances to a pure dimension devoid of space or time.

"Just ask her, Édouard." A deep voice from the opposite end of the table slices through our private universe.

I feel myself freefalling and crash-landing in the midst of the silent room where all heads are turned toward us.

It is Stevens who speaks. He gulps the last of his wine, then wipes his mouth on his sleeve. "The poor fellow has been in misery for days over Mademoiselle Berthe. That's why I brought him the painting of her." He slurs the comment to no one in particular and chuckles.

The painting that set Madame Manet on edge before dinner? *Mon Dieu*. I have done nothing to deliberately cause Monsieur Manet misery. Nothing to provoke a wrong message.

A clap of thunder erupts, as if we've angered the Gods.

In my peripheral vision, I see him still leaning on his elbow, only now his clenched fist has slid to the bridge of his nose, hiding his expression.

"My dear miserable friend," Stevens says. "She is right there at your fingertips. Just ask her."

Chapter Four

Our words must seem to be inevitable.
—William Butler Yeats

"You insult my daughter and offend me with your crass insinuations." Maman shoves back her chair and stands up from the table, wobbling a bit, glaring first at Stevens, then at Édouard. "Do you think Berthe a common model? Like your Olympia?"

Maman does not wait for an answer, but gives a curt nod to Madame Manet. *"Merci, Madame. Bonne nuit."*

Édouard gets to his feet, and I think for a moment he will not let her pass. The two square off, Maman *glaring,* Édouard silently imploring her to stay.

"Madame, *s'il vous plaît,* Mademoiselle Berthe is very beautiful. I simply wish to paint her portrait. That is all Monsieur Stevens was trying to say, although very poorly, I must admit. He meant no harm. There was no insult behind his jest. *Oui,* Stevens?"

The man, slumps down in his chair like a naughty child ruefully trying to render himself invisible. He shrugs. "Of course. I meant no harm. Please forgive me Madame, Mademoiselle."

With all the commotion stirring around me all I can think is *Édouard Manet wants to paint me.* All I can do is sit leaden in my seat, hands in my lap, trying to breathe. Stevens painted my portrait, yet somehow this is different.

I do not know whether to hug Monsieur Stevens or strangle him for laying the unmentionable wide open on the table for all see. I steal a glance at Edma, who looks simply captivated by the fiasco.

Degas frowns and studies his fingernails. "I do not understand the fuss. I certainly don't see any harm in Manet painting her. She knows she is a painter, not a model, even if she does afford her colleagues the favor of her likeness every so often."

Maman gasps. She lets loose a little cry and throws up her hands. "I am now quite sure I regret giving Monsieur Stevens permission to paint my daughter."

She storms out of the room. Edma and I follow. As does Édouard.

"Madame, please. Be reasonable."

"Reasonable?" I fear Maman might slap him. Instead, as bold as you please, she strides over and snatches up the gift Stevens presented to Édouard.

White knuckled and shaking, she grips the gilded frame. Instantly, her face turns an unhealthy shade of ash.

"Maman?" I murmur.

Edma and I rush to her side to comfort her. From the look on her face I fear she might faint dead away. Then I see for myself what has offended her so.

Stevens's painting.

Of me.

It is not the likeness that is so horrid, it is how he has inscribed it. The words are painted on the canvas bold and black, right above my head.

To Monsieur Ed. Manet.

My mother's face flashes like the lightning storm outside. "My daughter's image gifted like chattel to a man whose acquaintance I have just made this evening? A married man at that." She signals a manservant for our wraps and hats. "Unforgivable."

Madame Manet appears at her side and gently lifts the frame from Maman's hands and gives it to Eugène who whisks it away.

"Madame . . ." Her voice, low and discomfited, trails off as if she is at a loss for words.

Gustave places a tender hand on his mother's shoulder. All of us, except Degas and Fantin, stand in stony, hot silence.

It is what Maman did *not* say that screams loudest: *Your son is a man whose radical politics and reputation for a risqué sense of the appropriate trails after him like the unclean stench of a leper. I do not wish my daughters infected by him.*

A bouquet of purple hyacinths and a note arrive the next morning.

When Amélie presents them to Maman, Edma and I are sitting on the divan in the drawing room with sketch pads in our laps. Maman rests in her chair by the window and reads the letter with a face as blank as untouched paper.

Cradling the blossoms, Amélie stands slightly behind our mother and gives us a knowing smile.

An arched brow.

A nearly imperceptible nod.

Edma elbows me and mouths, "From *him*."

I bite my lip as my gaze flickers to Maman. But she is still scrutinizing the note through her lorgnette.

Amélie shifts the flowers so she can hold them out for Maman's inspection. Their pleasing scent fills the room, and I inhale the sweet expression of Édouard's regret.

Hyacinths, the flower of repentance. A symbol of atonement for one's misdeeds.

Maman inspects the bouquet through her glasses, but does not accept it.

After a moment's hesitation, Amélie retracts the flowers. "I beg your pardon, Madame, the courier awaits your answer."

Lips pursed into a tight rosebud, my mother lowers her looking glass and thrusts the card at the maid. "The answer is no. Return the flowers immediately."

Edma gasps.

My heart twists. "No? Maman!"

I scoot to the edge of the divan. The sketch pad falls from my lap as I hover in a half-sitting, not-quite-standing pose.

"They are beautiful." My voice is a squeak. "Please do not send them away. We . . . we could use them in the studio, arrange them into a beautiful still life."

My mother looks right through me. Just as she had as we boarded the carriage last night. Even if she had struck me it would not have hurt as much as seeing her blind rage.

My knees give way and I fall back into the cushions.

Oh, she says she does not blame me. Last night she proclaimed the fiasco Stevens's fault, belittled his disregard for proper decorum.

"Right in front of Madame Manet," she had said in the carriage. The black of night cloaking her disgust, but I knew the look. She wore it like a decorated soldier who had been wounded in battle.

As I counted the *clip-clip-clop* of the horse's hooves muffled by the squeak and rattle of the carriage, she ranted, "Right in front of Suzanne, as if she were not the wife. As if she would not care that her husband might be 'languishing in misery' over another woman. *Unnnnnnthinkable.*" Maman had drawn out the word, her voice an octave higher than its usual pitch.

I stared out the window for the duration of the trip, relieved I could not fully see her face. Or perhaps I was glad she could not see mine.

"It is a good thing your father was not with us tonight to witness such a slight against his own flesh and blood."

A small *oomph* punctuated her words as she threw herself against the seat back. Finally, it seemed the rant had flushed her bile. The rhythmic sway of the carriage, carrying us home through rain dwindling to a soft patter, lulled her into heavy stillness.

I know she blames me, even if she does not realize it herself.

I am twenty-seven years old and long past marriageable age. Even worse, I am a painter, a sympathizer of the disgraceful cretins who passed my portrait back and forth like a bawdy joke, an illicit amusement.

Pornography between married men.

If word of last night's incident gets out, my chances of finding a husband will narrow even further. The only reason it gives me pause is the potential repercussions Edma might suffer because of my antics.

She is changing, starting to come around with interest in Adolphe Pontillon. A navy man. A sensible man with whom she can make a life and have so many *bébés* to fill her world they will edge out everything except proper life.

As for me, sometimes I feel as if there is another Berthe who lives deep inside me. She is not the dutiful daughter or the quiet artist who dallies in paint for amusement, willing to forgo it for matrimony. This Berthe secretly hopes word that Stevens's prank has spread like syphilis through the brothels. With this Berthe, the very thought of forcing herself into a charade of convention makes her feel like a caged animal. She would rather die than be sentenced to such a dull life.

I am afraid of this Berthe because I try to be good. I try to do what is expected of me, but more often than I care to admit, she lurks in the shadows of my heart threatening to consume me and the upright life I try so hard to live.

"I am sure the courier will not wait all day, Amélie," Maman snaps. "Tell him to take these back to the person who sent them, *s'il vous plaît*!"

The maid hesitates, slanting a glance at Edma. *What have I missed?*

Maman frowns and claps her hands.

"*Tout de suite*, Amélie. Now!"

With a *swoosh* of skirts, the maid hurries out of the room.

"But Maman," I protest.

My mother gets to her feet and brushes past me without a glance. She is not gone half a minute when Edma grabs my hand and pulls me up and off the divan.

"Come. Fast."

In the foyer, we nearly run into an ashen-looking Amélie, standing with the flowers clutched to her breast, her back pressed against the wall as if she expects Maman instead of us. Her gaze darts around, then she thrust the note and flowers at me. Amélie tries to back out of the room, but Edma grabs her wrist.

"No, Amélie, stay." My sister's voice is barely a whisper, but it pins Amélie to the spot where she stands. "Ask the courier to wait while we write a reply."

My heart thuds. "Reply? What shall we say?"

Edma throws her hands into the air. "We cannot send him back empty-handed. We must say something."

Amélie disappears through the front door to detain the messenger. Edma grabs the note from my hand and opens it, and we huddle together to read it.

Dear Madam et Mesdemoiselles, I am mortified by last evening's unfortunate turn of events. I wish to call on you this afternoon to convey my most sincere apology. Yours respectfully, Édouard Manet.

Yes, regret.

A humble request for forgiveness.

I bury my face in the sweet-scented blossoms and inhale deeply until I feel my sister tugging at me again.

"Come now. We must work fast."

We pause at the entrance to the drawing room for a cautious glance about the place. To our good fortune, there is no sign of Maman.

Edma tosses the card on the desk and sets about foraging in the drawer for a pen.

I lay down the flowers and pick up the crème-colored linen card. I trace the top fold with my nail, teasing my way down the side until almost as if by its own will my finger slips inside the note and rests between Édouard's words. I do not open the card. Still, I can see the ghost of his script through the paper and somehow that is enough. I run the tip of my finger on the underside, along his writing, caressing each word. Instinctively, my finger pushes against the upper fold. At that moment everything crystallizes. If I push the tiniest bit, I will be inside.

Or I could simply lay down the note and walk away.

"Here, give that to me." Edma snatches the paper from my hand. The crisp edge slices my finger, leaving a clean, white gash.

I gasp and press the stinging flesh to my lips. The moisture only intensifies the discomfort.

Oblivious, Edma lay Édouard's note facedown on the desk. She dips the pen into the inkpot and glances up at me expectantly. "What shall we say?"

I bite down on the wound instead of answering her. The metallic taste of blood fills my mouth.

I shrug and wipe my wet finger on my blue skirt.

She frowns. "Here, *you* write." Edma thrusts the pen at me. "This is for your benefit not mine. It should come from you."

The reality behind her words startles me, as if someone has lit a candle in a pitch-black champagne cave.

I take the pen in hand. A drop of ink splatters onto the desk, narrowly missing the paper. My sore finger throbs against the pressure of my grasp.

Edma fidgets and worries the lace collar of her yellow dress. "If we invite him today, Maman will be furious. It will not be fair to subject him to her mood." She glances toward the door. "Another day. Tomorrow?"

"Amélie?" Maman's voice sounds in the hall just outside the drawing room. Edma and I jerk upright.

The flowers.

I yank open the desk drawer and sweep the blossoms inside, nearly clipping my sister's fingers as she drops Édouard's card among the contraband.

The scent of hyacinth lingers and the drawer still seems to vibrate its slam as Maman ambles into the room. We must look a guilty sight standing shoulder to shoulder behind the desk for no apparent reason.

Maman scowls. "What are you doing?"

At the same time Edma says, "Nothing," and I started to explain, "We are studying the angle of the room to use for a charcoal drawing."

Unaccustomed to lying, I drop my gaze from hers. Two stray purple petals lay atop the desk. They must have fallen as I swept the flowers out of sight. Bending forward, I cover the errant blossoms with my hand. I also hit the wet ink spot.

Maman watches us for a moment, then shakes her head as if she has resigned herself to being unable to account for the strange ways of the younger generation. "Where is Amélie? That girl is treading a thin line today."

Amélie. *Non.* My heart thuds. Maman will have a fit if she finds her with the courier so long after she told her to send him on his way and with no note or flowers. Given Maman's mood, Amélie's thin line would likely disappear altogether.

"Amélie!" Maman heads toward the foyer.

I squeeze my eyes shut and send a silent prayer that Amélie will think fast enough to formulate a plausible excuse for her loitering. I grab Edma's arm, and we brace ourselves for Maman's explosion.

But there is none. Only the sound of her calling for the girl in an increasingly shrill and more distressed tone.

"Amélie!"

"Oui, Madame?" Amélie's voice sounds from the kitchen, the opposite direction of the foyer.

Smart girl—she had gone out the front door and reentered through the back.

The ingenious girl had pulled it off, I would thank her later. I just hope she has told the courier to wait for the note.

I dare not look at Edma until Maman is out of the room and well on her way to the kitchen. I notice I've transferred the ink stain from my hand to Edma's sleeve. But there is no time to worry about it.

Edma jerks open the drawer. I grab Édouard's note—and the pen.

Please come Tuesday at four o'clock.

"Tuesday?" Edma protests. "*Non,* that's four days away. Tomorrow."

"Too soon. Maman will never receive him."

We hear our mother's voice in the hall again. Then Amélie's voice, louder than usual. "*Pardon, Madame,* just one more question regarding luncheon, *s'il vous plaît?*"

Maman's footsteps retreat.

My heart is in my throat, but I manage to choke out, "Edma, hide the flowers and distract her until I get back."

I hurry down the hall, taking care to tread lightly so the sound of my slippers do not give me away. Icy currents course through my veins. I hold my breath and pray Maman will not see me as I enter the foyer. Once safe in the entryway, I ease open the front door, then pull it to a soundless close behind me.

As I step from the foyer into the windy brightness of the day, it takes my eyes a moment to adjust. I hurry down the stone steps, across the walk and out the gate, where I nearly collide with a little boy who runs in front of me chasing his little dog down the street.

As I right myself, my hand instinctively tries to secure my hat. But there is none. Nor gloves, I realize, as a handsome couple strides by arm in arm. I feel naked standing on the city street in my housedress, my head bare, the gusty wind tousling my hair out of its chignon.

They are not neighbors, *merci Dieu.* In fact, I have never seen them in my life. But my, how right they look strolling together in the gentle warmth of the morning sunshine oblivious to my near mishap with the boy, unaware of all but each other.

Just as they pass, I glimpsed a nuance in the woman's expression, a mixture of aloof pleasure and worldly knowing, a subtle power in the tilt of her chin.

I follow their movement as they continue down the rue Franklin until they are silhouetted by the sun. The light burns my eyes.

The sun's glow reflects off windows and metal rooftops belying the storm that savaged us last night. It strikes me that fate is no more than a storm that blows through, upsetting everything in its path, until a random change of course propels it in a new direction, leaving us to pick up the pieces of our broken lives.

Movement out of the corner of my eye draws my attention to the manservant from last night's soirée. Slouched against the stone wall, he looks much younger than he appeared last night; a boy who has barely passed through the threshold of manhood. He straightens when he sees me and tips a quick nod.

I hold out the note. "Please deliver this to Monsieur Édouard Manet. *Merci.*"

He reaches out to take it from me. The light captures the ink stain that sullied my palm. My gaze flickers to the note and my writing, scrawled as dark and bold as a dirty secret exposed to the world.

In a dreamlike slow motion, he takes possession of the letter. I glimpse a flicker of amusement in his eyes, and it seems I can almost read his thoughts: flowers from a married man to a woman who is not his wife; notes with sweet sentiments flying back and forth. All fodder for folly.

I am probably not the first.

Instinct screams for me to repossess the note, but by that time he has already thanked me and turned away.

I should go after him or at least holler, "Tell him no. The answer is no."

But Maman appears at the gate.

"Berthe, what are you doing out here?" Her initial surprise settles into an angry line across her forehead.

Panic, like pinpricks, courses through me as I look from her to the courier who is growing smaller as he makes his way down the rue Franklin.

"You're flushed," Maman says.

She reaches for my cheek, but I draw back. Her eyes flash. "What is the matter with you? What in heaven's name are you doing out here all alone? No hat. No wrap. Really, Berthe."

Edma peers at me over Maman's shoulder. I glance from her wide, guilty eyes to my mother's, narrow and accusing.

"I needed . . ."

Wide and guilty.

"I thought . . . ."

Narrow and accusing.

"I needed . . . air."

"Why did you not go out into the garden instead of coming out here like this?"

Under the pressure of her scrutiny and too shaken to speak, I simply shrug and glance down the street. I have lost sight of the messenger. As I stand in front of my mother I try not to gulp air in greedy, unladylike breaths.

"Come inside at once." Maman steps aside to afford me room to pass. As she follows Edma and me up the walk to the house, she mutters the entire way. "Since last evening both of you have behaved strangely. All the more justification for avoiding that *man*. Yes indeed. Controversy breeds controversy. That is what I have always believed— Edma!"

At the top of the steps, Maman grabs my sister's arm. "Is this ink on your sleeve?"

I glance at the dark stain, blue-black, on Edma's yellow dress. I close my dirty hand and hide it in the folds of my skirt.

The next thing I know, Maman throws Edma's arm away from her as if it disgusts her. "Please go for a walk or go out into your studio for a bit. My nerves cannot tolerate the two of you. But change your dress first, Edma. You look like a filthy street urchin."

Still muttering, she pushes past us and climbs the steps to the front door.

Edma and I stand on the walk staring at each other in bewilderment as she disappears inside.

My sister does not have to say a word for me to understand what she is thinking. We are not used to deceiving Maman. If impulse is the devil's temptress, we are her pawn. Now we have four days to explain to our mother what we have done.

Chapter Five

Nobody ought to look at paintings, who cannot find a greater meaning than the artist has actually expressed.
—Nathaniel Hawthorne

ANTICIPATING Édouard's arrival on Tuesday causes time to stand still. For four days, the hours linger like life in a dream-spun impression that cannot live for being confined to the canvas. The days dawn and fade, sketching vignettes so similar that one falls into the next as colorful glass in a kaleidoscope shifts shape, but only travels around in a circle.

Tuesday, the stillness breaks. In a sense, the kaleidoscope smashes to the floor and all the shards fly free.

Edma and I have not yet told Maman about Édouard's impending visit. We are still searching for the words that never seem to present themselves, when Maman finds the hyacinths hidden in our studio.

I am sitting on the terrace a bundle of nerves, knowing what the afternoon holds when I look up and see her clutching the withered flowers like a ghost bride haunting the altar of her abandonment. I should take it for a harbinger of what's to come, but I am stunned into a strange heightened awareness that will not let me get past the moment—the jasmine is blooming on the terrace. The bush droops with the weight of the blossoms, as if its perfume is so heavy it causes the plant to pitch forward. I think I shall always associate the scent of jasmine with Maman's rage. Strange it would not be the hyacinth, but they have started to fade. When she throws the wilted purple bundle at my feet, several dried petals lift on the breeze and roll like tiny tumbleweeds across the terrace.

"What are these?"

The vibrant purple has dulled to a stormy gray. The old, withered stalks look like the protruding veins on my mother's wrinkled hands.

Maman is always in a nasty mood when Papa is away. He isn't due back until the next day. Her expression warns she might slap me if I do not answer her *tout de suite.*

"They are flowers."

She bares her teeth at me in a grimace that is equal parts disgust and impatience.

"I can see that, you stupid girl. Where did they come from?"

Stupid girl? I am stunned into silence. My mother has never spoken to me in such a manner. Never called me such a horrid name. She steps toward me, hovering, fueled by burning resentment. I stand up to meet her.

She is so close I can almost feel the moisture of her breath. Although I am not very tall, I stand a good head taller than she. My mother does not cower. She stares up at me demanding an answer.

"They are the flowers delivered from Édouard Manet."

Maman slaps me hard across the left side of my face. The blow smarts like a thousand nettles, but I will not let her see how much it hurt.

A wry smile pulls at the corners of my mouth, although I

am sure my eyes speak every sentiment I wish to convey. "Édouard Manet is calling today at four o'clock."

I believe she might strike me again, but she wavers.

"Je ne comprends pas?"

The sun disappears behind a cloud. The breeze picks up, and I noticed the air has chilled.

"I invited him."

Her gaze is a gauntlet thrown between us.

"You shall send him a note telling him he is not welcome."

"He thinks you are the one who sent the invitation. I wrote it on the back of the note he sent Friday, and I did not sign my name. If we rescind the invitation it shall reflect poorly on you."

I will my voice not to shake. Much to my relief, it does not. Maman stares at me for a long moment. I can almost see the thoughts calculating in her head.

She prides herself on being a superior hostess. This stems back to Papa's prefect days. She has refined entertaining to an art.

"Were you planning to tell me or were you just going to let him surprise me?"

"I was going to tell you, Maman. When the time was right."

She laughs. The sound is bitter like lemon. I wonder where Edma is and how she has managed to disappear at just the right moment. I shall not blame her. I am equally at fault here. In some ways I feel as if the largest part of the onus lay upon me.

Maman does not speak to me again until Édouard arrives. Of course, Edma and I make ourselves scarce, after I find my sister hiding in the kitchen. She heard Maman yelling at me on the terrace and had hidden out with Amélie. I consider berating her for being such a coward and letting me bear the brunt of our mother's anger, but it will not change anything.

Edma and I sit quietly. Amélie has left the room to prepare for our guest.

Although it is hard knowing Maman is cross at us, I feel better knowing the secret is revealed. It is as if the curtains have been thrown open so that light may cleanse a haunted room.

We know our mother will graciously receive Édouard. She will briefly hear what he has to say and will find a way to usher him out. He'll be standing on the walk before he realizes he was never welcome in the first place.

"So he wants to paint you," Edma says. "Is she afraid you will turn into Olympia right before her very eyes?"

Olympia, scandal's own mistress. It is rumored that Victorine Meurent, the beautiful woman who posed for *Olympia,* was Édouard's mistress. But she left him. For years now, he has had no regular model. I didn't realize he was searching for one. Perhaps he's not.

Still, I can't help but picture myself as Olympia, wanton and mocking, sprawled in serene impudence, with a thin black ribbon around my neck and a small slipper on one foot. The other foot, brazenly bare, tucked beneath the sole of my shoe, toes teasing, hinting at hidden promises yet to be discovered. If Maman knew, she would lock me away for the rest of my life.

"Mademoiselle Berthe, your mother wishes you to join her in the drawing room."

Amélie's voice shocks me back into reality. Edma grabs my hand.

He is here.

I had not heard his knock.

Somehow, he has slipped in unnoticed.

Edma rises to accompany me.

"*Pardon, Mademoiselle.* Madame wishes Mademoiselle Berthe to come alone."

Edma's mouth falls open, but she doesn't make a vocal protest. As I walk alone like a doomed woman to the guillotine, the other Berthe chants with each step I take toward Édouard.

Olympia, who looks the world in its naked eye without a blink of shame.

Was that how I looked Thursday night as Stevens goaded Édouard to ask me to sit for him?

Olympia, the mistress odalisque.

Is that how I look hesitating in the drawing room doorway as Édouard stands to greet me?

There are certain places in Paris I go to seek refuge. I love to walk along the *quai* near the Louvre. There is something very soothing in the way the buildings rise up near the river Seine, like tall, stately sentries standing watch over the long, straight line of old houses with their irregular rooftops and stone balconies jutting like drooping eyelids off the melancholy faces. It is my sanctuary. I always feel as if no harm can come to me here.

Seeing Édouard in the drawing room, I want to grab Edma and run to my haven near the Louvre. Alas, it is impossible, so I try to think pretty thoughts that will calm me: the boats moored along the river dipping and nodding without a care; the rhythmic song of the water slapping the embankment; the fact that Suzanne has not accompanied her husband on this visit—

That is not a pretty thought, and I should not dwell on it. Even if it is the truth.

I try to clear my mind, but Édouard looks stunning. I do not know if it is the way his navy frock coat turns his gray eyes a shade of deep blue or if it is just the pull of his presence that attracts me so, but as he takes my hand and bows, I find myself at a loss for what to say or do.

"Mademoiselle. So nice to see you again."

I look to Maman for direction. She motions for me to sit next to her on the divan. I am glad because despite her earlier anger, it feels safe, and I hope somehow it means she has forgiven me. Or at least that time has blunted the edge of her anger.

"Maman sends her regards," says Édouard after taking a seat across from us. His silver-tipped walking stick lay on the floor next to him. His elbows are propped on the arms of the chair. He steeples his long, slender fingers as he speaks. "She wanted to come, but I told her it would be best if I came alone."

Amélie slides a tea try on the table between us. Silently, Maman indicates for me to pour the tea. The room is so quiet, I pray my hand does not shake and cause the cup and saucer to rattle.

I manage to complete the task without disgracing myself and hand him the first cup.

As he takes hold of *la soucoupe*, he says, "Mademoiselle, I deeply regret what happened Thursday night. It was a disaster. A disgrace. Monsieur Stevens and I meant no harm to your good name."

Édouard looks me square in the eyes. His words resonate in earnest, an agitated swirl, as if a swarm of bees has taken formation in my belly. A few seconds pass before I realize I am still holding onto the saucer.

I let go. A small wave of tea splashes over the top of the cup.

Édouard has the good grace to pretend not to notice and turns his attention to Maman. "If necessary, Stevens will call to apologize himself."

"That won't be necessary," Maman says and changes the subject. "Monsieur Manet, before Berthe joined us you mentioned you have just returned from Boulogne."

Édouard sips his tea. He lowers the cup to the saucer resting it on this knee. "I have, indeed. In fact, Maman, Suzanne, and Léon are still there."

So that explains it. It was simply not practical for her to come. I was not sure if finding justification for her absence made me feel better or worse. But, there it was . . .

"They will stay for the rest of the month, but I will travel back and forth between Paris and Boulogne. I must work, and it is impossible to paint with the family in such proximity. Besides, Boulogne will not work for my next project." His gaze flicks to me, then back to Maman, who watches him, sizing him up as a judge decides the fate of a criminal.

"What is this next project, Monsieur?" she asks coolly.

"In Boulogne, one morning I was out for a stroll and happened upon the most interesting sight. It was a vision. A woman sitting high upon a balcony fanning herself. It reminded me of Goya's balcony painting. Breathtaking. I saw it in Spain in sixty-five. Are you familiar with the work?"

I nod. "I once admired an engraving of it in a book."

"It is a masterpiece." His eyes are full of wonder. He opens his mouth to speak again, falters, then blurts, "What Stevens says is true. I have longed to paint your daughter's portrait, Madame. I would be most humbled and most appreciative if you would allow her to join Mademoiselle Claus and Monsieur Guillemet in my own re-creation of Goya's balcony composition."

He strings the words together in one breath, as if pausing he might be robbed of the opportunity to finish. Then the three of us sit in thick silence staring into our teacups. The grandfather clock ticks a full fifteen beats before my mother says, "Berthe has quite a mind of her own. The decision is hers."

Maman will not look at me. She sips her tea and stares at a spot over Édouard's right shoulder.

"Mademoiselle, you would come into my studio first as a colleague, second as a *model.*" He turns back to Maman. "I use that term with all due respect, Madame."

Overwhelmed by the sick feeling that Maman was pushing me into my own trap, making me pay for my defiance, I cannot answer.

Inside me two Berthes war: one is the picture of Propriety. The obedient daughter. The proper lady, quiet and contemplative; the other is an impulsive woman I scarcely recognize—an ugly creature prone to being swept away, she is not so compliant, discreet, or pensive—an Olympia of sorts.

Lost in impulse's shadow, Propriety cannot find her voice. This delights Olympia. So does the thought of my being Édouard's model. Yes, the prospect delights and arouses her.

Impulse pushed me along the knife's edge and delivered Édouard to me this afternoon. It is impulse that makes me say, "Of course, I will be your model."

Chapter Six

There is no excellent beauty that hath not some strangeness in the proportion.

—Francis Bacon

No sooner has Édouard invited us to his studio on Thursday to begin the session and taken his leave, when Maman's anger sweeps through like a mistral menacing all in its path.

"You are a disgrace to yourself and your family."

I should have expected her anger. On a deeper level, I knew it was coming, yet I was too afraid to face it to even brace myself for the inevitable: that she would fly to pieces after I had betrayed her twice in one day.

She had seen him to the door, leaving me in the drawing room alone. Once the front door clicks shut, I rise from my seat on the divan and make for the sanctuary of my studio.

But I am too late.

Maman corners me. "You sit right there and listen to me." She thrusts her finger in my face and backs me to my place on the divan. "You will not humiliate this family."

The force of her anger seems to vibrate the house, but soon

I realize it is only her voice that shakes. I could more easily weather another slap across the face. I would have even preferred she drag me by the ear and throw me out into the street at Édouard's feet rather than face the bald realization of how much I had hurt her.

It is not what I intended, but feeding on itself, the circumstance has taken on a course of its own. The reality is a physical ache that manifests itself in the pit of my stomach, a by-product of the lump lodged in my throat that will not allow me to speak.

She gave me the choice and I took it.

Probably for the best I cannot say this, as this will only worsen the situation.

"I suppose you think you know what is best?" She is screaming at me. "You know what you are doing? How are you going to explain this to your father?"

I try to answer, but my attempt to speak against her barrage of questions is as useless as trying to walk against the winds of the mistral. I let her blow.

After a long while she winds down with, "What are you trying to prove?" I do not answer immediately. She must think I am mocking her with sullen silence.

"Answer me when I speak to you! I asked you what you are trying to prove?"

I cleared my throat. "I am not trying to prove anything, Maman."

Heat flames my neck and ears. I hope my mother will not notice. She shakes her head, disgust skewing her small features. "He is a married man, Berthe. You are a single woman. Have you become so blinded by selfishness you have forgotten it is not merely your own reputation at stake here?"

I knew it was not *my* future over which she fretted. It was Edma's relationship with Adolphe. The one bright spot she had pinned her dreams upon. Certainly more hope than I had given her.

"Maman, I do not know what you mean. Married or not, I have no ill intentions. I simply want to learn from Monsieur Manet."

"Learn? Learn what? You do not need another painting teacher."

"I am not looking for a teacher as much as I am looking for the inspiration I might receive by just watching him work."

"Ridiculous. Your father and I have invested far too much money in your lessons with *Messieurs* Guichard and Oudinot. If you must seek inspiration elsewhere, we are not getting our due from them."

She throws her hands in the air and talks as if someone else is in the room. "We spoil her. That is precisely the problem. I should not be surprised that she turned out this way. But I am surprised." She turns back to me. "Surprised and shocked and saddened. Because with all we have given you, all the leeway and latitude, you have become a person I do not even know anymore. A person I do not wish to know."

"How can you claim you do not know me, Maman? I am *your* daughter. I am an artist just as you and Papa have encouraged me."

Maman flinches, almost imperceptibly but I see her react to the sting. Then she refocuses her glare on me, even more piercing this time.

"Your father and I have encouraged you to be a proper lady."

I should let it go. I know better, but my ire is like a door forced open under pressure. No matter how I try to bar it shut, bile manufactured by the talk of my place in this world grows until it oozes out between the facade's cracks and crevices, until the door swings open and everything spills out.

"Proper? As if that were my life's purpose? It is not my fault I was born a woman."

My mother stares at me for a moment, cold and disbelieving. When she speaks, her voice is low and uneven, as if I have wrung from her all the energy she possesses.

"Berthe, we have afforded you advantages many a young woman would be delighted to have. Luxuries. The best clothing, the best upbringing, the best possible position to meet a man who will ensure your future. Many respectable young men call, yet you push them aside, when all you would have to do is —"

"What? What should I do, Maman? Sit upon the sofa waiting for a *proper* man to give me permission to live? If that is so, it is a dull existence. If that is all you want for me, then why, Maman, did you raise me to think? Why did you and Papa encourage me to have an opinion?"

She closes her eyes against my words. I know I have delivered the fatal blow in our verbal jousting match. Although all the bile has drained from me, I only feel worse. It is as if something, some bond or branch between us that once seemed immovable, has splintered. Panicking, my mind reels, searching for a way to mend the fracture.

"I am sorry, Maman. I never meant to . . . I never meant to disappointment you."

I am sincere. But she does not answer me. She simply turns, leaving me alone in the room with my words reverberating in the air.

Two days later, Maman accompanies me to Édouard's rue Guyot *atelier.* Would she have gone if Papa had not returned home? He did not mention the incident with Édouard to me, but I know she told him. How else would she have explained why she was not speaking to me after our argument in the drawing room?

I am sorry to give Papa such a stressful homecoming. I have missed him. Our house is not the same without him, and my mother has grown so tense.

But I do believe it is he who is to thank for Maman's accompanying me to Édouard's studio. He is a strong man. A practical man. He looks beyond the silly superficial dictations of society to the matter-of-fact. The fact that I can learn something from Édouard.

Ah, Papa, I really do not know what I would do without him.

Maman and I arrive late, or at least later than Fanny Claus and Monsieur Guillemet, the other models Édouard has engaged for the painting.

"Bon jour, bon jour!" Édouard greets us warmly. Maman is cordial, but aloof—for my benefit, I'm sure—as he takes our wraps and makes introductions.

Tall and distinguished, Monsieur Guillemet bows with a flourish and works a bit too hard, I must say, to charm us. I'm glad because his agreeable demeanor might melt Maman's icy formality.

Édouard presents Fanny Claus, a young violinist and friend of his wife, Suzanne. Apparently, she and Suzanne often play duets at the Thursday night parties at his mother's house.

Fanny Claus nods demurely. I am a bit disappointed when I realized both she and I have worn white dresses for the occasion. They are of vastly different styles, still I worry that the monochromatic sameness will not work for Édouard's painting and he will require one of us to change. But he will be the one to make that decision, I think eying, the short, puffy Mademoiselle Claus.

I would not go so far as to call her fat, but she is an unredeemingly plain girl. She has no neck to speak of and a long, pallid face with close-set black eyes that gave the appearance of two raisins pushed into rising bread dough. The simple white frock does absolutely nothing for her complexion.

"May I offer you some tea?" Édouard asks. "Or a cup of chocolate?"

"Tea, *s'il vous plaît.*" Maman pointedly turns her back on me, to talk to Madame Chevalier, Fanny Claus's chaperone, a formidable-looking woman wearing a matronly navy blue dress with a high, rounded waist and fitted sleeves with epaulettes.

I am looking at the paintings hung on the far wall. So many of them; it's difficult to take them all in. Portraits, still-life scenes, fruits, flowers, vegetables . . . Even more tucked in a little nook around the corner of a partition.

"Mademoiselle, what may I prepare for you? Tea, chocolate?" Édouard smiles.

"Nothing for me, *merci.*"

"Are you sure there is *nothing* with which I might tempt you?"

His voice is a velvet cloak, inviting me to abandon all my apprehensions and allow him to wrap me up in it. It steals my breath and sends my stomach into tight spirals.

Something flares inside me, challenging me to call his bluff. "Beyond tea and chocolate, Monsieur, what sort of temptation had you in mind?"

His eyes widen. I have rendered him speechless. Instantly, I regret being so vulgar. But as the feeling envelops me like the sticky summer air, I turn away to join the others. He detains me with a hand on my arm, stopping me with a simple touch. The others—I cannot see the others, but I can hear them chatting ignorant of our physical contact right behind them.

"There are a great many offerings with which I might endeavor to tempt you, Mademoiselle." His words are a sultry whisper, and he steps closer. "Right now, I daresay, is not the time. But I can make time, if you like."

I close my eyes against the feverish lurch of pleasure that springs forth in my belly. I am powerless to move away. Even if I could, I would not because then I would not be able to savor the nearness of him. His scent—a mixture of coffee and paint and another note uniquely Édouard—beckoning me to lean closer, until the course texture of his beard brushes my cheek.

I pull back, startled, reclaiming my personal space.

Édouard releases me without another word and disappears. I linger alone for a moment, trying to regain my bearings.

When I rejoin the others, he is bent over a small spirit-stove, where he has busied himself heating the water for Maman's tea.

Monsieur Guillemet's deep voice resonates through the room. A flutter of ladies' laughter erupts. I notice Fanny Claus looking at me. She doesn't smile, doesn't blink. The way her morbid raisin eyes bore into me makes me fidget. Had she sensed the exchange that took place between Édouard and me?

Nonsense. How could she?

Édouard bangs around, opening and shutting cupboards, setting out tea tins, a kettle, and cups. He seems in no particular hurry to get the painting under way.

I'm glad because I need to gather myself.

I am not the type of woman to swoon, but it would be a lie if I said his sudden frankness did not affect me. His offer to *make time* is a stone plunged into deep water, leaving my emotions rippling from the impact.

Thank God, Fanny Claus finally turns her boring black gaze back to the conversation. I lift my eyes to the vaulted, paned-glass ceiling to offer a silent prayer of thanks.

The clear view makes the studio appear larger and brighter than I had imagined. Although if pressed, I could not tell you the mental picture I had conjured of Manet's *atelier.*

I glance around Édouard's space—at the makeshift

balcony—complete with a piece of wrought iron—he has assembled near the wall of windows. I suppose that is where he will paint us. There's a dressing screen in the far right corner. How many women have disrobed behind its flimsy veil?

Leaned against the walls in stacks five or six deep are more canvases in various stages of completion. More paintings hung haphazardly here and there on the walls above a mélange of rolled cloth, clay pots, books, paint-stained rags, the accoutrements for a formal table setting, a copper kettle turned on its side, a silver candelabra.

Clutter in every nook and cranny—the sum of these parts equals the man who whispered of temptation and forbidden promise; a man I want to know much better.

I turn away from the place I had been looking, as if the motion will erase my illicit thoughts, to a window covered by a large sheet of muslin tacked to the frame. Midmorning light filters through. The determined rays stream in around the loose edges like the splayed ribs of an open fan. It reminds me of the fitful luminosity of the *Tintoretto* that had so captivated Édouard the very first day I encountered him.

I walk over to a worktable shoved into the corner against the far wall. The wooden surface is heaped with rolled canvases, discarded drawings, and dust-covered sketch books and volumes of literature.

I run my finger over the dusty cover of Baudelaire's *Les Fleurs du Mal.* A number of years ago, the poetry caused quite a furor, and some of the poems were banned after he stood trial for obscenity. I have never seen a copy of the book.

I glance over my shoulder and lift the volume from the table, thumbing through, stopping occasionally to read a verse or register a sentiment.

Why was it judged obscene? Based on the brief passages I read standing there, I do not understand. I glance up every now and again to assure myself Fanny Claus, or worse yet, Maman, is not watching me.

No. Fanny still has her back to me. Maman is still ignoring me. But my heart is thudding at the thought of her discovering my perusal of something so risqué, something judged *obscene.*

Why all the fuss?

Nothing about it upsets my sensibilities. Lightning did not strike me dead for opening it. I did not faint or feel sickened, or otherwise harmed.

But if it was judged obscene, what does it say about me that I see nothing wrong in it?

And what, too, does my fascination with Édouard's work say about my sensibilities? I can see grounds for raised eyebrows: He has painted nude women out of context. It is no wonder someone of weaker constitution would take offense.

Yet, I think him brave and heroic for being so modern, so willing to challenge the stodgers of the Academy.

What *does* that say about me?

If I cannot discern what's improper in something that has been judged obscene, might there be something inherently wrong with me?

I return *Les Fleurs du Mal* to its place and pick up a sketch book and flip through roughs of still lifes, the unfinished profile of a delicate-looking woman. But it is the full-length nude stretched out on a bed that gives me pause.

Olympia.

My breath catches.

A preliminary sketch? Even in its crude state its allure is undeniable. I stare in awe at the drawing for a moment and notice something different about it. It takes me a moment, but I realize she is lying in a different position from the finished painting.

In the final version, her legs are outstretched and her left hand covers her sex, but in this rendition, her right knee is shamelessly bent and her left hand rests across her body.

I turn the book to view the sketch from a different angle, and I recall the other day, Edma and me in our studio. How we dissolved into nonsense after Maman's severe disapproval of Édouard's visit. It is Edma's way to make folly out a grave situation. While I obsess over the unpleasant, she makes light of it. That's just her way.

True to form, I was sulking at my easel trying to work, trying to not think of how mad Maman was at me, when Edma started making silly remarks, taking on the voices of the men who had attended the *soirée* at the Manets' home on the Thursday prior. She was trying to make me laugh, but was failing miserably. I was growing quite irritable because she was making it nearly impossible for me to concentrate.

She held a paintbrush under her nose. I guess it was supposed to be a mustache, and she could barely keep a straight face.

She deepened her voice into a slurred, faux baritone, imitating Stevens's drunken antics. "Just ask her, or must I do it for you, you poor, poor miserable man?"

I don't know if it was the way her voice cracked during her ridiculous imitation of a drunken man that tickled me so, or the ridiculous way she looked with that brush balanced between her nose and upper lip, but I succumbed to her giddy buffoonery and said, "You want *misery*? I shall give you *misery*." I grabbed the paintbrush from her and pretended to fence.

Edma clapped.

"*Mesdames et messieurs,* I present to you the new Olympia."

I performed a dramatic, slow curtsy, waving my brush with a flourish.

Edma clapped louder, "Brava!"

The memory teased a smile to my lips.

"Do you like it?" Édouard's deep voice, all too real sounds behind me, and I snap the sketch book shut and return it to its place on the worktable.

The silence between us is a silken cord that binds me to him. It is too much, pressing down like a lover's body. All my senses meld together until I hear my own blood rushing through my veins; or perhaps it is his breath against my neck or his hands in my hair.

Yet when I turn to face him, he stands at a respectable distance. "I hope you do not mind my looking. I was just . . ."

His expression, a look of sultry longing, of want and raw need, catches me so off guard I cannot speak.

"Not at all. By all means, please look until you have had your fill." He picks up Baudelaire's book of poems and holds it out to me. "Would you like to borrow it?"

I do not answer because the studio's front door bangs open, and Madame Manet staggers through the threshold, holding a large picnic basket with both hands.

"Bonjour, everyone!" she calls.

Édouard hands me the book, which I take, for lack of knowing what else to do, and rushes over to take the basket from her.

"Maman, what a surprise. I had no idea you were coming today."

I set down the book, knowing I cannot bring it home. I cannot even allow myself to imagine the scene it would cause in the carriage on the way home. Fully expecting Suzanne to trail in after Madame Manet, I move away from the table to join the others, feeling more than a little indiscreet at having lost myself in Édouard's belongings.

"I thought I would bring your lunch." Madame Manet greets Maman. "I brought enough for an army. There is plenty for everyone."

Édouard closes the door.

No Suzanne.

Why did she not accompany Madame Manet? Why would she let her mother-in-law bear the burden of the long journey and transporting the food alone?

Édouard sets down the basket and kisses his mother on the cheek. "What a surprise. How very kind of you to come all this way, Maman."

Madame Manet beams and retreats to Maman's side. "Madame Morisot, I am so very happy to see you here today." She hesitates, and I wonder if she will mention the unfortunate events at the soirée, but she does not. Probably for the best, because I'm not sure how Maman will respond.

Instead, she asks her son, "How is the painting progressing?"

"We have not yet begun. But I was just about to suggest we get to work." He looked at me. "Shall we?"

He drags a chair to the balcony setting, and indicates for me to sit. Once I am in place, he lifts my left arm to rest on the makeshift railing. My body hums at his deliberate touch. Yet, there's nothing personal in it. It's all in the name of work.

He steps back to look.

"Mademoiselle, if you please, tuck your skirt underneath you so we might see the legs of the chair. Mademoiselle Claus, would you be so kind as to help her fix her train so it flows nicely over the back?"

Fanny Claus does as she's asked, but to accomplish the task, I must stand so we can turn the chair back so it will not obstruct the line of the dress.

When I sit, Édouard studies me for a moment, brows knit. I wonder if he is displeased with what he sees, with both of us being dressed in white gowns?

He says nothing but, "This painting will take several days. Are you prepared to wear the same dresses for the duration?"

I nod. "Will they not get dirty, monsieur?"

He strokes his beard and turns to Maman and Madame Chevalier. "Mesdames, would it be possible for the mesdemoiselles to wear a different dress tomorrow and bring the white frocks with them? They can leave them here to change into each morning. Mademoiselle Morisot is right, if they wear them back and forth every day, I am afraid they will get soiled."

My eyes dart to the dressing screen, and my breath catches at the thought of undressing behind it. Then my gaze shifts to Maman to gauge her reaction.

Madame Chevalier looks to Madame Manet, who seems undaunted by the request. Maman stares at me with narrowed I-told-you-so eyes, as if the suggestion has flown from my lips.

"As long as you are comfortable with the idea, Madame Manet," says Maman. "I suppose I am, too."

Much to my surprise, Madame Chevalier agrees, and that is the end of the discussion. Fanny Claus and I will be dressing partners, for there was no possible way we can navigate the buttons that run the length of the back of our dresses.

"Angle your body to the right, but look slightly to the left."

I do exactly as he instructs.

"No, too much. Back to the center. Just a bit. Yes, there. Good. Good. Hold that."

He turns to his worktable and comes back with an armful of items, among them a red fan and a necklace. He hands me the fan, then walks around behind me and slides a slip of black velvet around my throat.

I only catch a glimpse, but I see the choker consists of a heart-shaped medallion strung on a piece of ribbon. I feel his hand working at my nape, and I wonder if the choker belongs to Suzanne or whether it is just a prop he keeps in the studio for just such an occasion.

After he finishes tying, he walks around to the front. "Hold the fan in your left hand and bring it up so it rests on your right arm.

"Yes, that is it. Perfect! Hold that pose while I arrange the others."

It takes him an instant to accomplish the task. He directs Fanny Claus to stand next to me, and places Monsieur Guillemet in the middle, slightly behind us.

With my face angled away, it is hard to see the props he has selected, but I get the idea from conversation.

"Mademoiselle Claus, let the umbrella fall across your body, anchoring it with your left arm. Bend your arms at the elbows, like so." He demonstrates. "And act as if you are putting on these gloves."

His instructions for Monsieur Guillemet are as simple as, "Stand between the two ladies, *s'il vous plaît,* with your arms like so."

Édouard bends both arms at the elbow, one slightly higher than the other, as if Guillemet is walking midstride.

I believe Manet is about ready to start, but he frowns and walks over to the worktable and rummages around for a while, then comes back with the homeliest hat I have ever seen—a close-fitting cap with a big, ugly dried pompon of a flower pinned to it.

For a split second I fear he will pull it onto my head as fast as he slipped on the necklace. Alas, it is Fanny Claus who wins the pleasure. I hear Édouard rustling around next to me, but I dare not turn my head to look and lose the perfect angle he has assigned me.

I smile to myself, as I can only imagine how ridiculous her long, expressionless face must look in that unfashionable hat.

Maman, Madame Chevalier, and Madame Manet sit in the background chatting. They do not prove to be a distraction to

Édouard during the morning's preliminary setup, but as the wears on, and he begins to put charcoal to canvas, he grows visibly tense, occasionally looking over his shoulder at them.

"Are you all right Mademoiselle Berthe?"

His question startles and embarrasses me out of my trance. Although I have been daydreaming, I know very well he has not asked after the others' well-being.

I adjust my pose, but try to sit straight. True, I am growing tired of holding the same position, but I won't complain. I knew what was expected of me before I agreed to the task.

"I am fine, *merci*."

Although, I suppose I forgot how exhausting it could be to sit in one position for hours. I heard Monsieur Guillemet fidgeting behind me.

"Antonin, please stop moving about. I am trying to capture your pose."

Guillemet groaned. "My friend, we have been here for hours, it seems. I believe I speak for everyone when I say we need a rest."

"Bear with me for a few more moments . . ."

Édouard's words trail off, and his "few more moments" stretch on like a river meandering without an end.

I gaze at the fan until my eyes water. My arm is falling asleep and I want so badly to shift, but I do not dare after Édouard reprimanded Monsieur Guillemet. Careful not to move, I glance at Maman and try to catch her eye. I want her to know I am concerned about her comfort after sitting for such a long time. Surely, her back hurts.

"Mademoiselle —" Édouard looks up. "Mademoiselle Berthe, I realize your kindness to pose for me is taking you away from your own work. I do appreciate it. Are you planning on entering anything in the Salon this year?"

"It is only July, Monsieur. Too early for me to decide."

"*Au contraire, Mademoiselle,* it is never too early to have a goal in mind."

I am embarrassed by his attentions. He had been so quiet until now. His sudden interest in my plans, our conversation in general, seems too conspicuous.

I am glad he has me angled away from Fanny Claus. That way I do not have to look at her, or what might be worse, I do not have to make an effort to not look at her.

"Perhaps it is a good thing I do not have a goal in mind. For if I did, I should not be so content to sit here and ponder it when time in the studio would be the only action that would help me reach that goal."

He nods. "Very well then. Here's to not having a Salon goal in mind so that I may freely monopolize your time."

He laughs at his own wit and I smile back. I could only guess what the other two are doing, as neither of them makes a sound.

It strikes me that aside from the overly loud talking, Madame Manet has not interrupted him even though it must be nearing lunchtime. I thought certain Édouard would suggest a break soon, but he seems lost in his sketching, tossing the occasional annoyed glance over his shoulder as the ladies laugh a little louder than they should or get carried away talking at the same time. They seem to be having a grand time. I am glad because Maman looks less like she is burdened by the obligation to be here for me and very much like she is enjoying the company of new friends.

"There, that should suffice for today." Édouard sets down his charcoal stick and steps back to view his work. "We shall reconvene tomorrow for a longer day."

I am not at all sure if I want to see how he interprets me. I cannot say why, other than we seldom view ourselves as others do. One's personal interpretation seems so intimate, although

I've never thought of it that way before. I am not quite sure I am prepared to know how he views me, silly as it seems. Eventually, I will know.

The others move about. The three elder ladies crowd around the easel.

Maman peers through her lorgnette and cocks her head to one side. From her pursed mouth and knit brow, I can tell she is not quite sure what to make of Édouard's morning work.

"Well, like all things, I guess this, too, will take time." She lowers her glasses and looks at Madame Manet. "Your son obviously knows what he is doing."

The words come out more like a question than a statement, but Madame Manet does not seem to take offense.

She simply smiles and nods. "Please eat lunch before you go. I brought plenty for everyone."

"Thank you, but we cannot stay," says Maman. "We must get home."

Although I am not aware of any particularly pressing matter, I am relieved that Maman does not want to stay.

Édouard is unpacking the basket and setting the feast on one of the less crowded worktables. "What is it that pulls you away?"

"My son, Tiburce, is arriving this afternoon." Maman looks at me and smiles. "And we are expecting a caller. A gentleman caller. Berthe will want time to get ready."

Chapter Seven

. . . I've dreamt in my life dreams that have stayed with me ever after, and changed my ideas: they've gone through and through me, like wine through water, and altered the color of my mind.

—Emily Brontë

OBSERVATION is a powerful tool. Generally if I trust this sense, it does not steer me wrong. Edma confirms as much the afternoon I return from Édouard's studio. She pulls me out for a walk and we take the carriage down to the Quai du Louvre. At first I believe she has taken me here because she senses the tension between Maman and me—she knows how this stretch of the river Seine calms me. Yet, once we walk down the incline from the street to the waterfront—out of earshot of the driver—she bubbles over with excitement.

"Léon is Suzanne's son," she says. "I have been dying to tell you this all day."

I blink. "No he's not. Léon is her brother. Madam Manet—"

Edma shakes her head. "Wait until you hear this—Fantin and his sister stopped by today while you and Maman were out. One conversation led to another and he happened to mention Léon's relationship to Suzanne. So that can only mean Manet is the father."

"Edma, it makes no sense. The boy is in his teens. Édouard married Suzanne only a few years ago. If he married her for the child, why would he wait so many years to do so?"

Edma shrugs. "Fantin said the wedding was a big surprise to everyone. Not even his closest friends knew of his relationship with her. One day he went away, the next he came back married. Even Fantin does not understand. So you see the only explanation can be that Léon is *their* son. He married her out of obligation, not because he loved her."

Suzanne and Édouard's son? It does not make sense, but Edma seemed to have it all figured out.

"That's quite scandalous, indeed, Edma. But, the fact remains that even if Léon is their son—which I do not believe—and even if Édouard married her a dozen years after the fact, they are married and even explaining away the marriage does not make Édouard more available to me."

In fact, the realization accomplishes nothing but casting me in a foul mood, and I think it best to change the subject. "The way Maman carried on this afternoon about *gentleman callers*, one would think there was going to be a wedding in *our* family's future."

Edma blushes a pretty shade of pink as we stroll along the quai. She does not comment, but her silence—and dreamy smile—give me pause.

"Is there something you would like to tell me?" I ask.

She shrugs. Noncommittal.

"Has Adolphe—"

"Oh, no no no. He has asked me nothing."

Yet, something in her smile suggests more, something she is not telling me. It has been days since we've had a chance to talk. I feel distant and disconnected from her. As we walk in silence, I also feel secure that she will tell me in due time if there is something more. She does not keep secrets as I do. Everything about Edma is forthright.

"Maman made believe the gentleman caller was for you?" she asked.

I nod.

"And you said nothing to the contrary?"

"Of course not. She is already furious with me. If I had corrected her in the company of others, our mother's anger would have opened heaven and earth. Do not look at me as if I took the coward's way out."

"But why? Why would she do that other than to thwart any *improper* intentions she fears might be fleeting through Édouard's mind?"

That familiar sensation of tight spirals swirl in my stomach—the same as when he'd teased me earlier about temptations and making time. "*Fleeting* would be the word of emphasis, Edma. If the man has ever entertained a single thought about me, I'm sure it was just in passing."

"You fancy him."

I laugh as a slow burn simmers on my neck. I open my fan and start fanning. "I suppose Adolphe shall ask Papa for your hand all too soon. Possibly early fall? Perhaps even late summer?"

"Do not change the subject, Berthe. We are not talking about Adolphe. We were speaking of Édouard. From the looks of him at dinner Thursday night, I am confident Monsieur Manet fancies you, too. Surely he has entertained *several* intentions where you are concerned. But it is much too early to label his intent completely improper."

My pulse races. I fan faster and take deep breaths to steady myself.

"See there?" She releases my arm.

I turn my head so she cannot see my expression and quicken my pace.

"Please do not hide your feelings from me." She touches my sleeve. "Me of all people, Berthe. I will not judge you, because if not for Adolphe, I, too, would be drawn to the irresistible Manet charm. Although it would be for naught because it is evident he has eyes for only one lady. And that lady is you."

I gasp—more out of relief than shock—and glance at my sister through the lace on my hat.

"Tell me your feelings. Tell me everything. I have never seen you this taken with a man."

I do not know what to say, much less what to make of the jumbled emotions knotted inside me. But Edma waits. I suppose she would wait all day for me to speak.

"I have never seen such an expressive face as his. . . . I think he has a decidedly charming temperament, which pleases me immensely."

We walk on in silence for a moment until I finally blurt, "I suppose if he were not married I would find him attractive. Alas, it is hopeless. Suzanne has claimed him and that is the end of that."

"When has unavailability ever precluded desire? Berthe, have you ever seen a more unsuitable pair in your entire life? No wonder the poor man vibrates with discontent and, I daresay, *longing* when he gazes at you."

I stop. Squeeze my eyes shut against the warmth spreading through my body. A slow thaw melts the icy wall covering my heart.

"It is hopeless, Edma. If this is how I am perceived in his

company, I am ruined. It could have negative repercussions for you, too."

"Do not worry about me. What is to be will be. For both of us."

How I envy my sister's confidence. I feel as if I am standing on a rooftop contemplating a leap. I can no more choose my feelings than I can choose to stay on the roof if a tile slips and sends me sailing.

"What do you plan to do about this?" she asked.

"It is not as if I have a choice in this matter."

"*Au contraire,* sister dear. You are in complete control. For that, I envy you."

Her words floor me. I stop and gape at her. "I do not know what you mean."

She laughs. "You know perfectly well what I am saying, and you of all people should not feign shock. False astonishment does not become you. You have said yourself it is not fair men are afforded all of the pleasures and women carry all the burden. If a married man may take a mistress, what is wrong with an unmarried lady taking a *monsieur*? Have you never thought of taking a lover?"

Her words transcend the clatter of the carriages rattling by. I glance around, hoping no one heard her. "Edma, do keep your voice down. You know perfectly well I cannot do as you have suggested."

"What? Why can you not take a lover? Will you not even say the word? *Lover.* Say it, Berthe."

"Shhhhh!"

I quicken my steps, but my sister keeps pace.

"Come now, Berthe. Do you never have *certain* . . . feelings?"

"Of course I have feelings, Edma. Do not be ridiculous."

"Berthe, I am speaking of feelings that can only be satisfied by a man's touch. You know what I am saying. . . . Your soul is much too passionate to pretend you feel nothing. It would be a crime for you to live not exploring those passions because you thought it improper. That, my dear, would not be living."

What she says holds so many preposterous grains of truth, but my dear sister could direct, from high upon her comfortable prematrimonial perch. She is in love and I am sure from her perspective, my taking a lover looks lovely and romantic and sinfully exciting.

I do not respond, but merely stare straight ahead hoping I am not as transparent as I feel. Knowing fully that by not responding I am giving away the answer that resides in my heart.

"Berthe, your strength is nothing to be ashamed of. I admire you for not giving up on your art to bend to convention—God knows it is not the easy path. If I were stronger, I might be so inclined to devote my future to art and—"

"And what? Lovers? Rather than taking a husband?"

She nods and we laugh.

I am at once happy and terrified and buoyant and hopelessly, hopefully overwhelmed by the new possibilities blossoming inside me. I have not felt so alive since—since the day I first laid eyes on Édouard.

Edma threads her arm through mine and gives me a little squeeze. We stroll along the Seine in silence.

A lover . . . *Hmmm.*

The sun shines on Paris—its wide boulevards and shiny new construction glint in the afternoon light as if she has shed her dingy gray cocoon and donned a brilliant new coat. Every place I look reveals something glittering and new. Yet I know very well nothing has changed since the last time I walked this bank.

It's the same cobblestone embankment, the same plane trees with their deep green leaves and peeling bark, the same Pont des Arts connecting the Right Bank to the Left.

Only this time, my eyes are fully open.

I tilt my head to take in the tall buildings rising over the water, standing watch over us. The breeze tickles my face and the river laps against the boats moored along the embankment, as if all things natural and manmade have joined together to welcome me to this beautiful new world. I cannot help but smile as I breathe in the sweet scent of Edma's perfume mingled with the acrid smell of the waterfront.

For the first time in ages, I breathe easily.

"Tomorrow is Maman's receiving day," Edma says. "I shall go with you to Édouard's to allow her to stay home. Perhaps that will quell her peevishness. With her absent, you might be able to relax. Would be a pity if he painted you like this."

Edma grimaces. We laugh.

"Would be a pity for Maman and you to be sparring with each other during Tiburce's homecoming," she adds. "If I go with you tomorrow, the two of you will be less likely to quarrel. Just leave it to me. I shall arrange everything for you."

At home, an anxious-looking Amélie meets us at the front door. "I have a most urgent message for you, Mademoiselle Berthe."

"What is it?" I ask.

"Pardon moi, Mademoiselle." She look over her shoulder as if to assure no one else is near. "But could we step outside into your studio? For privacy."

Edma shoots me an urgent look and the three of us walk across the garden to the studio.

"Come in," I say.

Amélie opens the door and quickly closes it behind her

once we were all inside. She reaches in her pocket and withdraws a small leather-bound book.

"You had a caller, Mademoiselle."

"Who?" Edma asks. "I am not expecting Adolphe for another hour. Tell me I did not miss him."

Amélie shakes her head. "Monsieur Manet left this for you."

My blood runs cold at the mention of his name and even colder when I see the book is the volume *Flowers of Evil* I had perused in his studio.

"Is he still here?" I ask, hopeful in spite of myself.

"He could not wait. He just handed me the book and asked me to be sure to give it to you. There is a note tucked inside the cover. He told me to alert you to the fact."

I open the book and see the crisp crème-colored linen paper sealed with red wax bearing the initial *M.*

"Does Maman know of his call?"

"No, Mademoiselle. Please forgive me for not informing Madame, but—"

"No apology necessary, Amélie. You made the right decision."

Relief spreads over the girl's face. She nods. "If there is nothing else, I shall return to my duties in the kitchen."

"*Merci*, Amélie."

I tear open the note and read it aloud.

"Dear Mademoiselle, you left in such haste you forgot the book. I took the liberty of delivering it to you. Keep it as long as you like. Yours faithfully, E. Manet."

"Why would he bring it to you if he is going to see you tomorrow at the studio?"

I can tell by the look on her face she is not asking a question, so much as proving a point. Still, I shrug.

Edma laughs. "Unless he was hoping to intrude on your

'gentleman caller.' Persistent. Obviously a man who knows what he wants. But his timing is bad."

She shakes her head and *tsk-tsk-tsks* as she walks over to the window. "Oh poor, poor Édouard. To be cursed with such a bad sense of timing. 'Tis the undoing of many a great lover."

Lover. The word upends my belly, causing my hand to fly to my stomach in self-defense.

"Edma, stop it. If Maman hears you she will have a fit."

My sister toys with an arrangement of yellow mums sitting on the window table. "You must admit persistence is a very attractive quality."

I cannot deny it, but it does not mean I must admit it. I have confessed enough today. Instead, I stare at his book in my hands.

"What is the book?"

When I do not answer, she crosses the room and plucks it from my hands. She gasps and her eyes fly wide. "It is banned, is it not? Where did he get it?"

She pages through it quickly, pausing now and again to read snatches of verse.

"How you would please me, night without your stars,
Which speak a foreign dialect, that jars
On one who seeks the void the black the bare . . .
A dream, a form, a creature, late,
Fallen from azure realms, and sped
Into some Styx of mud and lead
No eye from heaven can penetrate . . ."

"Oh Edma, who cares if it is banned? It is innocuous. Just a collection of poetry. I do not need some moralizing windbag saving me from myself by dictating what is right and what is wrong."

"You should give it back to him. Take it back tomorrow and tell him it does not interest you."

"I do not want to give it back."

Edma arches a brow.

"If you are worried about giving Maman reason to have a fit, this will surely set her off if she discovers it."

"Then she must not discover it. And she will not if no one makes her the wiser."

Edma's mouth falls open and she hands me the book.

"I would never tell her. Do you accuse me of not being able to keep a secret?"

"Of course, I do not doubt you, Edma." She alone is the one constant in this world of shifting light and shadows in which I find myself captive.

Yes, Edma I can trust. Myself, now that is another question.

I listen at the drawing room door as Edma approaches Maman about accompanying me to Édouard's the next morning.

"It will free you to stay home with Tiburce and greet your guests."

As I suspected, Maman is none too pleased. "I should think you would care to stay home and spend time with your brother, too."

"Who will accompany Berthe?"

"Berthe is twenty-seven years old. She is not a child anymore. Since she seems to think she knows what she is doing, I resign myself to this situation. Let her go alone for all I care."

"Maman, surely you do not mean it."

No, she doesn't. What she actually means is I should be the one to stay at home, too.

"Edma, I am at my wits end and I do not know what else to do with her. I have spoken to your father about your sister's headstrong ways. He feels I should just let her be. She seems to value her painting above all else. It is to the point where I have started to question her mental faculties, but your father will not hear of it. If you are so inclined to accompany your sister, so be it."

With that, Maman washes her hands of the situation and redoubles her wall of stony silence toward me, grumbling to Edma about the hardship our absence will cause, since she will only have Amélie to rely on for service when her friends call. We usually serve the tea and cakes while she entertains, but she is relatively safe in her friends discovering exactly where Edma and I have gotten off to because her friends are from different circles than the *avant-garde* who populate Manet's circles.

Maman seems to like Madame Manet, *mère,* well enough. Her sanctions against the sitting are purely for my punishment. Because yesterday Maman knew when she bid everyone *adieu* that she would not see them tomorrow. She has certainly done this purposely to force me to choose.

Maman or art.

I will not be tested.

Later, as Edma dresses in preparation for Adolphe's visit, I sit in the chair in our room captivated by Édouard's book. It is the epitome of modernity. I read, spellbound, a poem entitled, *Le Balcon:*

Mother of Memories, mistress of my dreams,
To whom I am in love and duty bound,
You will recall, as red the firelight gleams,
What fond embraces, what content we found,
Mother of memories, mistress of my dreams . . .

I sat up straight in my chair not believing what I had just read. A poem called *The Balcony* in a book hand delivered by a man who was painting my portrait in a work of the same name.

"Mother of Memories, mistress of my dreams . . ."

"Should I take Madame Manet to visit Maman tomorrow during her receiving time?" Edma holds up a pretty deep-blue gown, then one of white silk adorned with tiny pink flowers.

"Don't be ridiculous," I say, glancing up from the page. "Maman will never forgive you if you leave me unattended."

"I suppose you are right. She may say she no longer cares, but she does."

She had settled on the blue dress and starts to change. "What shall I do the whole day? I will go mad if must I sit there talking to the chaperones. I'm sure I have nothing in common with them."

"Sitting is what a chaperone does. And that is what you have agreed to do. *N'est-ce pas?*"

She gives me a brooding look.

"May I at least read the book he loaned you?"

I snap it shut and cover the slim volume with my hands as it lay in my lap.

"Do you really want to sit with Madame Manet and company and read *Les Fleurs du Mal*? I am sure Édouard has other books you may borrow." My grip tightens on the book. "But not this one, Edma."

Chapter Eight

Compare with me, ye women, if you can
I prize thy love more than whole mines of gold
Or all the riches that the East doth hold.
My love is such that rivers cannot quench,
Nor ought bet love from thee, give recompense.
—Anne Bradstreet

THE next morning, I awake feeling as if my youth has been restored. My refreshment is not merely the benefit of a good night's rest, but culled from a deeper source. Something vital has awakened inside me—a newfound awareness roused after living unconsciously for far too long.

I am full of clarity and new life and feel as if I could conquer the world. Or at least the indecision that has plagued my world since meeting Édouard Manet one week ago.

Still in her dressing gown after I have been ready for more than a half hour, Edma is maddeningly slow. I am fully set on going alone if she does not hurry. With white dress in hand, I double the skirt over my arm so it will not drag the floor and tuck Édouard's book into the folds.

"Come, we must leave now. What is taking you so long?"

"Berthe, it is not even half past eight. We do not have to be there until ten o'clock. What is your hurry?"

"I want to arrive before the others."

I stand in the foyer for another ten minutes before my sister finally graces me with her presence. She looks fresh, if not a little harried as I help her with her bonnet. We call good-bye to Maman and are on the steps when our mother appears at the door.

"It is only half past eight, why on earth are you leaving so early?"

"We wanted to get an early start so Monsieur Manet can set to work faster," I say.

"You have not had breakfast."

"No we have not," Edma grumbles.

In fear that Maman will detain us—or worse yet find some reason to keep us from going—I grab my sister by the elbow and start walking. "No sense in troubling Amélie. She has enough work this morning preparing for your guests today. Manet will give us tea or coffee when we arrive."

By the time I finish, we are outside the gate. I can no longer see Maman. I do not let go of Edma's arm until we were safely settled inside the carriage.

Once we are on our way, the cool morning air calms me, and I set my white dress, with the book tucked securely inside, beside me, settled back and relax a bit.

Edma's mood seems to have not suffered from my pushing her to hurry. "I daresay, Maman must not be too concerned about us going," she says. "If not, do you think she would have been so agreeable?"

Agreeable? Hardly. Yet, I guess she was more agreeable this morning than she was yesterday when she scarcely said three words to me. But I could tell she was still none too pleased with me. "The source of her good mood, no doubt, was Adolphe paying you a call."

Again.

Edma blushes a pretty shade of pink at the mention of her beloved's name and chatters on about him as the carriage rolls us closer to Édouard. I am happy to let my sister carry on about Adolphe's gestures and expressions, his small tokens of affection, how he talks in future tense when he speaks of life and the exciting possibilities that await them.

She leans in and lowers her voice. "Yesterday, you asked if I was anticipating a proposal. Don't be surprised if he asks Papa for my hand before fall sets in."

I knew it was coming, yet I couldn't fully bring myself to face the possibility of Edma leaving.

It is unspeakably selfish to wish my sister to stay with me—two old maids happily painting side by side in our studio. Alas, knowing she would move off with Adolphe wherever his career might beckon them—he was a military man, after all—knowing I will no longer have the privilege to see her every day makes me want to weep.

I swallow the pang.

What would I do without Edma? We have never been apart. We were happy for our elder sister, Yves, when she married. It suited her. She does not paint and worked toward matrimony as determinedly as Edma and I work at perfecting a painting for the Salon.

When Yves left, marriage was a dim light on the horizon for Edma and me. Now it glared as menacingly as a comet aligned to hit the earth. She is not only my sister, but my best friend. The thought of living without her is almost unbearable.

Her eyes shine. "Tell me, what you think of him, Berthe? Would you find him a suitable brother-in-law?"

Tears sting my eyes, and I look out the window until I am sure I have them under control.

She sounds so happy.

"Edma, anyone who makes you happy, makes me happy."

She smiles, serene and confident, a woman content in love's glow. We ride along in silence until she finally asks, "Have you thought anymore about what we talked about yesterday?"

Her question makes me flinch. I shake my head hoping not to seem startled.

"Are you nervous?"

"Nervous? Why on earth would I be nervous?"

Edma shrugs. "I just supposed . . . Well, I just thought—"

I hold a finger to my lips. "Edma, be practical. You are caught up in the thrill of love, but Adolphe is a single man Édouard is not. Do not encourage me to long for that which I cannot have."

I slide my hand between the dress's silk layers to the book. Its solid form reassures me.

Edma smiles, but her eyes hold a sweet sadness—as if she grieves for all the unrequited lovers haunting mankind. For a quick moment, I hope I am not seeing my own emotions mirrored in her eyes. I look away and sit back with the echo of my words ringing to the rhythm of the horse's hooves on the cobblestone streets. Suddenly, I do not feel quite as sure of myself as I did when I awoke.

"This painting of Édouard's—who else is posing with you?"

I tell her of the stoic Fanny Claus and how she is a friend of Suzanne's, and of tall, funny Monsieur Guillemet, and how the idea for the painting swept Édouard off his feet.

It seems that the idea does not only intrigue Édouard, Degas is at Édouard's studio when we arrive. I am none too happy to see him, as I hoped to have a few moments alone with Édouard before the others arrived to discuss the book.

You can't bring it up in front of the others, says Propriety.

But why care what the others think? urges Olympia. *Just talk to him about it.*

Impossible, says Propriety. *Not in front of the others.*

Édouard greets us warmly.

"Bonjour, Mesdemoiselles," says Degas. "I have come to see what all the fuss is about. To judge for myself if all the commotion Manet has created over his new masterpiece is worthy of the ruckus."

"Ruckus?" I smile at Édouard. "What is he talking about?"

Degas smirks and studies me—a lazy, appraisal raked from my face, down to the hem of my skirt.

"May I take the dress from you?" asks Édouard.

I tightened my grip on the book hidden beneath the fabric. "Just tell me where to put it."

Édouard motions for me to follow. Heels clicking on the marred wooden floor, I follow him behind the dressing screen.

"You may leave it here." He stands just inside the panel, his body blocking the opening, standing much too close to me.

I pull the book from the folds of the dress.

He smiles. "Did you have a chance to read it?"

I nod. Nerves make my arm twitch and my elbow knocks into the screen. It sways, but does not fall—*merci Dieu.* It reminds me that although we are tucked away out of sight, Edma and Degas can most assuredly hear every word we exchange.

I press the book into his hand, glancing up at him a moment before I drape my dress over the top of the screen.

My mind skitters back to yesterday, to his playful teasing, and my blood rushes with temptation that beckons me to lean into him again. The silence in the outer room is so obvious it roars.

Now, do you understand why it is frowned upon for ladies to go out without a chaperone? quips Propriety. *Especially in the company of a handsome man who has a habit of invading one's personal space.*

He smiles at me, tenderly—as if he knows Baudelaire has

said everything we might say to one another—a look that pierces my defenses. He slips the book into his pocket and rejoins the others.

I linger behind the screen and close my eyes to the sound of his voice talking to Edma and Degas. I do not hear what they are saying, so much as the melody of their voices floating up and out on the air as I gather myself.

When I walk out from behind my cover, Edma is saying, "On the way over this morning, Berthe told me about the painting. That it is modeled after Goya's *Balcony*?"

Édouard tells about coming upon the scene on his walk.

"It was beautiful." He looks at me and I wonder if no one else feels the energy bounding between us.

"It was an omen," he continued. "I was immediately overcome by the sensation that I must re-create it. That I must make it my own."

Degas' laugh—a dry, brittle *hrumph*—startles me. Arched brows frame the flat planes of his face, which stretch down to a diminutive bowed mouth set in a permanent scowl. His small round eyes dart here and there, questioning and watchful, seeing everything.

"Show us the canvas, Manet," says Degas, his voice colored shades of gray.

"Oh, yes, may we see it?" Edma urges.

Édouard strokes his beard. "I can hardly say it is suitable for viewing. I have only invested a half day's work in it. I still have a long road ahead."

Degas does not relent. Finally, Édouard drags out the easel. He angles the canvas so we can view the bare-bones sketch of yesterday's scene.

I am surprised and very pleased to see my form is the most detailed of the three.

Degas draws closer, stroking his clean-shaven chin, making

interested noises such as, *"Hmmmmm,"* and *"Umm-hmmm."* I thought his brows could not possibly arc any higher, but they do, like tiny umbrellas opening over his small eyes.

"*Oui,* Manet. *Très bien.* I am sure you plan to work very hard on this one." He looks at me. "For she will surely prove a challenge. But that is what you live for, is it not?"

His insinuation makes me bite my bottom lip. We all ignore him as we would a naughty child who has spoken out of turn. If we do not acknowledge his gauche behavior, perhaps he will stop.

But he does not.

"Manet is a master, no doubt," he says to me. "Do not let him monopolize your time. He will if you give him the opportunity."

I glance at Édouard, who is frowning and staring at the canvas. "I have no idea what he is babbling on about. He is a cynic and a pessimist. Pay him no mind."

"Ah, true, my friend. I may be guilty of all charges, but you are married. I do not know which of us bears the greater burden."

With his finger, Édouard smudges a line on the canvas. Then picks up a piece of charcoal and begins to draw.

"Thanks to you, my dear friend, the rest of us have no burdens, since you do us all the favor of carrying the weight of the world on your shoulders." Édouard steps back to assess his work. "Although I have often wondered if mankind might not be better off if you were to relieve yourself of your worries, if even for a day, and enjoy the company of a good woman. We would certainly find you more agreeable."

Degas snorts. "I have no time for fools of either sex. From what I gather, Mademoiselle Berthe, you are much like myself, a purist at heart. Take my word for it and watch yourself around this flatterer."

Édouard laughs as if Degas has made a joke. He turns the canvas to the wall.

"*Ah,* but Monsieur Degas, I am not so naive to fall prey to *petite flatterie,*" I say. "In fact, I was wondering whether Madame Édouard Manet would honor us with her presence today. I should love to get to know her better."

It is a lie, and I am sure Édouard knows it, but I do not care. I have no burning desire to know Suzanne, today or ever. But I must put Degas, that disagreeable little man, in his place. He has a lot of audacity insulting Édouard in his own studio and suggesting that I might be so weak that I cannot take care of myself.

Degas looks down his pointed little nose. "Will we see your lovely wife?"

Édouard has busied himself readying his supplies. "I do not know, Degas. Please feel free to call on her in Boulogne and inquire after her schedule if you wish."

Days turn into weeks. Weeks push close to a month and the sittings stretch on. Maman has grown tired of spending her days sitting in Édouard's studio. After the first week, Madame Manet made excuses as to why she was otherwise detained. Edma, too, had other things to do. After strict discussion with Madame Manet and Madame Chevalier, Maman decides it is perfectly fine for me to go to the sittings alone, with the understanding that Madame Chevalier will be present.

After all, Fanny Claus and her chaperone will be ample supervision for a woman of my age. She does not say it that way, but the meaning is implied.

As is the meaning behind the sighs and cross demeanors of Fanny Claus and Monsieur Guillemet. Their restlessness grows more acute as each day drags on. The vague hints of displeasure blossom into bitter protests about the amount of time Édouard is taking. But their complaints seem to roll off him as a carriage wheel spins over cobblestones.

I do not mind. Time with him in his studio is time well spent. Édouard and I talk and laugh and discover so much about each other.

We discuss Baudelaire—depravity and vice or the poet of modern civilization? He entertains me with stories of the times Baudelaire came to the Thursday night soirées.

"Ma *mère* did not know what to think of him at first," he says. "Later she longed for his company."

"How I wish I could have met him."

Édouard tilts his head to the right and peers at me around the canvas. His gray eyes smoldered. "He would have been captivated by you."

He is charming and absolutely proper—not a hint of impropriety, much to my dismay. After all this talk of Baudelaire and indecency, I long for just a hint of something more, but *non*, he is the perfect gentleman.

How utterly frustrating. Still, I would not mind if the sessions stretched on indefinitely. The minutes that stand between us when we are not together weigh heavy and endless. The days with him are far too short.

Madame Manet had taken a temporary respite from the Thursday soirées, since she, Suzanne, and Léon are still in Boulogne. It is probably for the best. I wonder at Édouard's separation from her. I suppose an artist's wife gets used to the models and the long hours her husband spends away. Suzanne has her spy. We are under the watchful eye of little Fanny Claus, who I'm sure provides Suzanne with detailed reports.

Finally about forty days into the painting, while we are taking a short rest to stretch our limbs, Fanny Claus walks over to the canvas, as bold as you please, and looks. Édouard has turned it toward the wall and I watch her scoot the easel back as if he had invited her to do so.

Her face falls. "I am finished, Monsieur Manet."

She yanks off her gloves and tosses them aside. "It is plain to see you have eyes for only one subject in this painting. You will do fine without me."

Édouard had been making a pot of tea. He stops and gapes at her.

"Mademoiselle Claus, I am sorry if I have offended you. But I must confess, I do not understand why you are angry. Each of you is important to this composition. Perhaps I have detained you too long. For that I apologize. If you feel you must go, by all means, please go."

She leaves.

But later, when I take a good look at the painting, Fanny Claus's words ring true. The exquisite detail in which he has painted my image makes the vague sketches of the others look even plainer, as if they are merely marking space on the canvas.

Surely he will go back and paint them in more detail later. Looking at us for the past month, surely he has had enough time to commit our features to memory. But if the truth be known, I am secretly gratified to see the painstaking detail he has spent on me.

To think there was once a time when we were strangers; when Édouard Manet was just a name on a magnificent painting. Now I come to his studio as a friend. We discuss art and God and politics and the world in which we live. He considers my opinions and does not think less of my strong convictions.

Why did we not meet before he married Suzanne?

Chapter Nine

In studious awe the poets brood
before my monumental pose
aped from the proudest pedestal,
and to bind these docile lovers fast
I freeze the world in a perfect mirror:
The timeless light of my wide eyes.
—Baudelaire, "Beauty"

I ARRIVE at his studio the next morning, alone, as I have for the past two weeks, but a little later than usual. I am the first to arrive.

"I feared you had deserted me, too." Édouard looks anxious standing in the midst of his studio, but does not seem the least bit bothered by the fact that we are *alone* without the benefit of a chaperone.

I set down my handbag, unnerved and exhilarated by this realization. Fanny Claus was cross yesterday, but I did not think she would leave so abruptly.

"Of course I would not desert you." My words sound far more certain than I feel. "Aren't the others coming today? Did I not get a message that you canceled the session?"

"They are finished." He shakes his head. "I still have much work to accomplish before I will deem this painting complete. Alas, I suppose I have imposed on everyone long enough. You may leave, too, if you choose."

His words release me, but his eyes ask me to stay.

I know I should go, because if we are discovered alone together, it could be disastrous, even in its innocence.

I know this, but still I hear myself saying, "I did not come all this way to simply turn around and go home."

We stand shyly for an awkward moment, and I fear I might come apart for how clumsy I feel.

Then he smiles. "I was hoping you would say that. Here, come and sit for a moment." He pats the arm of the divan. "Let us have some tea before we get to work."

He moves to the kitchen to start the water as he has done every morning since he began this painting. I perch on the edge of the sofa and glance around the studio, seeing it with new eyes—the dressing screen with my lone white dress draped over the top just as I had left it. Fanny Claus's gown is gone.

Today, I am on my own.

My gaze trails from the easel pushed into one corner to the rumpled covers on the unmade bed on the opposite side of the room.

"Did you sleep here last night?"

"I did. I worked on the painting well into the evening and it made no sense to go home to an empty house, with Suzanne, Léon, and Maman still in Boulogne."

It pains me to hear *her* name pass his lips. But something dangerous bubbles at the thought of her being so far away—that they have been apart for so long. The sensible Berthe warns, *Watch yourself. You should leave if you want what's best.*

I can scarcely hear the caveat over the memory of his whispered promise that first day in the studio—vows of temptations more sinful and pleasurable than rich chocolate. What, in addition to tea, did he have in mind today?

More important, am I ready to discover the answer?

I stand with a start. "I suppose I shall change." Cringing at the tiny squeak that masquerades as my voice, I retreat behind the dressing screen.

I close my eyes, take a deep breath and force myself to consider the consequences of staying with him today. I need only bid him *adieu* and walk out the door.

I have imagined being alone with Édouard, even longed for it in my most private fantasies, but never, no, no, *never* have I dreamed I would arrive at this situation.

Emotion and longing merge and crest like a wave propelled by wind. A strange funnel swirls in my belly and my eyes fly open. I have no more control over these feelings than I have over the sea flowing onto the shore.

I reach back with both hands and began unfastening the tiny buttons on my dress. As I worked the first one free, Édouard rattles the teakettle. With the next, he draws the water. With the third, he sets the kettle to the fire.

Button by tiny button, I work myself free, hitching up the fabric to conquer the hard-to-reach places, until the dress falls to the floor.

Édouard coughs and drags the easel to the middle of the room. I hug myself, closing my eyes and running my hands down my bare arms to quell a shiver.

Oh, how scandalously free I feel standing here like this. Terrified and liberated, undressed and alone with this man. I touch the partition's cloth. The shield that hides my nakedness from Édouard's eyes wavers beneath my trembling hand. And the knot in the pit of my stomach slowly unfurls.

I lift the white dress off the rail. Édouard seems to stop moving. The room is suspended in a reverent silence as I bury my face in the silky white. It has picked up the scent of Édouard's studio. I breathe in the aphrodisiac for a moment before slipping it over my head.

The organdy flounces fall over my body like a lover's hands urging me out from behind the screen.

"Would you help me with the buttons, please?"

Édouard sets down his palette and wipes his hands on a rag. He does not say a word, but watches me as he tidies himself, as if he knows precisely what I am asking of him.

As he moves toward me, I feel it—an almost indiscernible click as the magnet of him pulls at the pin of my heart and everything snaps into place.

I grip the edge of the partition, but he places his hands on my shoulders and turns me so he can get to the buttons.

He brushes aside a wisp of my hair that has fallen from its place. His fingers trail across the nape of my neck. I inhale quickly, a short, sudden little gasp, and a shiver shadows the trail of his fingers. My head tilts in the direction of his hand, and my sleeve slips from one shoulder.

For the span of a breath he does not touch me, and I do not move. I let the fabric stay as it has fallen, exposing the top curve of my breast that lay like an overripe fruit, atop the edge of my stiff corset.

His hands settle on my shoulders light as a whisper. One hand perfectly still, the thumb of his other traces the exposed skin—a soft, barely-there caress that gives me permission to pull away . . . or not . . .

I lower my cheek and dust his hand with the murmur of a kiss. He strokes my jawline, my cheek, my bottom lip—gently tracing it with the pad of his thumb.

His other hand, just inside the back of my dress, traces the vee of bare skin to my waist, then around to my belly. His hand splays the expanse of my stomach, to the underside of my breasts, and he pulls me firmly against him.

His body responds.

He slides a finger down my collarbone to the fleshy fullness at the top of my breast and presses his lips to my neck. My breath quickens to short, silent gasps. As I arch back, his finger brushes my nipple. I nearly cry out.

He turns me to face him, weaving his hands in my hair, exploring the hollow of my neck, trailing his tongue over my earlobe. I fear I will explode from desire, but he lowers his mouth to mine—I start at the feel of his beard, surprisingly coarse against my sensitive lips, a sharp contrast to the smooth wetness of his lips and tongue.

Fully, deeply, ardently, he kisses me, moans a deep, throaty sound of satisfaction that is unexpectedly animal, and I melt deeper into his kiss allowing myself to sink into his body. I savor his taste—coffee and a hint of peppermint—the hard feel of him and how safe I feel in his arms as the rest of the world melts away.

How I had longed for this kiss.

How many nights had I dreamed of being in his arms? Feeling his body pressed to mine, yearning for the lingering seconds he would look into my eyes just before his lips touched mine for the first time.

He pushes down my other sleeve and steps back allowing just enough space between us, so the dress slides down my body and pools at my feet like a white cloud.

He eases me down onto the dress, behind the screen. His mouth never leaves mine as he explores delicate places never before touched by a man.

I think I hear a woman's voice in the far reaches of my consciousness.

He tears away from me, and gets to his feet in what seems like a single, fluid motion.

"*Bonjour,* Édouard! Are you here?" Suzanne calls out mere seconds before her footfalls announce her presence inside the studio.

Chapter Ten

What's the earth
With all its art, verse, music worth
Compared with love, found, gained and kept?
—Robert Browning

I STAND trembling behind the screen afraid to move, afraid to breathe. All I can think is how symbolic this is of my life—wanting that which I cannot have. Craving that which is forbidden me. Yet I ignore common sense in search of the illusive to fill the void that seems to grow larger every day.

I am ashamed to think I believed I might find it in a married man.

On the other side of the screen, Édouard mutters something about taking a walk. "Perfect timing that you should arrive now. I was preparing to go out. Won't you join me?"

I hope his face does not reflect the tightness in his voice, and I wonder if Suzanne is suspicious.

"Édouard, I have only just arrived. Might we sit awhile so that I might rest from my journey?"

"Haven't you been sitting since you left Boulogne? I would think more sitting should only tire you further."

The dress I wore here is hanging over the screen. If I attempt to pull it down, she would surely see it. That won't work.

The hem of my white dress is sticking out beyond the confines of the acceptably patrician. Do I dare pull it back and attempt to dress, or do I stand here in my underwear banking on the possibility that Édouard will be able to get her out and away from the building so that I might make my escape.

There is only one exit. Right now, Édouard's wife stands squarely between me and my freedom. My heart pounds so furiously that it is almost uncomfortable.

"Aren't you expecting Mademoiselle Claus and the others? I should quite like to see her. That's one of the reasons I came today."

"In that case your timing is quite bad. Yesterday, your friend, Mademoiselle Claus quit the painting. Leaving me quite in a lurch. Without her, there was no need to detain the others. So I am left to my own devices."

Quite convincing.

I wonder for a moment if Fanny Claus might have told Suzanne that she and her chaperone would no longer be in attendance. Did Suzanne think it in her best interest to appear in person to check on matters? But the logistics are nearly impossible. It is highly unlikely that Fanny Claus would have had time to send a note to Boulogne in time for Suzanne to receive it and travel.

No, it was merely coincidence. Or perhaps something even more unsettling—a wife's intuition.

All I can do is wait and hope that intuition does not alert her to question the blue gown thrown haphazardly over the screen or hang up the white dress that has *fallen* to the floor.

* * *

"Amélie promised I would find you here."

"Édouard—" His voice seems to echo in the Louvre gallery. It sends a jolt up my spine that makes me sit straighter. I flinch, ashamed at having uttered his given name. Too familiar. I am losing myself again.

Edma peeks out from behind her easel and smiles. "Monsieur Manet. What a pleasant surprise."

"*Bonjour Mademoiselle,* I did not realize it was you hiding behind the canvas. How lovely to see you." A pregnant pause. "Both of you."

The musée feels tremendously vast and cold despite being crowded for a Thursday. In addition to Edma and me, one other painter copies the Rubens. In the short time he has been here, a handful of onlookers have strolled by pausing to scrutinize our work. Looking from our easels to the masterpieces on the walls, they utter inane comments as if we are deaf or too dumb to comprehend their criticism.

It will be hard to speak to him after yesterday, but I desperately need to talk to him. He knew, and he found me, sought me out, rather than leave me in fits and knots over the outcome of Suzanne's surprise visit.

Edma is watching us. Her eyes dart from Édouard to me. I have not told her of yesterday's events. I have not told her because it will not happen again. I am ashamed. Ashamed at having narrowly escaped and at the perverse thrill I get now thinking about his hands on me.

It is wrong.

I shall not put myself in that position again. I thought Suzanne would never agree to go with him, but finally after a bit of persistence she did.

Édouard is quite a persistent man.

"What brings you to the Louvre today, monsieur?" she asks. "Business or pleasure?" She giggles. I cringe. It's so out of character for her to act like a silly, smitten girl.

I grip my paintbrush so hard my knuckles go white.

"My business is personal in nature actually."

He speaks to her, but his gaze is fixed on me.

Edma sets down her pallet. "I see. In that case, I shall get back to work and leave you to your personal business." She stands. "In fact, I find I need a closer look at the folds in Marie de'Medici's dress for this study. If you will excuse me."

"Certainly." He sounds as relieved as I am at having the chance to talk alone.

Behind Édouard's back Edma makes a face at me, then covers her eyes with her hands before wandering over to a painting hung on the far wall, different from the one from which we are working.

"I had to see you," Édouard says. "Are you all right?"

I shrug still unable to process the myriad of emotions coursing through me. I am at war with myself: *You are so foolish for longing for him as he stands right in front of you,"* says Propriety. *Even after you spent the past hours fretting, feeling dirty and used, over nearly being found out.*

Yes, but underneath it all, says Olympia, *despite everything that has happened, you hoped he would come today. And he did.*

That alone eases my melancholy as a piece of bread can save a starving man from dying of hunger.

I glance at Maman, sitting on a bench across the gallery. She has dozed off reading her book.

Yesterday morning after fleeing Édouard's studio, I apologized to her. I walked in, found her, and said, "This standoff has gone on far too long. I have behaved foolishly. I want things to be as they always have been."

She forgave me.

But only after I told her my days of sitting for Édouard Manet were over.

She agreed this war between us had gotten out of hand and seemed relieved to call a truce. She said she holds no grudge against Édouard. She was angry with me over my choices. The way I have chosen to live my life.

I shudder to think what damage our relationship would suffer if she only knew the choices I had really made.

"It will never happen again." I murmur the words, a little cooler than my initial reception of him, and resume painting—same Rubens I was working on that day I first met him.

Sure, taunts Olympia. *You will not let him walk away. You desire him too much.*

But Propriety scolds, *After foolishly giving yourself over to him for his balcony painting, you have sorely neglected your own work. If you are to be a painter, you must paint. If you long to give into the temptation to flirt, you should choose a more appropriate man.*

You have renewed your focus on painting. Sadly, as it stands, you will not have work ready in time to enter the Salon. Perhaps next time you will not behave so stupidly, squandering my time.

"Berthe . . ." He steps closer, holding his hat. "You fled in such haste yesterday. I wish you had stayed. I came right back after Suzanne left."

My hands shake as I paint. "Stay? Do you know how close we came to being discovered? How could I have behaved so foolishly?"

When I finally fled, I was so unnerved I did not even button my gown. I simply wrapped my cloak around me and fled, as fast as I could. When I got home, I went straight up to my room, removed the dress, and put on my nightclothes, telling Maman and Edma I was not well.

The terrible part is that despite near disaster, the feel of his kiss is still fresh on my lips. Yesterday as I ran away and today as I cannot. They tingle with desire even as he stands here, and I tell him, "It will never happen again."

I lay down my brush, but do not look at him. If I do and see longing in his eyes, I will crumble and that would be catastrophic. Hiding and running; fearing discovery. His studio is an open door. Anyone can walk in. If there were not something inherently wrong with me, that he is married should have been enough to have stopped me. We should never have arrived at the problem of being forced to hide our passion and hope against all hope that we would not be discovered.

"It was not right for me to stay with you alone in your studio. I should have left when I discovered Mademoiselle Claus was not coming back." I press my hands to my face and see Edma trying to act like she is not watching us. She looks away when she sees me. "Your wife must have known."

"She does not know. And will never know what happened between us."

I remember his hands on my body, his lips on my neck, and I shudder. "It should have never happened, and I would thank you to take your leave, Monsieur."

My voice, a hissing whisper, trembles, and I pick up my brush again.

He glances at Maman, still sleeping, and I know he is concerned about waking her. I'm concerned, too. It's bad enough my sister is seeing this exchange. *Merci Dieu* no one else is close enough to hear.

"Berthe, please. I must see you again."

"To finish what you started?"

"It is not like that."

"Then how is it, Monsieur Manet?"

Footsteps sound from the gallery entrance behind us. I glance back to see Degas approaching.

We fall silent.

Wonderful. Just wonderful. The last person I want to see right now.

"Manet? It is you. I am not surprised. Every time I see you now, you and Mademoiselle Morisot are together. *Hmmmmmph.* Is this your work, Mademoiselle?"

"Yes it is." The words were a warning, daring him to give me an opinion. I am in no mood to abide his biting sarcasm.

Degas steps closer to the canvas, bends down to look. For the first time since making his acquaintance, a new expression passes over his jaded face. I cannot label the look exactly, but his features soften as he gazes at my painting.

"*Bon. Très bon.* This is excellent. Better than most men. Manet mentioned you have talent, but I had no idea."

"See?" says Édouard. "Didn't I tell you?"

I scowl, feeling as if I have been set up. Manet would have Degas come along and flatter me to soften my continence in case I was in a bad mood after yesterday. I feel quite sickened at the possibility that he has told Monsieur Degas about yesterday's rendezvous and near mishap.

"Did Monsieur Manet ask you to meet him here today?" I ask.

Degas' sardonic glare eclipses his former look of near respect. "I beg your pardon, Mademoiselle?"

I glance at Édouard, who is stroking his beard.

"Did he ask you to . . .?"

Degas is no longer looking at me, but at my canvas.

"If you are asking if I told him of your remarkable ability to paint, the answer is yes," says Édouard. "But no, Mademoiselle, I did not, as you imply, bribe him to come here today to remark as such. He is simply calling talent as he sees it and admiring it, as he should."

Maman lets out a snore that echoes in the gallery. She stirs, but does not awaken.

"Do you show in the Salon?" Degas asks.

"I have in the past. This year I will not have time to get anything ready." I purposely do not look at Édouard, because the statement makes me think of all the time I have recently spent in his studio. And how it ended with me standing before him with my dress down, my defenses low, and his hands holding my body against his.

"Well, it is too bad for them, but it is not a tragedy for you. The Academy rules the establishment with too lofty a hand. The art world needs something more than the Salon. We need an outlet that does not bind us to play by their rules."

"What else is there besides the Salon?" Manet asks.

Degas rubs his chin contemplatively. "That is what some used to say about studying outside of l'École. But you, Manet, can attest to the fact that some very fine artists have come from outside the hallowed halls of l'École des Beaux-Arts."

Manet nods.

"The same will soon be said about the Salon."

Manet chuckles. "What? Do you think you can change the face of art in Paris?"

Degas looks as if he will spit. "Not the face of art, just the manner in which it is viewed. Mademoiselle, Manet, would you be interested in discussing this at greater length?"

Manet shakes his head. "I get into enough trouble with the Academy without organizing against the system."

"You, Manet, are a coward. Mademoiselle, are you interested?"

"I would love to hear more."

If Degas knew how to smile, I suppose he would do so now. Instead, he lifts those umbrella brows and nods.

"I shall organize a luncheon at my home and send word. Until then, *bonjour.*"

He walks away, leaving us alone.

"Will you go?" Édouard asks. "If you do, I, too, shall attend."

"Monsieur Manet, *s'il vous plaît.*" I stand up. "You do not understand. We cannot do this. I cannot—"

"*Non,* Berthe, *s'il vous plaît.* It is you who do not understand. What happened between us yesterday was not something I smirk at. Nor do I think less of you because of it. I think you are an incredibly talented artist who also happens to be an incredibly beautiful woman. Even if we cannot enjoy a relationship of pleasure, I certainly hope we can share a friendship of equals. That is, if you are able to do so. If not, if you think less of me after what happened yesterday, then I beg you to consider how you would label me if the tables were turned. It is only fair. You are welcome at my home and my studio anytime. *Bonjour, mademoiselle.*"

Three days later, Maman and I attend Degas' luncheon. Édouard and I stand face-to-face once again. I did not think he would come. But here he is, and I am happy.

As promised, Degas has rallied his friends, who meet regularly at the Café Guerbois to discuss such matters, but they moved the meeting to his home so I could join them as it would not be proper for a lady to waltz into a café. I had quite a time convincing Maman that luncheon with six gentlemen was appropriate.

I don't understand what they might discuss at the Guerbois that would so offend my feminine sensibilities that we will not discuss here today. Someday I might have a mind to walk into a café just for the sake of doing so.

Or maybe not. When I think about it, it does not hold much appeal. In the meantime, here we are, seven artists and one slightly put out Maman, gathered together to talk about the dire state of the Parisian art *communauté* and how we—a group of virtual unknowns, plus one well-established rebel—can change the world.

I am not hopeful.

Besides Édouard and Degas, I sit with Camille Pissarro,

Frédéric Bazille, Auguste Renoir, each of whom I have never met, and Claude Monet, whom I remember thanks to an error at the Salon a couple of years ago when his surname was mistaken for Édouard's.

"Manet was not at all flattered to have some youngster poaching off his ill-gotten fame," Degas says, as we sit around the table enjoying bowls of steaming potato-leek soup. "He was especially peeved when Monet's mundane seascapes got more attention than his latest outrage."

Monet grumbles over the *mundane* label Degas has slapped on him, but then laughs with the others. Édouard simply rolls his eyes. I wonder if he has taken offense at being called *old* when Monet is scarcely ten years his junior?

"Now, look at the lot of you," Édouard finally says. "Resorting to my old diversionary tricks, hoping to beat the system at its own game. You do me proud."

"Yes, Ed, and we are so pleased you changed your mind and decided to join us today," says Pissarro. "When Degas said you declined, I thought you had mislaid your rebellious streak. But here you are. There is hope for this world, after all."

Édouard's glance slides to me.

My stomach spirals.

Hope? Perhaps.

We chat over lunch. I can barely eat because my stomach is a jumble of nerves at seeing Édouard again.

But he is pleasant enough and sits next to me and makes an effort to engage me in conversation. I cannot help but believe he was sincere about wanting to be my friend.

After the intimacy we shared, all I could dwell on was that he would not be my lover.

Now, I find reassurance in how he wishes to be my friend. If he were going to brag about his conquest he would have done so already, and the men at the table would certainly not be talking to me as a colleague.

What has happened between us is our secret. Somehow it seems more valuable.

"The art they show at the Salon is produced by trained monkeys," Monet says, when Degas' housekeeper, Zoë, serves the apple tarts. "Each one copies one another, afraid to try anything new."

"It is true," offers Renoir. "Even the critics attest there is better work at the Salon des Refusés than in the Salon. When was the last time you saw a truly original piece at that exhibit?"

Édouard clears his throat. "The Salon of 1863, artwork entitled *Déjeuner sur l'Herbe*."

He smiles at me and leans back in his chair, his hands splayed on his vest.

"The critics deemed you a disgrace to morality," says Degas. "But at least it is modern. There has been nothing noteworthy since Delacroix and Ingres. We need to take control. Do things differently."

"Being different for difference's sake? It just seems so artificial." I regret asking the question as soon as the words are born.

"She makes a very good point," says Édouard. "You must remain true to your soul. If you scribble on canvas like a monkey merely with the intent to be different, you are no better than the monkeys who conform to the system."

"I think it boils down to a question of modernity." Bazille's voice is big for such a quiet man. "It is time we stopped living in the past and strive to bring modern art up into the modern world. We must move forward and leave the past behind."

Chapter Eleven

I want to breathe
you in I'm not talking about
perfume or even the sweet o-
dour of your skin but of the
air itself I want to share
your air inhaling what you
exhale I'd like to be that
close two of us breathing
each other as one
— James Laughlin

JANUARY 1869

IMPULSE draws me to Édouard's studio. I have not seen him in two weeks, since that day at Degas' home. True to his word, he left contact up to me. A very real part of me feels empty without him. After being used to seeing him nearly every day for more than a month, I miss him.

I am taking a chance by calling alone, unannounced. There is always the possibility he will not be there or will not be alone. I must risk it because I will not know peace until I see him again. If he is in, it would be fate's way of telling me I am supposed to be there. If he is not in—well, I shall turn and go.

I pull my coat collar closed and sink my hands deeper into my muff as the carriage rattles over the Boulevard Malesherbes. I believe the Café Guerbois is not far from here. I am tempted to ask the coachman to drive by, but a few restless snow flurries fall through the carriage window, and I shiver against the cold. As curious as I am to catch a glimpse of this exclusive male enclave, it must wait for another day. Maman is ill. I have taken the carriage into the city to fetch a remedy from the apothecary. There was no one to accompany me, so I have gone alone.

The shop is just around the corner from Édouard's studio, and I cannot resist dropping in to say hello. To show him I harbor no ill feelings after what transpired a fortnight ago.

Heat rises up my neck at the thought. Yet, when I get out of the carriage, I can see my breath.

Before I allow myself to contemplate my actions—to lose my nerve—I climb the forty-eight steps to the *atelier* and stand at his door.

I knock, shove my chilled hand back into my muff, regretting my impetuousness. But the door flies open so quickly I gasp and wonder if he is expecting someone else, or going out—but, oh . . . the look that sweeps over his face when he realizes it is me knocking at his door.

"Bonjour," I say. "Were you just leaving? I can call another time."

He wears a white button-down shirt tucked into trousers. His shirtsleeves are rolled to his elbows and there is a splotch of crimson paint on his forearm. I am surprised to see him dressed so casually and so lightly for such a cold day. But it suits him. Even in this casual stance he looks *magnifique.*

"Even if I had an appointment with Napoléon himself, I should not go now that you are here. Come in, Mademoiselle. Please, come in. Oh, it is great to see you. Would you believe I was just this minute thinking about you?"

"You flatter me."

"The truth is you have not left my mind since I saw you at Degas' table, more beautiful than the roses of the centerpiece."

I smile and try not to let myself be carried on the wings of his flattery. Alas, how else does one reply to such a sentiment?

He bows, sweeps his left hand in a motion beckoning me inside. I follow, feeling as if something inside me that has been broken a long while is finally beginning to heal.

His studio is chilly and I shove my hands deeper inside my muff. "Why do you not have a fire? You will catch cold. Maman is terribly ill. That is why I am out today. To fetch her medicine."

He stands there, a dazed smile on his face, until finally he blinks, as if clearing his thoughts. "I am sorry your mother is unwell. If you are too cold, I will set a fire."

"Oh, no please don't go to the trouble."

"It is no trouble, really. Normally, I would already have the stove blazing, but I just got in."

"Were you away?"

He nodded. "Boulogne. The family is still there."

"I see." My heart pounds.

"I return because I have too much work to do."

I feel victorious, for I remember the little deal I had made with the heavens. It is a good sign to find him here. I could have so easily missed him. If I had called yesterday or tomorrow, I might not have found him in. As he starts the fire in the *poêle,* my eyes search all the familiar spots in the room.

The balcony set is still standing, and I am glad. I want to believe he left it up on purpose. But then again, it has not been so terribly long ago that he was working on the painting. Since the last time I was here. My gaze latches onto the dressing screen, and my stomach lurches at the memory of what transpired between us that day I was last here. I look away.

"How is the balcony painting coming? You must be nearly finished by now?"

"Almost. Would you like to see it?"

I nod.

As he lights the fire, he indicates a canvas on an easel toward the back of the studio.

From far away, I cannot see much of a difference in Fanny Claus and Monsieur Guillemet's images. They look the same as the last time I saw the painting. However, my likeness is considerably more detailed.

Well, that's what they deserve for walking out on Édouard. It makes my blood tingle to think of the time he has spent perfecting my image, and I can't help but wonder what he thought of as he painted me.

Heat flames my cheeks at the memory.

And here I am. Back again.

I set my muff on the sofa and start to remove my hat, but another canvas catches my eye.

Turned upside down and propped against the wall, is a portrait of . . . I cock my head. Suzanne and . . .?

I squint at it as I walk over and lift the small piece, only about 70 centimeters across and not quite as high. It is indeed Suzanne, a ghastly reproduction of her in profile sitting at the piano looking as broad as she is tall and fully the triple-chinned, dumpy hausfrau.

Even more shocking is the figure painted directly behind her. I turned the picture upright so I can view it, and recognize Édouard, slumped on a divan looking lost, staring into space with the unmistakable look of bored discontent.

The painting is truly bizarre and makes me feel very uncomfortable, as if I am walking into the midst of a feud.

"Degas' handiwork," Édouard says vaguely.

He looks none too pleased, and I can't tell whether he dislikes the unflattering nature of the painting or if he thinks me nosy for picking it up.

"The man has some gall," he murmurs and slams the stove door.

I wonder if this is Degas' attempt to paint from modern life rather than romanticizing art—as his compatriots preached so adamantly the other day—or if somehow, it is a commentary on the state of the Manet marriage.

I believe it is the latter. Why else would Édouard react so violently? Especially when the canvas was a gift.

It is on the tip of my tongue to comment on the former—opening a discussion of Degas' and Monet's ambitions to show outside of the Salon—when Édouard snatches the painting from my hands, and like a madman, takes a paintbrush to it, smearing an ocher rectangle down the far right quarter of the canvas, blocking out the piano and Suzanne's face. Curiously, he leaves half her body visible as well as the image of him lolling on the couch. He also takes care to leave Degas' little red signature scrawled in the bottom right corner.

"There," he says after he has finished. "That should teach him."

I am so stunned I cannot speak.

He removes a still-life painting of a bunch of asparagus from the wall and hangs Degas' family portrait in its prominent place.

The scene disturbs me in a way that knocks me off balance. Or is it because I've come here today, tempting fate, when I know better.

"I should go."

I go to the couch and collect my muff and start toward the door.

"Stay just a while, please?"

I hesitate. I have never glimpsed this unpredictable, angry side of him. It frightens me so much I'm not sure it is safe to stay.

He must be reading my thoughts. "I'm sorry. Degas makes me so angry. Sometimes he oversteps the bounds of appropriateness."

The spell is broken, and any fanciful thoughts I might have entertained have been trampled under his tirade. So I stand, wearing my hat and coat, clinging to my muff, as he pours tea.

"Come sit. I know you don't have much time, you must get back to your sick Maman, but please indulge me for fifteen minutes."

I remove my hat and coat and sit upon the big red divan, my dress puffed around me like a giant white cloud. I twist my body toward him so that we might finish our conversation.

"Stay just like that" he says, picking up his sketch book. He draws a few quick marks, then gets up, rummages through a drawer in a chest across from the bed and pulls out a red fan—the same one I held in *Le Balcon*. He hands it to me. Steps back to look, then kneels and tugs the hem of my skirt up so my black slipper shows prominently.

"What are you doing?" I pull my foot back, but he grasps it firmly and returns it to where he originally placed it.

"Don't move," he says. "I want to paint you just like this."

"Édouard, I must get back—"

"I know. Just allow me a few moments to capture you just like this."

I cannot resist. So I make small talk while he sketches, determined to lighten the tone.

"I have come with news. My sister, Edma, is engaged to be married."

He smiles. "Is she?"

"I believe you know the fellow. Adolphe Pontillon?"

"Pontillon? You're joking? He is an old navy comrade of mine."

"He proposed just last week. We expected it sooner, but his military unit shipped out for a month. Our house is all aflutter with wedding plans and such."

"When is the special day?"

"In late February or early March. They have not chosen the date just yet. I suppose with Edma's wedding, she will not be part of the new modern movement now. Degas and company will just have to understand." I stiffen at having uttered his name and hope it doesn't cause Édouard's bad mood to return.

"Why not?"

"Edma will give up painting once she marries."

"Why would she do that? Why would she throw away such talent?"

I have asked the same question myself numerous times, and I am thrilled to hear him echoing my sentiments.

"Are you saying you would have your wife be a painter?"

"My wife is not a painter, so I cannot answer that question. But if my wife painted, I would consider it my duty to be her greatest source of inspiration." He arches his brows. "I would not be doing my duty as a husband if I did not encourage her."

There's implied meaning in that statement, says Olympia.

Propriety ignores her.

His gaze lingers on my face and his hand pauses, charcoal on the sketch pad. "You look so . . . . so beautiful . . . in your white dress and black ribbon, sitting there with your cheeks pink and flushed. I want to remember you this way always."

See! See there? says Olympia.

My pulse pounds. I desire him so much it is torture, and for this brief moment he is mine. We two are the only beings in the world. I savor the moment and its lush sensuality.

"Are you painting much these weeks, since I no longer hold you captive in my studio?"

"Oui. I am concentrating on my copy studies at the Louvre, as I will not have time to finish something for the Salon jury to consider."

"Nonsense, if you get to work you could easily have a masterpiece together well in time for the jury."

I shake my head. "It is doubtful with Edma's wedding dominating every waking moment."

He frowns. "Do not let others distract you."

I lift my eyebrows at him and resist reminding him that he is the one who usually dominates my time.

He laughs. "I saw that look on your face. How terribly inconsiderate of me, Mademoiselle, to monopolize your time when I am warning you against just the such. I understand that you have work to tend to and precious little time in which to do it. It is not often a woman enraptures me. When that happens, the whole world seems to slip away."

What did I tell you? says Olympia.

A sensation like a whirlwind lifts the pit of my stomach and takes flight inside me.

"Really, I do not mind. If I did, I should not be sitting here right now."

He smiles.

"So your sister is getting married," he says absently. "And you?" He says the words so vaguely, I do not understand what he means.

"Pardon?"

"Do you have a bridegroom on the horizon?"

"*Moi?* Getting married? Of course not."

"I am delighted to hear that."

His seductive smile stirs something inside me. I do not like it, because it is something he should not be toying with if we are to remain friends in the pure sense of the word.

"Why are you delighted that I should not give myself to another, Édouard?"

He does not answer me. I am not comfortable with the direction the conversation is taking.

"I should leave."

"Not yet. Please?"

I can neither stay in hopes of a companionable visit nor can I summon the will to rise and take my leave. So I sit silently counting the beats between his looking at me and the paper as he draws. Until finally his eyes linger on me, straying from the rhythm.

"You realize they're all mad for you."

It was more of a statement than a question.

"Pardon?"

"Especially Degas, I could tell what was on his mind when he came to the studio to see *Le Balcon.* And when he delivered *that* painting." He nods to the altered canvas on the wall. "Beware of him, Berthe."

Interesting, since that is precisely what Degas said about him, says Propriety.

"You are angry over Degas' painting, Édouard. It has nothing to do with my friendship with Degas. So please do not pretend that it does."

"It should not have anything to do with you, but he has made it so. He painted that portrait of Suzanne and me because of you, so that I would remember my place."

"Well, you should. You are married. Degas and I are not. He is my friend. And even if he is a little gruff, he is as safe as a kitten."

Édouard slams down the sketch book.

"He is the world's worst misogynist, and even though he is enamored with you he is incapable of expressing it properly, much less loving you the way you deserve to be loved."

"Pray, tell me exactly how I deserve to be loved, Édouard?"

He takes my hand and pulls me up from the chair so we stand face-to-face. I believe for a moment he will kiss me, but he does not. I am more disappointed than relieved, because he has awakened something in me that will no longer sleep, something that longs for more and will not be satisfied with just the occasional visit where we passionately fall into each other's arms fearing we will be discovered.

"We cannot do this," I murmur. Yet, he does not back away, does not release me. "You will not have me, yet you do not want anyone else to have me. It is the worst of inhumane treatment, Édouard, because I do deserve to be loved."

Chapter Twelve

"Everything that was no longer exists;
everything that is to be does not yet exist."
— Alfred de Musset

FEBRUARY 1896

Dearest Berthe,

I have never once in my life written to you. It is therefore not too surprising I was very sad when we were separated for the first time. I am beginning to recover a little, and I hope that my husband is not aware of the void I feel without you. He is very sweet. Full of attention and solicitude for me. Please be happy for me.

Yours Always,
Edma

My Dearest Edma,

If we go on this way, we shall no longer be good for anything. You cry on receiving my letters, and I did just the same thing this morning. Your letters are so affectionate, but so melancholy, but I repeat, this sort of thing is unhealthy. It is making us lose whatever remains of our youth. For me this is of no importance, but for you it is different.

This painting, this work that you mourn for, is the cause of much grief and many troubles. You know it as well as I do.

Come now, the lot you have chosen is not the worst one. You have a serious attachment, and a man's heart utterly devoted to you. Do not revile your fate. Remember it is sad to be alone; despite anything that may be said or done, a woman has an immense need of affection. For her to withdraw into herself is to attempt the impossible.

Oh, how I am lecturing you! I do not mean to. I am saying what I think, what seems to be true.

Affectionately,
Your sister Berthe

MARCH 1869

I try to pretend Edma is merely away on holiday without me, but I do not succeed in fooling myself into a better mood.

I have not seen Édouard since that cold January day at his studio. He did not come after me with a plea of friendship, and

I certainly did not seek him out only to have him tell me we will never be. I do not trust myself alone with him anymore. I certainly will not throw myself at a man who does not want me. It is all for the best that I have a million tasks to tend to, important work that went undone as I helped my sister prepare for her marriage to Adolphe.

After all the celebrations surrounding the wedding, I am in no mood for another soirée, especially one where I am expected to assist Maman in serving as hostess to Édouard and his family among nearly thirty other guests for the informal gathering.

Alas, Maman is in a festive mood having succeeded in marrying off her second daughter. She seems on a mission to create a matrimonial trio. I suppose she believes she stands a better chance of striking a match for me if she casts me in the company of eligible men. So she has taken it upon herself to invite every unmarried man I have ever mentioned, including Eugène Manet, which means she also extended an invitation to Édouard, Suzanne, and Madame Manet.

They all come.

As well, in attendance are Degas, Pierre Puvis de Chavannes, Fontin (who is still nursing heartbreak over Edma's nuptials), among others, including several unmarried men who work at the ministry with Papa.

At least Maman is playing fair—an equal number of interesting, creative fellows offsets the dull business-minded professionals whom I fear will bore me until I nod off as they rattle on about industry and finance and other dry subjects, which hold absolutely no interest for me.

Without my dear Edma, I scarcely know what to do with myself and hide in the kitchen, helping Amélie.

It's an informal affair. Hors d'oeuvres and drinks, which Amélie ran herself ragged to prepare. Small consolation, it's not a dinner party. Still, I wonder why Maman cannot just leave it alone.

She walks into the kitchen, sets two empty wine decanters on the table, and starts barking orders. "Amélie, we need more canapés and the carafes need to be refilled. Please be more vigilant so that they are not drained empty. It looks bad when my guests have to ask for refreshment."

The poor girl shoves a tray into the oven, wipes the perspiration off her forehead with the back of her hand, and starts to fill a plate with hors d'oeuvres.

"Berthe, why are you in the kitchen when we have guests in the drawing room?"

I pour a bottle of wine in the carafe. "Because I prefer Amélie's company to the thirty intimate friends you have invited over tonight. Maman, I am sick to death of parties after all we have just been through for Edma's marriage."

"This soirée is for your benefit," she says. "Please come with me and be sociable. Perhaps you, too, will find a husband. There are plenty of eligible men out there. Surely there's someone out there who suits you."

If you only knew, Maman. I blink back the urge to voice my thoughts and say instead, "I am not looking for a husband, Maman. Marriage is not something I will enter into unless I am in love."

Amélie bangs the oven door shut.

"It is far better to get married with compromises than to remain independent and in a position that is no position at all," Maman quips. "Within a few years what is left of your charm will pale, and all too soon, you will have far fewer friends than you have now. Tonight, you have your choice of any man in the room."

In other words, the bloom is wilting on the vine. I should present myself to be picked while the picking was good.

When I do not respond, she says, "Go along, you have not greeted the Manets. Please do make an effort, Berthe."

As Maman and I enter the drawing room, my gaze connects with Édouard's. It is true. I have not yet spoken to him. I realize it is the mark of a terrible hostess.

A young man whom I do not know—probably someone from Papa's office—is playing a lively Mozart concerto on the piano. As I make my way over to greet the Manets, I see Degas.

Good. I shall talk to him instead. I suppose a good hostess would make obligatory greetings, not tying herself to one guest until she's made her rounds. But hostessing, as with *wifeing*, is not my strong suit, and I do not have the energy or the inclination to make the rounds. I'll opt for a long visit with Degas, whom I have discovered is always good for a dry laugh. He, of all people, will see the irony in Maman's pitiful attempt to marry me off to the first man who would have me.

I steal a glance at Édouard, who still stands near the door talking to Fantin. So Édouard believes Degas to be mad for me.

How ridiculous.

"Bonsoir, Monsieur."

Degas stands. "*Bonsoir, Mademoiselle.* Lovely to see you tonight. I trust you have been well?"

We talk about our work, Edma's wedding, and the progress he and Monet have made arranging a show independent of the Salon.

"Our hardest task seems to be finding a gallery that will host such an event. We have had no luck."

"Now that my sister's wedding is over, perhaps I can help."

"That would be very kind of you." He reaches into his coat pocket and removes a slender, rectangular object I soon realize is a fan. "Here, I have brought you a gift."

I open it and realize it is not just an ordinary fan, but beautifully hand painted in watercolor and brown ink. It portrayed a group of Spanish dancers and musicians.

"Did you paint this?"

He nods. "You see here, this depicts the romantic poet Alfred de Musset." He leans in closer—but there is nothing improper in his gesture—and points to the figure. I feel Édouard watching us as we talk. "You know of Musset, yes?"

I nod. "The writer. He enjoyed quite a passionate liaison with George Sand."

"Oui, this is she." He points to a figure drawn opposite Musset.

Degas' gift gives me pause. Why a painting of Musset and Sand? If I let my mind wander, it could pick out all sorts of suggestions—commentary on my affinities . . . But how would he know? Or Degas' affinities? It is curious how Manet and Degas have avoided each other tonight.

"Have you spoken to Monsieur Manet and Suzanne?"

"I have not." Degas swells like a big toad. "He is no friend of mine."

"What is the matter?"

"He is a vandal, an ingrate. *Quelle horreur!* I gave him a gift and he defaced it. I presented him with a family portrait I had painted myself. I go to his *atelier* to find he has painted over it."

I did not dare confess I was there the day Édouard did so. I also do not dare question the underlying meaning implied in the portrait or the fan. Oh, Degas, what kind of innuendo? I tap the fan against my palm.

"Watch out for him," Degas says. "Manet cannot be true. He has an inherently fickle nature and cannot be trusted."

His insinuation makes me uncomfortable. I do not like being in this position. Even if I am keeping my distance from Édouard, both men are my friends.

"Monsieur Manet is a gentleman."

"Come now, Mademoiselle, open your eyes. His behavior is as clear as the crystal chandelier that hangs from your ceiling. He has designs, but they are not so well hidden as he might think."

"*Bonsoir, Degas,* do I hear you taking my name in vain?"

Édouard appears, smiling. I am relieved because he can defend himself if Degas continues to persecute him. I will not be responsible for the task.

Degas talked on as if he had not heard Édouard approach. "You claim Manet is a gentleman? Since when? Did he finally decide to spin moral fiber?" He turns in mock surprise. "Ah, Manet, there you are."

Degas is angry, and after the display of temper I witnessed in Édouard's studio, I fear they will get into a brawl. "Monsieur, your timing is impeccable. We were indeed talking about you."

"Were you?" Édouard takes my hand, raises it to his lips, and meets my gaze. "Mademoiselle, it is a pleasure. It has been far too long."

"Monsieur."

He lowers my hand and taps the fan. "This is lovely. A present from an admirer?"

"An ardent admirer," Degas purrs. "Hand painted expressly with the demoiselle in mind."

The tone of his voice sends a most unromantic shudder up my spine that makes me open my eyes wide and turn away from Degas.

"How have you been?" I ask Édouard.

His gray eyes seem a couple of shades darker, and he glares at Degas, who wears a most irksome little smirk.

"I have been very well, *merci*. Busy, but well."

"I'm sure you have," Degas says. "What, with the beautiful Mademoiselle Gonzalés in your studio every day. How goes the painting of her?"

Édouard tenses. "It progresses."

"A new commission?" I ask.

"No," says Degas. "A new student. A lovely young creature at that."

I go numb. "I thought you were too busy to take on students?"

Édouard shrugs. "Generally, that is true."

"Unless they are young and vivacious and ethereally beautiful," says Degas.

Édouard stutters. I have never seen him so unnerved.

"This is the first time I have accepted a student in my *atelier.* Her father is Emmanuel Gonzalés the novelist. He asked me to give her lessons as a favor to him. She shows promise."

Degas wheezes a dry, throaty laugh. "Not to mention she is twenty years old and stunning. She has huge—" Degas started to make a gesture at chest level, but gasps as if he had just realized a woman was present and moves his hands up to encircle his eyes, "— big, big brown eyes that have simply made Manet the fool. Oh and such a haughty will. But it comes naturally as the world seems to grovel at her feet. Right, Manet?"

Édouard does not smile. In fact, he looks as if he is exercising great restraint to hold his tongue and not strike Degas.

Fat Suzanne is at the piano now. She is playing her Chopin, eyes closed, as if she does not have a care in the world. I cannot decide if she is blind or stupid or if she had gotten so comfortable in her cushy station that she has resigned herself to not give a damn about her husband's antics.

I have grown tired of both Degas and Édouard. They may enjoy stabbing at each other, but each lance simply glances off the intended target and impales me. I am tired of playing the fool. Enough!

"Excusez-moi, Messieurs."

I slip out the terrace door and head toward my studio. So

the ethereal Mademoiselle Gonzalés has been keeping Édouard *busy.* He has replaced me with someone new, someone young and beautiful and more exciting than I.

While I know I have no claim on Édouard, what was I supposed to believe when a few weeks earlier he had paid court to me with charm and devotion? But he did not follow through. Shouldn't that be enough of an indication that he is simply a flatterer?

And I am a fool for believing there was something more in his eyes.

The full meaning behind Degas' words—*Manet's inherently fickle nature and he cannot be trusted*—dawn hard and fast.

I feel like an idiot, as if I have not been paying attention and have suddenly painted myself into a predicament that can only be resolved by starting anew.

Very well, then.

Mademoiselle Gonzalés can have Édouard. My best defense will be to keep my distance from him.

In my dark studio, the air is quiet and lighter. I do not light a lamp, but stand there alone in the darkness. The glow from the house shines bright, and I walked over to the window to look out at the night.

In that solitary moment it becomes ever so clear that I have failed at everything that matters. I failed Maman by my unwillingness to compromise—to get married and give up this *silly hobby,* as she called it, for the respectable life of a proper lady. I even failed myself for nurturing feelings for a man I cannot have. Worse yet, since meeting him, I cannot seem to finish a painting. I am floundering, adrift on a vast sea of nothingness.

If I am going to be unhappy, why not resign myself to an unhappiness that makes Maman happy? Why not go in and select the first man on whom my gaze lands and let him be the one? Through the window, I gaze at the party happening amidst the golden glow of candlelight. People eating and drinking, laughing and talking.

A solitary figure standing off from the crowd catches my eye. Eugène Manet stands alone. The party seems to buzz around him, yet he stands a pillar of silence, keeping to himself.

Tears well in my eyes. I know I could no more go in there and choose a husband at random than I could escape my hopeless life by jumping the garden wall and making a clean getaway.

I will be better off telling Maman I have a headache and calling it a night. Although, she will be furious at me for leaving her to tend to the guests alone.

I pick up a new cotton rag Amélie has draped over my easel and wipe my eyes, glancing at Edma's easel, standing empty and abandoned in its usual place, as if she will be back any minute. It makes my insides ache.

But just as Edma has chosen her path, I, too, have chosen mine. I never travel the easy route. I should know that about myself by now.

A faint knock on the door startles me out of my thoughts. Édouard pushes open the door and steps inside.

"Ah, so this is where you disappeared. I—"

"Monsieur, please. There is no point."

"Degas presented a most inappropriate picture of my arrangement with Mademoiselle Gonzalés. I felt I must—"

"It does not matter. It is your business to settle with your conscience and your wife."

"She is nothing to me."

"Who is nothing—Suzanne or Eva?"

When he does not answer, I whirl around to face him. He stands so close my shoulder brushes his chest as I turn. He does not step back. The edge of the windowsill presses against my bottom. Golden light from the party casts his eyes the color of a stormy sea.

I do not know why I do it, out of desire or out of sheer anger for the way he has been trifling with me. I lean in and pressed my mouth to his, fast and hard.

His hands slide around my waist, move up my back, raking into my hair, and he deepens the kiss.

His taste once so foreign has become familiar, a taste I crave that melts my determination and dissolves my defiance. This is expressly the reason I should not kiss him.

I push past him, without looking back and flee into the garden, running headlong into Eugène Manet.

"Excusez-moi, Mademoiselle."

He grabs me to cushion the impact and for a moment we stand in an awkward embrace. Tucked into the fold of Eugène's strong arms, I feel Édouard's kiss fresh on my lips, the coarseness of his beard prickling my face. I jerk away from Eugène, half expecting Édouard to come barreling out of my studio.

Of course he does not.

He is much too suave to make such a grave mistake and give himself away.

Eugène steadies me with a hand on my shoulder. Even in the dim half-light of night I can see that he is flushed from our contact.

"Are you all right, Mademoiselle?" he asks.

"Yes, Monsieur Manet, I am fine. Please forgive my clumsiness. I was not watching where I was going."

"No, Mademoiselle, the fault is all mine."

We stand in awkward silence. Until he says, "Such a lovely party. It is quite nice to see you. I have often thought of paying you a call, but . . ."

His voice trails off and he stares at the ground, not at me. I cannot help but compare his shy reserve to his brother's brash boldness. My heart fills with such sadness, for a moment I believe I might dissolve into despair.

But I will not give Édouard the satisfaction.

Instead, I focus on the differences between the brothers. Eugène is taller than Édouard, gentler, and more sincere in manner. I suppose it would be a crowded house if two dominant personalities commanded the spotlight.

"Shall I escort you back to the party?"

He offers his arm. I remember the soirée at his mother's home that night he escorted me to dinner. Oh, how different things were then. A pang of remorse grips me.

If I could go back and relive the weeks in between, would I change the outcome?

I shiver against the cool night air.

What was the use of pondering such nonsense?

"I would like that very much, Monsieur. *Merci.*"

I take his arm, and we walk in heavy silence to the party.

Chapter Thirteen

I know your heart which overflows
With outworn loves long cast aside
Still like a furnace flames and glows,
And you within your breast enclose
A dammed soul's unbending pride;
—Baudelaire

APRIL 1869

My Dear Edma,

I see from your letter that you are enjoying the sunshine as we are, and that you know how to benefit from it. Spring is a lovely thing; it makes itself felt charmingly, even in a little restricted corner of the earth like the garden. The lilacs are in bloom. The chestnut trees are almost so. I was admiring them a little while ago. Papa listened to me, then put an end to my enthusiasm by immediately forecasting the end of all these splendors.

I am wondering what I should do with my summer. I should be glad to come to you on condition, first, that it will not inconvenience you, and second that I shall find opportunity to work. My inaction is beginning to weigh upon me. I am eager to do something at least fairly good.

I understand that one does not readily accustom oneself to life in the country and to domesticity. For that, you must have something to look forward to. I know Adolphe would not appreciate my talking in this way. Men are inclined to believe that they fill one's life, but as for me, I think no matter how much affection a woman has for her husband, it is not easy for her to break with a life of work. Affection is a very fine thing on condition that there is something besides with which to fill one's days. This is something I see for you in motherhood. Do not grieve about painting. It is not worth a single regret. There is one worry you are rid of. For the past month I have not seen a single painter.

The Salon opens soon. I considered writing Manet a note to ask him for an admission card. Alas, I hesitate to do so.

I often imagine myself in your little home and wonder whether you are happy or sad. I suspect you are both. Am I wrong?

Affectionately,
Your sister Berthe

Édouard dropped by today, but I was not at home to receive him. I believe the fates have made it perfectly clear there is no hope for us. We cannot pretend to be merely friends, yet I cannot put him out of my mind. Even in light of Eva Gonzalés.

The friendship Maman and Madame Manet have developed makes it increasingly difficult to avoid him.

I suppose I cannot evade him indefinitely. Maman already believes there is something wrong with me and has tried to persuade me to see a doctor to treat my malaise.

One bit of news that did brighten my spirits was when Degas dropped by with word that Édouard's painting of Mademoiselle Gonzalés is not progressing well. Degas says he cannot seem to get the girl's face right. After more than a month's work, he grows quite frustrated.

I suppose this means Édouard and Degas have mended their rift over the altered family portrait. I did not ask for fear it would reopen the wound.

April 1869

You are right, my dear Berthe, in all you say to me. It is disheartening one cannot depend on artists. You may call me crazy if you like, but when I think of any of these artists, I tell myself that a quarter hour of their conversation is worth as much as many sterling qualities.

Continue to write me your gossip as you call it. I have nothing better to do than decipher it.

Affectionately yours,
Edma

May 1869

For the first time in six years I did not submit work to the Salon. You can imagine my trepidation about attending. At one point, I even contemplated forgoing the event altogether. But Édouard—in a devious plan—sent Maman a note inviting us to the Salon opening to view my likeness in *Le Balcon. Celebration to follow at the Manet home immediately afterward.*

Maman was as excited about the unveiling as if it were her portrait.

"After all the time I spent waiting while he created it, a piece of me is attached to it."

She has miraculously developed a case of amnesia about the turmoil surrounding it. Given Maman's disposition, it is much better to have her embrace the occasion than not.

It had been nearly two months since I have seen Édouard. He called several times. But I managed to avoid seeing him, with hopes that time would eventually quell my feelings for him.

Although I do not know if I am ready to face him, I have decided to accompany Maman to the opening, as an obedient daughter should.

At the Salon, on our way to room *M,* a painting at the top of the grand staircase snares my attention; a piece by my friend Pierre Puvis de Chavannes. I stop to admire it.

"Berthe, Monsieur Puvis de Chavannes is such a charming fellow. I have no idea why you do not encourage that relationship."

Maman lifts her quizzing glass and looks at the painting. "No talent for art, but he is handsome and wealthy. A decidedly good match for you."

I do not answer her. Puvis may be wealthy and handsome as she calls him, but he is too old. It must be his aristocratic air that makes him seem as old as the throne. But come to think of it, he is nearly twenty years my senior—*ack!*—he's Maman's age. No wonder she finds him so attractive.

I am not in the mood to debate tonight, so I do not answer her. Thank heavens Carlos Duran and his wife approach, and divert her attention.

Soon we make our way to room *M* and are standing before Édouard's *Balcon*. He is nowhere to be found.

Maman stands much too close viewing the painting through the narrow lenses of her quizzing glass. "Well, it looks much the same as the last time I saw it. One would think he would have gone back to finish it."

"Maman!" I glance around in horror, hoping no one has heard her. "If this is how he chose to submit it, then it is finished."

"I am entitled to an opinion, and mine is that I do not think it looks finished."

I stare at the work in amazement. It looks larger than life hanging on the wall, in a prime location. He has painted me in splendorous detail. Fanny looks dowdy. Monsieur Guillemet looks stiff, and . . . Édouard has added a new figure, barely visible amidst the blackness of the open terrace doorway. A boy with a serving tray. Merely a ghost of an image, scarcely perceptible in the background.

"Bonjour, Madame, Mademoiselle." Degas sidles up next to me.

"*Bonjour Monsieur Degas,* Berthe and I were just commenting on Manet's painting. Rather unfinished, do you not agree—oh, there is Madame Arneau, I must speak to her. Babette! Yoo-hoo, Babette."

The woman waves.

"May I entrust Berthe to your good keeping, Monsieur?"

"Of course."

"*Merci,* please excuse me." She hurries off, soon swallowed by the crowd.

Arms crossed, Degas contemplates *Le Balcon*. "I would certainly say it is finished. So much so it seems the epithet *femme fatale* has been circulating among the inquisitive," he murmurs.

"Pardon?"

Degas regards me with his bored, intolerant expression that always makes me fear his next word will be, *"Imbécile!"*

"People have branded you a *femme fatale,* Mademoiselle."

I do not know how to respond. I snap my gaze from his face back to the painting.

"An alluring woman." Degas spits the words as if they leave a bad taste in his mouth.

"I know the meaning of *femme fatale,* Monsieur. It is just, I am more strange-looking than . . . alluring."

Degas' demeanor softens. "One could never brand your beauty strange. You are quite lovely. Léon, now he looks strange."

I glance around, expecting to see Suzanne's son nearby. Yet I cannot pick him out in the crowd. Degas' attention remains fixed on the canvas, a distasteful scowl now wrinkling his brow. Then I realize —

"Is that Léon in the background of the painting?"

Degas arches a brow at me. "Who else?"

I squint at the image. "Oh, I see." Actually, I do not see, but I will not admit so much to Degas. "It is interesting how Monsieur Manet painted him. He is barely there."

"Barely there." Degas smirks. "That is a very good way to put it. I suppose that is how the Manet household would like him to be. If not absent altogether."

His words make me uncomfortable, and I recall Edma's revelation that Léon is Édouard's son. Although Degas could probably shed some insight, I do not want to appear to perpetuate gossip. I will have to be subtle.

"Monsieur Manet does not care for his own godson?"

"Godson? *Ha!* Who told you that?"

"Madame Manet."

He snorts. "Yes, I am sure that is what she would have you believe." He wheezes a dry, humorless laugh. Léon is no more Manet's godson than Edma is your goddaughter."

What? What on earth is he carrying on about? The way he baits me, as if I know nothing, grows so tiresome.

"I am well aware that Léon is Manet's son, Monsieur. But the boy is what—about fourteen years of age? Why did Manet wait so long after Suzanne gave birth to marry her?"

Degas' mouth twists into a perverse little smile.

"That, Mademoiselle, is what everyone wonders. Especially since he did not give the child the Manet name."

One arm wrapped around his middle, he strokes his chin with his free hand. "Of course there is the question of *which* Manet is the father. To keep things simple the family prefers to refer to Léon as Édouard's *godson*. It cuts down on the nasty gossip, you see?"

No, I do not see. He is talking in riddles again. When he does this, I've learned I'm usually in for a wild ride before I discover where his dramatic innuendos lead.

Degas studies me with a look of sadistic amusement. "Can you not figure it out, Mademoiselle? Think about it."

"Monsieur Degas, s'il vous plaît. What are you saying? Just tell me." I let my exasperation bleed through into my words. For all his good qualities, the man can be quite enigmatic, and I am in no mood for games.

But before Degas can respond, Édouard appears like an apparition materializing out of the crowd with his mother, Léon, and a young woman I do not recognize tagging along behind.

Degas leans in. "Although I still do not understand what compelled him to marry his father's mistress. He could have acted as the boy's godfather without going to the extreme of tying himself to a woman he does not love."

His father's mistress? Unfathomable. Had they shared her? Passed her about as they would a communal flask?

When Édouard sees me, he bypasses several well-wishers and comes immediately to my side. "It this the demoiselle of the hour!" He bows and kisses my hand. "*Ah,* it is good to see you. You have kept yourself hidden away from me far too long."

My mind races back to that night in my studio, and heat spreads across my chest and up my neck. I utter a silent prayer that no one will notice, and much to my relief, Édouard is busy greeting Degas.

"Madame Manet. Léon." I nod to his mother and the boy. Léon returns the greeting and wanders over to examine a wall of paintings. As I watch him, Degas' words are fresh in my mind. *Léon is no more Manet's godson than Edma is your goddaughter.*

What on earth does that mean?

"Berthe, my dear, you look lovely," says Madame Manet. "Everyone has given positively glowing reviews of *Le Balcon.* You do Édouard proud." She offers the compliment, but seems distracted by the hordes buzzing around us.

It feels strange receiving praise for a painting of which I had no part in other than to sit and stare into space. I don't much care for the passive role.

"She is my good luck charm," Édouard chimes. "I have already had an offer for the painting, although it pains me to think of parting with it."

"I'm sure you will heal quickly if the price is right," says the young woman. She is quite beautiful and something in the way she looks at him makes me a little shaky.

Édouard smiles and nods an appreciative touché.

"Mademoiselle Berthe Morisot, may I present Mademoiselle Eva Gonzalés.

Oh.

"Enchanté," she says. "You are as lovely in person as you appear in the painting."

So this is the infamous Eva Gonzalés. She is quite poised for one so young. Even at my age, I do not possess half the confidence she radiates. I cannot suppress a pang of envy at her arrival at Édouard's side. How has Suzanne taken to Édouard's little ingénue?

"Merci," I say. "I understand you are the subject of his work in progress?"

Her brilliant smile falters, but reappears in the blink of an eye. She glances at Édouard. "I believe he has put me on hold for the moment."

"Oh, Monsieur Manet, why?" I exaggerate my concern, and I think Édouard is well aware.

"Let me say it is not progressing as I had hoped."

Eva's eyes darken a shade. She pointedly turns her charm on Degas.

I am just as happy because Édouard offers his arm and we stroll past a few paintings.

"Have you just arrived?" I ask.

"No we have been here since the opening. We were searching for you."

My breath catches. And I steel myself against the charm that always manages to weave its way into my defenses. I fortify my wall of self-preservation by reminding myself that I am merely a fresh dalliance. Obviously, the bright, shiny Eva Gonzalés's company seems a bit tarnished these days. Oh, the wonders a brief absence seems to work on the heart.

"How are the master and pupil getting on?"

He groans.

"I am about to go out of my head. She is a very demanding girl. Chatters incessantly. I went to Boulogne last week simply to escape her."

"Then why do you not turn her out? Tell her you have too much work to do. I seem to remember you telling me that was your reasoning for not taking students in the first place."

"If it were only that simple. The good news is that her papa returns next week, and we shall discuss the situation. Anyhow, the change will be mutually beneficial. I believe she grows tired of this old man's company."

I turn and glance at my likeness from across the room. The intensity of it startles me, and I pause to let the pins-and-needles feeling subside.

"I noticed you painted a figure into the background of *Le Balcon.*"

He turns, follows my gaze, and holds himself a bit straighter.

"Yes, do you like it?"

I nod. "Very subtle. It's Léon, *non?*"

"Oui, I thought the background needed a touch."

"He is a fine looking boy. He's Suzanne's *brother*?"

Édouard nods absently. He has turned his back to the painting to look at a landscape.

"Why does the boy not live with his parents?"

"His father is no longer living, and it is best for him to stay with Suzanne. Did you see Fantin's etching?"

I shake my head no.

His father is dead? Oh, well. Someone is not telling the truth. I wonder who?

"I am not surprised," he says. "The painting is hung so high I think people will strain their necks trying to view it. Poor man; not very good placement."

"Where is your wife tonight, Édouard?"

"She stayed at home. She does not care for large crowds. I suppose she will view the Salon after the first rush fades away."

We linger a bit in front of paintings we like and mutter

comments such as "ghastly" and *"quelle horreur"* under our breath about those we dislike. Yet, my mind is only half on the critique.

His father is dead, *hmmm*. "When did you meet Suzanne?"

"Oh, many years ago. It was right after I returned home from Rio de Janeiro, while I was in the navy. She taught my brothers and me to play the piano in exchange for room and board."

"*Hmmm,* I thought your mother said she came to France at the urging of Franz Liszt?"

"She did, but soon fell upon hard times." He stops walking and gives me a knowing look. "Mademoiselle, affairs do not always go according to plan."

I wish more than ever I could hear his thoughts.

"Then she met my father who took pity on her and took her in."

"And when did you marry?" I am more determined than ever to fish a confession out of him. For once I want him to be honest with me and take responsibility for the people in his life.

Édouard narrows his eyes, gives me a quizzical look. "October, five years ago. Why the inquisition?"

I shrug. "It just . . . " I quickly perform the mathematics. So Léon would have been eight years old when Édouard and Suzanne married. Why did he wait so long?

"Do you love her?"

Édouard blinks. A muscle in his jaw works.

"Mademoiselle, she is my wife."

"I know she is your wife, but do you love her, Édouard?"

I am well aware that I am speaking in Degas-like riddles, and I wonder if Édouard can decipher the core of what I am asking.

He runs a hand through his hair. "Love takes many forms,

dons many guises. In fact, there is much speculation about the lovely dark woman in *Le Balcon*. Just stand back and you will hear them wondering. Several have speculated that this beauty is Manet's love. 'Does he love *her,*' they ask?"

My breath catches as I await his answer. But I feel a hand on my shoulder. No! Not now, I want to yell.

"Berthe?" When I turn, Maman's brow is stern and heavy. "You monopolize Monsieur Manet's time. I am sure many eagerly await his attention. Why don't we take a turn about the Salon and view the rest of the show?"

Édouard bows to her slightly. "Madame Morisot, what a wonderful idea." He offers his arms to both of us. "Shall we?"

Chapter Fourteen

Let me not to the marriage of true minds
Admit impediments. Love is not love
Which alters when it alteration finds,
Or bends with the remover to remove,
O, no! It is an ever-fixed mark,
That looks on tempests and is never shaken;
—William Shakespeare

MAMAN excuses us from the Manets' after-Salon soirée claiming a headache. In the carriage afterward, her anger pours out like spilled red paint.

"I see what is going on, Berthe." Maman frowns. "I am no idiot. Neither are the revelers spouting '*femme fatale*' and 'lovers.' *Lovers,* Berthe*?* Is that what you wanted people to think as you paraded around the Salon with him?"

You don't care what people think, spouts Olympia.

Don't you dare admit that to your Maman, says Propriety. *You should be ashamed.*

Propriety wins. I remain silent.

"I encourage you to go to Edma in Lorient until this nonsense blows over. The change of scenery will suit you, and I do hope time away will quash any notions you might harbor about encouraging Monsieur Manet's attention."

It is no use arguing with her. Besides, I miss my sister terribly and want to see her. Adolphe is away. It will suit Edma and me to have some time together. The fresh air and sunshine will clear my head. I am ready to paint, to be productive. Rather than feeling sorry for myself over my lack of showing in the Salon, I am more determined than ever to produce something worthwhile.

Lorient is a wisp of a town. One might easily overlook it if not for the harbor. Compared to Paris, it seems a lifeless place. Adolphe's naval duties have brought him there. The giddy newlywed, Edma followed without a second thought.

I step off the train—the lone passenger to disembark—and sense the monster driving Edma's torment. All browns and grays, it is a pitiful place. Few trees and even fewer flowers. As I stand alone on the platform inhaling the sharp, briny air, I wonder for a moment if I am the only person awake—or even breathing—in this awful place.

Finally, Edma bounds around the corner of the depot, a blur of yellow dress and dark hair, her skirts kicking up in her haste.

"Berthe, you're here! Oh, you're here!" Breathless, she embraces me as if the harder she holds me, the more she'll regain of the life force that has drained from her over the two months she has languished here. "Your train is early. I wanted to be here when you arrived."

"I have only just turned up." I pull back to look at her. "Oh, how I have missed you."

"And I you."

My eyes well. I blink fast to keep tears from spilling onto my cheeks. As the train chugs away, it seemed to blow a tedious sigh at the sheer dullness of the place.

It is unseasonably dry and warm for April. The sun has baked the dirt street into a pattern of desiccated cracks. The carriage rattles along the naked, dusty path through the center of town. The harbor's gray water sits as flat as a sheet of glass, languidly reflecting the Lorient's dull palette of noncolors from the anchored boats and the short, sandstone wall that snakes along the waterfront like a dead serpent. In the distance, the sea roars low and discontent.

Edma's house is but a short walk from the station, but she has hired a hack to collect my trunks and valise. When I left Paris, I was not sure how long I would stay, so I packed for the long term. The length of my visit will depend on how long Adolphe is away and how much work I can accomplish. But the sight of my dear sister pleases me so, once the carriage arrives at the modest white two-story house Edma calls home, leaving is the farthest thing from my mind.

"Here we are." A hint of humility whitewashes her words. She hesitates at the front door and plucks a dead bloom off a riot of red geraniums planted in the window boxes and lets the withering petals fall to the ground.

"I hope you will be comfortable here."

"Edma, with you, I could be comfortable in the wild. Anywhere, as long as we are together."

Her mouth curves, but the smile does not extend to her eyes. She opens the front door, and we step inside.

Pausing in the entryway, I blink, coaxing my eyes to adjust to the darkness, eager for a first glimpse of my sister's new life—the faded light blue paint adorning the vestibule; the scuffed wooden floor; and most curious of all, "Edma, there is not a single painting on your walls. Why not?"

She frowns and looks about as if noticing the discrepancy for the first time.

"I will send for some of my canvases in due time, but I

need to figure out what will best suit this place." She takes my hat and gloves and sets them on the wooden table in the entryway. "You might say the house and I are still getting acquainted."

She looks down as she speaks. Not only has she quit painting, it seems she has divorced herself from art altogether.

The driver stands behind us with one of my trunks hoisted up on his shoulder.

"Where shall I deposit this, Madame?"

"Please take it upstairs," Edma says. "The first bedroom on the right."

"Edma, why didn't you tell me? I could have brought your canvases."

She throws her arms around my shoulders and sobs. "Oh, Berthe, I am so unhappy. Adolphe is always away. If this is married life, I—"

She buries her face in my shoulder and weeps.

I pat her back, "Hush now," take her by the shoulders and hold her out so I can see her. "I am here now. You suffer from too much solitude, that's all. Everything will be fine now."

She wipes her eyes, but the tears still well and spill. "I don't know what is wrong with me. I'm sorry. You are here, and all I can do is cry like a baby."

"I do not want to hear another word of it."

I put an arm around my sister's shoulder and walk her into the sitting room. The driver's footsteps descend the stairs and stop at the front door. He clears his throat before calling a hearty, *"Bonjour, Madame, Mademoiselle."*

Edma holds both hands to her face and swipes at her eyes. I grab my handbag and settle with the man while she pulls herself together.

By the time I finish, Edma has recovered.

"I suppose you are hungry," she says. "I'll ask Dominique to fix you some lunch."

"No, Edma. You know how travel always upsets my system. I'll just take a cup of tea and that will be fine."

She smiles, seems relieved. "I have had no appetite. The sight of food nauseates me. So if you are hungry, do not hesitate to ask Dominique to prepare you something."

"Edma, do not make a fuss. I will be all right now that I am here with you. Everything will be all right. What I would like more than anything is for us to sit down and catch up."

The waterfront is the only place remotely interesting enough to even think about painting. I arrange Edma on the short sandstone wall. Her pink scarf and blue-green umbrella add color and soften the hard lines of the harbor, bringing a spark of life to the dreary scene.

"Put your right hand on the wall," I say. She complies, even smiles. In the past twenty-four hours, her mood has lightened considerably. Although she still refuses to pick up a paintbrush.

"That is no longer my life. There is no sense in adding to my frustrations," she says.

I start to argue with her, but Edma cuts me off.

"All too soon I will have much more to keep me busy."

"I thought Adolphe was not returning for three months?"

"That is right, and he will ship out again less than a fortnight later. My future occupation is a bit farther coming. Still, I have much to prepare."

She pats her belly and a weary smile tugs at the corners of her mouth.

"Do you mean—"

She nods.

I drop my charcoal and run to her. No wonder she was so melancholy about being alone.

"You're pregnant?"

I hug her again and again.

"I am not certain, but all indications point that way."

"Why did you not tell me last night?"

"I had made up my mind not to say anything until I was absolutely sure. I have not even told Adolphe or Maman, for that matter. I should probably not have told you until I know for sure." She puts a hand on her belly. "But I know in my heart I am."

"And I should have been furious if you had not told me."

We laugh. "Please do not speak of it until after I have told Maman. You know how she gets. It would be a disaster."

I hug her again.

"I am going to be an aunt. Oh, I cannot believe it. Tante Berthe. I love the sound of it."

I pick up my charcoal and Edma resumes her pose. As I watch her sitting there, a beautiful pink rose amidst the lifeless gray backdrop of still water and empty boats, a bittersweet pang pulls at me. I glance at Edma's belly. A child is growing inside my sister, just as Édouard's son had grown inside Suzanne.

A seed planted by love.

Tangled in the myriad of emotions that have surfaced since I met Édouard, part of me aches for the child I never knew I wanted until he came into my life.

Looking at my sister, so full of life, it is quite clear that she has moved on with her life.

This is how I decide to paint her: with her back to the cold, ugly harshness of the world. A rose that has blossomed and is thriving in the prime of her life.

My Dear Bijou,

Your father seemed to be deeply touched by the letter you wrote to him. He appears to have discovered in you unsuspected treasures of the heart, and unusual tenderness toward him.

In consequence, he often says he misses you. But I wonder why. You hardly ever talk to each other. You are never together. Does he miss you then, as one misses a piece of furniture or a pet bird? I am trying to convince him to the contrary, that it is much better not to see your poor little face bewildered and dissatisfied over a fate about which we can do nothing. It is a relief. This is what we have come to think, and we conclude that it is much better for you to be with Edma. That you two should remain together for a while.

I visited Manet, whom I found in greater ecstasies than ever in front of his model Gonzalés. He did not move from his stool. He asked how you were, but I suspect he has forgotten all about you for the time being. Mademoiselle Gonzalés has won all of Manet's attention. She has all the virtues, all the talent, all the charms. She is an accomplished woman.

Last Wednesday there was nobody at the Stevens's except Monsieur Degas, who sends his regards.

That is all for now,
Maman

I crumple Maman's letter. Why isn't she content with four hundred kilometers separating Édouard and me? Why is she still so afraid of what might happen that she finds it necessary to rub my nose in the news that he has forgotten me in my absence? That Eva Gonzalés holds him captive in her spell?

I stand at the window and gaze out at the harbor, at the lonely boats and the still, glassy water. I once read that water was a symbol for life. But here it seems dead. Is it an omen? The death of dreams and lives.

In Paris, the city breathes for you when you wish to give up. It gives you no choice but to live.

Perhaps I shall give into the death of Lorient and say here with Edma forever.

After four full days of work on the canvas, the painting is beginning to come to life. Edma, too, seems excited by it. I enjoy her company. The weather is exquisite, and she insists on accompanying me every day to the harbor to pose.

"Berthe, this is almost as good as being in the company of our friends. I have missed the Salon so much."

"Did I tell you I spoke to Puvis on opening night?"

Edma shakes her head.

"I had spent most of the evening with Édouard. He was in such high spirits, very excited about how the public had received *Le Balcon*. For about an hour he was leading his mother and me all over the place when I ran headlong into Puvis, who seemed very happy to see me.

"He was trying to persuade me to meet him at the Salon again the next day because he couldn't stay that night—had just dropped by and was getting ready to leave. While I was talking to Puvis, I completely lost sight of Édouard. I was mortified. Puvis left. Édouard had wandered off. Suddenly I was alone in the midst of the crowd. I was so embarrassed to be walking around the place on my own. When I finally found Édouard, I reproached him for leaving me."

"You didn't."

"I most certainly did."

"What did he say?"

"I believe he was a bit put out. He told me I could count on all his devotion, but nevertheless he would never risk playing the part of my nursemaid."

"You're joking?" Edma laughs, a great big guffaw of a laugh, which tickles me, too. Oh how I love the sound of my sister's happiness. It warms me like nothing else can.

"Sounds to me as if Monsieur Manet was none too pleased to see Puvis," she says. "Did they speak?"

Her insinuation makes me smile, and I look up from the canvas.

"They were cordial—just barely, though—exchanged polite words, but the next thing I realize, Édouard is gone."

"He left on purpose." Edma twirls her umbrella. "My, my, what a temper if he is not the center of attention."

"Oh, I do not know if it is like that."

The conversation trails off. Edma wears a wistful expression.

"I love hearing all these stories. Consider me crazy if you like, but when I think of all those artists, I tell myself that a quarter-hour of their conversation is easily the equal of solid quantities."

"I suppose." I blend some blue in with the green to create a shadow in the foreground of the scene. "They usually have something interesting to say. It's usually laced with a bit of scandal." I tell her what Degas said about Léon. Edma's eyes grow wide and she sits up straight.

"I can only guess that he married her to give the child a home," I say.

"But not his name?" Edma asks.

I shrug. "He is an honorable man." I want to add that their marriage does not mean he loves her as a husband loves a wife, but I refrain.

Edma sits thoughtfully for a while, tipping her face up to the warm breeze. "What does not make sense is that he married her so long after the boy's birth. What do you make of that? Didn't Madame Manet say they had been married five years? And the boy is in his mid-teens."

I nod as I blend white and red to the shade of her scarf and touch it to the canvas.

"Then that means he was nearly ten or eleven years old when they married. And why pass him off as his godson? Something does not make sense, Berthe."

I chew the handle of my brush for a moment, weighing my words. A cool breeze blows in off the harbor. I have pondered the same puzzle myself almost daily since that evening at the Salon. Alas, I have found no logical explanation save Édouard being a man of honor. Since answers will not annul the marriage contract, I have decided to leave it at that. Never mind the way he looks at me or worse yet, the way he kisses me into a stammering state of confusion. No, those are not traits of honor. Not when a man has pledged his life to another.

Yes, it is much easier to stop at honor and just leave it alone.

I gaze at the results of my four days labor. Never have I been so pleased with my work. It's as if the energy pent up during my months of paralyzing idleness has been stored, culminating in this piece.

"It feels sublime to be back on track," I say. "I would so much rather produce one good work than an entire Salon full of mediocre scribbling."

"Good, then shall we call it a day?" She stretches. "My back hurts from sitting on this hard wall."

"Yes, let's go. We've been here a long time."

I feel guilty talking about my triumph in the face of Edma's artistic purgatory.

But then I stop. Why should I feel guilty? She has a baby on the way—the thought takes me by surprise and sends little shivers down my spine.

Even if Edma did not wish to pick up a brush again, I hope she will at least consider adorning her walls with a few canvases.

I will paint her something new before I return to Paris. I consider leaving this one, but I want to hang onto it and submit it to the Salon next year. It was disappointing to not have an entry this year—it was one thing to be rejected, but it made me quite disgusted with myself to know I didn't even try.

Inaction—the worst of diseases.

I glance at the painting as we walk up the dirt road. In a way it is symbolic—that everything that is meant to be always works out as it should. Edma has her baby. I have my painting.

"Who is that?" Edma says.

"Who?"

I shade my eyes and follow Edma's gaze up the road to the porch of her house and see the figure of a man sitting on the porch steps.

At first I cannot see clearly because the sun is in my eyes. At four o'clock, the sun is on its downward grade in the western sky. It shines brightly, silhouetting the visitor. Without trees, the unfiltered light plays havoc on my vision, and I think it might be Adolphe returned home early.

I squint into the light and for the span of a beat, my heart stops. *No, it can't be—*

"Édouard?" I whisper.

Surely not—a strange swirling sensation begins in my stomach, and my head swims. Surely the light is playing tricks on my eyes.

"I believe it is he," says Edma. "Berthe, he has come to see you."

I quicken my pace as well as I am able, lugging a large canvas and easel. Edma has my paint box. It is no challenge for her to pass me. As we draw closer, Édouard stands and removes his hat.

"*Bonjour, Madame Pontillon. Et mademoiselle* . . . I am so happy to see you. I feared I had missed you after coming all this way."

He steps forward and relieves me of my easel. I am suddenly very conscious of the work that had so thrilled me only moments ago. I angle it away so he cannot readily see it.

"Bonjour, Monsieur," says Edma. She sets my paint box down on the step. "I hope you have not been waiting long. We have been out making the most of this beautiful day."

He smiles. "You look well, Madame. I have just recently arrived. Mademoiselle, I am happy to see you have been working. Please, may I see what you've done?"

What is he doing here?

I hesitate, gripping the edges of the canvas with both hands, careful not to smear the wet paint. The breeze lifts the scent of the oil and it reminds me of the last time I was in his studio. I wonder why. It is the same pungent scent that surrounds me most every day of my life. But suddenly it personifies him.

He reaches out and with a gentle hand turns the canvas toward him. He's quiet for a moment, then a slow smile spreads over his face.

"This is a masterpiece."

I recall a time when Degas remarked at how Édouard admired the work of his friends, and once Maman warned me to beware of the difference between a man's personal compliment and his professional evaluation. Yet, my heart lifts as a leaf soaring on the breeze.

"You possess such talent," he says. "I stand in awe of you.

I would gladly have this in my personal collection. Name your price."

Edma laughs. Claps her hands like a child.

I take a step backward, because it suddenly feels as if he is standing much too close. "Do not be ridiculous. I cannot sell it to you. The paint is not even dry." I am stammering, and I hate myself for it.

"What brings you to Lorient, Monsieur?" Edma asks, as if sensing my agitation. Her bemused expression suggests a mere fraction of the feelings coursing through me.

"What brings me here? Why Mademoiselle Berthe, of course."

My skin tingles.

Edma makes a sound like, *Oh!* "Well, if you will excuse me. I shall just go inside."

The door clicks shut behind her, but opens again. Edma sticks out her head.

"I thought you might want to go for a walk, but please come in anytime you like."

She disappears inside, leaving me alone with Édouard.

Chapter Fifteen

The stars and the rivers and the waves call you back.

—Pindar, Greek

LIGHT the color of amber glass reflects off the lone tree in my sister's yard. The hue deepens into a rich shade of burnt umber where the setting sun reaches through the leaves to caress the branches and trunk. Twilight usually leaves me feeling wistful—melancholy even—homesick for places I've never been, achy for some indefinable something I could never put my finger on.

This evening, as we stand on Edma's porch, Édouard offers his arm. "Shall we walk?"

"That would be lovely." As I lace my arm through his, I feel akin to the light—I am all at once mellow and fluid and hot.

This evening I finally feel as if I have found that for which I have been longing my entire life.

We walk in silence for a long time before I ask him, "Why did you come?"

"Mademoiselle, you disappeared. I waited for you to write

to me. But I waited in vain. Finally, I had to send Fantin to your Maman to do a bit of detective work to discover your whereabouts. And here I am."

He places his hand atop mine in the crook of his arm. I cannot believe he has gone to so much trouble to find me. If Maman's letter was true, I wonder how he escaped the enchanting Eva's death grip.

"Maman wrote that you have been quite busy with Mademoiselle Gonzalés. I did not write because it sounded as if you did not have a moment for anything else."

Édouard narrows his eyes. His brows knit into a bemused frown.

"That is not true. Would your sister mind if we were gone so long to take a turn around the harbor?"

I shake my head. "There is no one within four hundred kilometers who will mind."

Again, we stroll in silence. I wonder what he had told Suzanne of his trip to Lorient. *If* he has told her. And how long he plans to stay. Did he intend to ask Edma for a room for the night?

All these questions swirl in my mind, but Maman's comments about *the eternal Mademoiselle Gonzalés* surface high above them all, pushing the others to the side. I decide I will not let him sidestep the issue with the diversion of a walk.

"Relations are going well with Mademoiselle Gonzalés?"

He shrugs. Then after a moment's hesitation, shakes his head. "No. As I told you at the Salon, she is very young and demands constant attention." He wrinkles his brow as if the mere thought causes him pain. "I do not have the time or patience for that."

"Is that so? Maman wrote that—let's see, how did she put it? That she found you in greater ecstasies than ever in the presence of the captivating mademoiselle."

"I do not mean to dispute your mother's good word, but *au contraire*. When she visited my studio, I was working furiously to finish the mademoiselle's portrait." He waves his hand in disgust. "I have done as much as I intend to do with it. Yesterday, I informed her papa that the arrangement is finished."

I try not to smile. Try to stroll along as if we are discussing the weather and other banalities. But I find myself enraptured by the strange pleasure of standing so close to him—in public, without fear of happening upon an acquaintance who would delight in telling the world about what she has witnessed.

His hand is still on mine, tucked in the crook of his arm. Those we pass regard us as if we belong together—man and wife out for a stroll on this beautiful, warm spring evening. We do not see many people, but those we pass smile and tip hats in gracious greeting. Édouard holds himself in an erect manner that suggests he is proud to be seen with me.

I have the sensation of knowing what it is like to belong with him. Yes, it would be like this if we were married.

I stop wondering why he come to Lorient. Leaning in a little closer to breath in that familiar smell that is Édouard—the lingering scent of linseed oil, and wool and man. For a few beautiful, timeless moments we are one, and I lose myself in the blissful illusion as we walk together toward the harbor.

The air smells of a salty sweetness I had not realized before. Looking again at the cracks in the road, I recall the first day I set foot in Édouard's studio, when the air smelled fresh and the world felt new and full of possibilities.

Before we reach the water, he veers off the parched road past a row of identical white plaster houses to a grassy knoll I did not notice yesterday when I arrived.

Finally we stop at the top of the hill beneath the shelter of a weeping willow tree.

Dust motes dance in the golden sunlight that filters through the flowing branches, highlighting the new green that mingles with patches of the lingering winter brown.

He sits on the grass and tugs me down next to him. My stomach pitches because I think for an instant he might kiss me. Instead, he settles back on his elbows and simply gazes at me, through half-open eyes, his leg touching mine.

I arrange my skirt around me, more for the sake of diversion than anything else. When I glance up, it is obvious that he likes what he sees, but the intensity with which he studies me makes me uneasy, as if he is comparing me to every woman he has ever beheld.

I do not mind holding myself up to comparison when the competition pertains to something within my control, but I have always shied away from contests of a personal nature because the rejection that follows hits too close; it's too private. I can always fix a canvas or paint with different colors or in different venues, but I cannot change the person I am. And that is fine, for I have never desired to be anyone else—especially right now.

It is much easier to turn away before a suitor's interest fades. That way I never have to watch the interest dim. It never becomes personal. They never come back. Never pursue or try harder. They crumble and fall. And I know it is for the best. For the relationship would have fallen eventually.

A flock of birds screech as they fly by in formation.

But here is Édouard. Steadfast and persistent. He keep following. No matter how fast I walk away, I turn around, and there he is.

"I enjoy looking at you." His voice is a husky timbre, and his leg shifts closer to me. "I enjoy being with you."

I am exhilarated and frightened all at once.

What would he do if I reached out and took what I wanted, like a common whore? That is how Suzanne captured him—although it is hard to imagine her being so bold.

Édouard and I share the same madness, the same visions, and disgust for the impostors who claim to paint the truth. That is how we come together—in truth and beauty. Not by one snagging the other. Trapped into a life together by virtue of a child.

"Why do you call Léon your godson when he is your son?"

Édouard sits up but does not quite meet my eyes.

"He is not my son."

Annoyance bubbles up inside me, threatening to burst into a full-blown distaste.

"You do not have to pretend with me, Édouard. I know that is why you married Suzanne. No?"

I reach up and turn his chin so he must look me in the eyes. He seems to pale a shade.

"No, that is not why I married Suzanne."

"Why then?"

"It is complicated, and I do not want to spoil our time together by talking about it."

"Does it mean you love her?"

He covers his face with his hands and rubs it as if he can scrub my question away.

If he can't answer the question are you really going to sit here with him like this? says Propriety. *You shouldn't be alone with him in the first place.*

I get to my feet and start to walk away.

"Wait. Please, do not go."

I stop but don't turn around. "I do not wish to compromise myself. Especially with a man who loves another."

I take a few more steps.

"That is not it. Please stay and I shall tell you."

I return to my seat beside him, leaving more distance than before. Once I am settled, Édouard sighs and looks at me as if he might shed a tear.

"I have never shared this with anyone outside my family." He plucks a blade of grass and smoothes it between his fingers. "Léon is my brother."

I gasp, recalling Degas' words that I did not fully believe. "I do not understand."

He swallows, and his throat works through the emotion.

"When I was in the navy, my father fell in love with a young woman . . ." He hesitates and picks at the grass again. "That woman was Suzanne."

He meets my gaze and holds it.

"He was married to my mother, and she had given him three sons, so he could not very well leave her. So he brought Suzanne into our home under the guise of teaching my brothers and me piano. My mother did not like it, but she would not go against her husband's decision. About eight years before my father died, Suzanne gave birth to a son. It was all very hush-hush. She went back to Holland before she started to become heavy with the child, and returned with her *baby brother.* My mother was livid. She did not want Suzanne to return, but my father was heartsick without her.

He even contemplated leaving to be with her until my mother relented and agreed to Suzanne's return. It would have been a scandal if he had divorced my mother for Suzanne or given the boy his name, so everyone played along that Léon was her brother."

He paused and drew in a ragged breath.

"Then my father died. That was six years ago. My mother had absolutely no use for Suzanne and was ready to throw her and the boy out into the street.

"I could not talk any sense into her. It was as if all the anger pent up over all the years that my father had loved this woman in my mother's house had broken loose.

"She and the boy had no place to go—no money, no friends. She was a good person, Berthe. Even if I had given her money, what kind of existence would she have been able to provide for her child?

"So I married her."

I sit in stunned silence and worry the pleat on my skirt into place. Then he reaches out, and traces a finger along my cheek.

"I was thirty-two years old. I thought I might as well save her from a horrible fate. Because I had never been in love . . . until now."

My breath comes in shudders. His hand trails from my cheek, down my neck, my shoulder, my arm, grazing the side of my breast. The caressing sweep, finally resting on my thigh.

"I love you, Berthe. I have since the first day I saw you at the Louvre. Sometimes I fear I might go crazy for wanting you."

I look at his hand on my leg, at the broad fingers and short clean nails and think this is something, because most painters have rough dirty hands.

His are clean.

My throat is too tight. A fullness blossoms in my belly, leaving me breathless until tears come to my eyes.

Like me, has never loved until now.

I place my hand on his hand. He spreads his fingers so mine fall alongside his. He closes his hand snug against mine and pulls my fingers into his palm, taking possession.

If a person asked me why I loved him I would have asked why is the sky blue? Or why does honey taste sweet? My feelings for him are as organic as the willow tree above us, running more steadfast and deeper yet than its roots below us.

Now I am certain he feels the same for me.

He leans in and kisses me, full and gentle. His tongue parts my lips and thrusts deep inside my mouth in a tender urgency that compels me to melt into him. He tastes of passion and peppermint, just as I remembered.

He eases me back onto the grass, and I know my life is about to change, irreparably.

I have never had a man's hands upon my body, until his. I have certainly never known a lover—as we lay fully clothed with the sun setting over the western harbor, darkness sets in and cloaks us with the indigo night.

His hard body moves atop mine, and I feel I will burst from sheer need if he does not take me.

When it comes to it, he hesitates, pulling back, looking deep into my eyes.

"Are you sure, Berthe?"

My breath catches at the sound of my name passing his lips.

"I do not want you to do anything you do not—"

I pressed a finger to those lips. "*Shhhh,* I want nothing more."

I pull him to me and he answers with a groan that escapes his kiss. Then he shifts to the side and lifts the skirt of my red dress and my petticoats, exposing my bare legs. Somewhere along the way my shoes have fallen off, but I do not recall when or where. I forget them instantly and lay in glorious half nakedness watching him undo his trousers to free himself.

He strokes my abdomen down to my inner thighs, kneading my womanhood until the bleakness that has tethered me for as long as I could remember releases and my spirit rises up inside me like a giant balloon and bursts.

I cry out.

"You are so beautiful," he whispers before his mouth comes down on mine and he enters me.

Chapter Sixteen

I love in you a something
That only I have discovered—
The you—which is beyond the
You of the world that is
admired by others
—Guy de Maupassant

A FULL moon hangs high as Édouard walks me back to Edma's house. Lying with him under the weeping willow tree, watching twilight give way to a curtain of night as the moon climbs high, time seemed as irrelevant as the number of stars dotting the beautiful indigo sky.

I could have been perfectly content to stay under that tree, naked in his arms, forever—talking, laughing, loving, again and again. Alas, he finally pulls me to my feet, helps me into my dress, and we walk down the hill, warm in the cocoon of our newly expressed love.

My canvas and paint box are still on the porch. I move the painting out of our way to give us room.

"Please come in," I say. "Edma will let you stay the night."

He shakes his head. "I should not want to prevail upon

your sister." He takes my hands. "And I would not be content to sleep alone in a cold bed with you so nearby. I shall stay at the inn and take the train back to Paris tomorrow."

Knowing I could not go to the inn with him, a hundred horrid questions flood into my mind. Why must he leave? Will I see him tomorrow before he goes? If not, when will I see him again?

What's next, Édouard?

Panic, cold and sharp, stabs my insides, and I wonder how he can stand there so calmly when inwardly I am coming undone.

"It looks like you sitting there." He nods toward my canvas of the harbor. "Every time I see that painting, I shall remember this day."

"Oh, that sounds like good-bye." I hate myself for uttering the words. They sound so depressed, so needy.

"No, Berthe, it is just the beginning." He pulls me to him and kisses me. I want him as fervently as I did the first time he had taken me. "You had best go inside. Your sister is probably worried about where you got off to with me."

As he walks away, he stops at the bottom of the steps and turns back to blow a kiss.

What now, Édouard?

As I watch him disappear into the salty Lorient night, I know I will risk everything to be with him. I am tempted to go after him, to share his bed, make love to him as the sun rises and blesses our union.

But I do not.

Instead, I stand for a moment in the cool darkness, my heart breaking into a thousand tiny pieces hinged together by the glue of a promise—that this is just the beginning.

The house is dark when I let myself inside. No sign of Edma. She must be asleep and I am disappointed because I want to talk to her. I want to share with her every marvelous detail—the reason Édouard had married Suzanne; that we have loved; that we are in love.

I am different now. Fully a woman and it was every bit as wonderful as I could have imagined. The only thing I need is for Edma to encourage me that the future holds bright possibilities—that Édouard will divorce Suzanne and marry me.

I listened at the top of the steps and hear only the quiet of the house—the occasional satisfied creak and groan of the old home settling in for the night. If she is with child, she needs her rest. I decide not to awaken her and take the painting and my paint box straight up to my room to retire for a restless night, dreaming of marriage and babies.

Yes, perhaps I will give Édouard a child. I lay my hand on my belly, tender with the memory of his fullness. My body aches, but it's a good ache, and I wish Édouard were here to hold me right now.

I drift off to sleep thinking that if Édouard has planted his seed inside me tonight, my life would be complete. . . .

When dawn finally rouses the daylight, I dress quickly, fueled by the hope that Édouard will pay a breakfast call before he departs, and I go downstairs eager to tell Edma everything.

But she glares at me when I enter the drawing room.

"Where did you go last night?" she hisses.

I blink at her tone.

"If you are speaking of yesterday evening, I was with Édouard. You know that."

"And you know very well that is what concerns me. I was worried sick about you—you . . . you were gone for hours. It was dark. I was so worried something had happened to you."

Something did happen to me and it was wonderful and the

only thing I wanted more than sharing it with my sister was for Édouard to be here with me when I did.

"Oh, Edma, don't be ridiculous. Nothing bad happened. I was with him and—"

"Exactly. What are the townspeople to think? My sister cavorting about with a married man doing God knows what."

"I beg your pardon. The townspeople do not know me and have no idea of Édouard's marital status. Since when does that matter to you? I seem to recall a conversation—a day when we strolled along the quay—in which you encouraged me to pursue him despite all scorn and impropriety. Were you not sincere?"

She looks as if I have slapped her. Her mouth opens, then closes without an utterance. A feeling akin to dislike flickers through me.

"Answer me, Edma, why did you encourage me to seek my pleasure if you were not sincere?"

Her face crumples into a mask of astonishment. "Is that what you did out there? Seek your pleasure?"

"I did." I spat the words and let them reverberate in the cold space between us.

Edma closes her eyes, and I think for a moment she might faint. But when she opens her eyes, I see the unmistakable glare of disgust.

"How could you, Berthe? This may not be Paris, but I still must live here."

"Why the change of heart, Edma? Why did you encourage me to confess my feelings for him if you were only to sneer at me in disgust?" My voice has risen to a scream, but I cannot help it. This is not my sister sitting here. The woman might resemble her, that's where the likeness stops. My sister is warm and accepting and understanding. This imposter with her wedding ring and foul attitude is someone I do not wish to know.

"Were you taunting me—because you thought I would not have the guts to find the same happiness you have with Adolphe? Do you not want me to know that happiness?"

Movement in the doorway catches my eye. Dominique cowers, looking in askance.

"Do not worry, Dominique," Edma says. "Everything is fine."

I wait for the maid to leave. "No everything is not fine. I shall leave this morning on the train."

"Berthe—" Her words bounce off my back as I bound out of the room.

If I hurry I can catch the eleven o'clock train to Paris. Édouard will be so surprised to see me.

I cannot manage the trunks. So I stuff as many of my things as possible into my valise, grab my canvas, and set off on foot for the station.

Edma tries to stop me, but I kiss her and say, "It is best this way. I do not want to upset you in your delicate condition. I shall send for my belongings at a later date."

With that, she lets me go. Relations are still strained, and I hate to leave her this way, but I do not want to be subjected to her judgment. I guess I should have predicted this to happen. Edma is the good girl, the one who always does what's right, who always encourages me to go where she did not dare. And I always did because I was . . . Well, I was *not* the good girl.

On the short walk to the depot, I shove aside my sadness of fighting with Edma and focus on all the things I wanted to say to Édouard. That I love him. What we shared yesterday was the most beautiful thing that has ever happened to me. That I never want us to be apart again.

My stomach is all aflutter with the thought of his kiss when I arrive at the station, fully expecting to see him waiting on the platform as if he expected me.

But he is not there.

He is probably finishing his breakfast and will appear shortly. I purchase my ticket and sit on the bench—waiting.

The ticket master is talking to someone who never appears on the platform. It is not Édouard's voice. I discern that right away. A handbill lifts on the wind and blows down the tracks until it lodges in a clump of greenery.

The sun rises higher in the clear blue sky. Until in the distance, the faint rumble of the train announces the eleventh hour.

Still no Édouard.

As the train screeches and snorts to a stop, I slip inside the depot, and approach the ticket counter.

"Excuse me, Monsieur. Is this the only train to Paris today?"

"It is the only one left today, Mademoiselle. The other left at six o'clock this morning."

My blood runs cold.

"Did a gentleman board the train early this morning?"

"Oui, Mademoiselle."

I hear the conductor call, "All aboard."

"Merci, Monsieur."

He nods. Heavy with sadness, I turn and board the train for Paris alone.

Chapter Seventeen

It is terrible to desire and not possess and terrible to possess and not desire.

—W. B. Yeats

I HAVE been back in Paris two days and have not heard from Édouard. One minute I am convinced he is not aware of my return. The next minute I am sure he regrets what happened between us and avoids me.

If he's attempted to contact me in Lorient, and receives no answer, he might harbor the same doubts about my feelings. I have no idea what Edma will tell him, if anything, for I have not even heard from my sister since I left. I have no idea if she remains furious with me or, for that matter, what she plans to tell Maman of my visit.

Upon returning, I simply informed my mother I left because I was not able to accomplish enough work in Lorient to warrant an extended stay and there had not been enough time to write her of my departure. It is not a lie. Beyond painting the Lorient harbor, my inspiration dwells in Paris. Except possibly also in a certain weeping willow tree in Lorient, which I intend to paint someday. For now, I prefer preserving its memory in my mind rather than committing it to canvas.

Maman accepts that rationale. Her mood has lightened considerably since before I left for Lorient. I imagine her smug over revealing Édouard's rapt attention toward Eva Gonzalés. But neither of us acknowledge this is the source of her improved disposition. I simply concentrate on how Édouard has relieved himself of the young, beautiful pest. I prohibit myself from dwelling on the possibility that somehow Eva has managed to worm her way back into Édouard's life and that is what detains him now.

I hang the harbor painting in my studio, where I can readily view it and recall Édouard's words—*Every time I look at it, I shall remember this day.*

Usually, it helps to look at the painting. Other times it serves as a reminder of how difficult matters have become since that day. The lone figure sitting on the cold stone wall, waiting . . . the longer I sit in this house, a prisoner of my solitude, the more difficult the situation becomes.

As I pace the confines of my studio, walking between my easel and the sad stand where Edma used to paint, I realize the source of my angst does not solely stem from missing Édouard. I am sad over the way Edma and I parted.

If I am to fully recover my sanity, I must make amends with her. I do not mind being the first to reach out.

I wander into the drawing room and find Maman reading. She glances up from her book. "*Bonjour*, my dear, Bijou."

It has been ages since she has called me Bijou. "*Bonjour, Maman*. You seem happy today."

She lowers her embroidery into her lap. "It is nice to have you at home. Until you left, I did not realize how quiet this house would become without my children."

It is a strange remark because I am not so talkative that my absence would make a noticeable change in our home's atmosphere. I sit down at the desk and pull out a sheet of stationery.

Maman watches my every move.

"To whom are you writing?"

"To Edma."

"You miss your sister. I guess that is to be expected. I am glad you had such a good visit that you cannot wait to correspond with her. After you are satiated with work, you should go stay with her again."

I nod and pull a pen from the desk drawer.

"I do quite like the painting of Edma at the harbor. That alone was worth your trip. If you refuse to concentrate on finding a husband, I am glad you are at least painting again."

I wish Maman would stop chattering. I have no desire to venture into the volatile terrain of potential mates. It turns my mind back to all the plans Édouard and I have yet to make. How long will it take Maman to recover after Édouard and I announce our plans?

Maman and Papa are getting old, and I do not relish disappointing her. But I cling to the hope that she will eventually embrace Édouard as her son-in-law and view our union as happily as if Édouard had not made the mistake of marrying Suzanne.

I set pen to paper hoping Maman will realize I cannot chat whilst I compose.

My Dearest Edma,

Please do not be angry with me. I am sick over the manner in which we parted. Please find it in your heart to forgive me and to understand. I have never felt this way for anyone before.

Much love,
Berthe

Committing the words to paper releases some of my anxiety. I should write Édouard a note to tell him I have returned. I slip another sheet of paper from the desk.

"I learned a valuable lesson while you were gone, Bijou." I glance up to find Maman looking at me over the top of her glasses.

"What is that, Maman?"

"I underestimated you, my dear. It is not your fault that the public misread the meaning of Monsieur Manet's *Le Balcon*. After observing him with Mademoiselle Gonzalés, I have no doubt you are perfectly innocent. He is a philanderer and a flirt who needs no encouragement when it comes to attractive, vulnerable young women. You did nothing to entice him. I was wrong to blame you."

A funnel of angst swirls in my belly. The sound of her voice grates on my nerves as she sits there so smug and sure that her assessment is the only correct answer.

I want to scream that she is wrong. That she knows noting of Édouard's intentions. Nor of the situation. He is not a philanderer! He is not a flirt!

He loves me.

And I love him.

"I think your departure to Lorient has firmly set him in his place. I believe after seeing him that day in his studio—the way he fawned on that young girl right in front of his wife—he realizes his flattery will get him nowhere with you. Suzanne was visibly shaken by his actions. Madame Manet had me touch Suzanne's hands, saying she was feverish. The source of her fever was obvious."

Fear as intense as a living thing dances through me, and I believe for a moment I will succumb to my anguish right before her. I cannot bear to be in the same room with Maman and her incessant prattle. I rise from the desk, Edma's letter and the clean sheet of paper in hand, and walk toward the door.

"Where are you going?"

"To prepare this letter to send."

"Leave it here, and I shall see that Amélie takes it for you."

If I do, she will read it.

But I manage to murmur, "I am not quite finished with it. I shall give it to Amélie when I am done."

"Save the letter for after lunch. It is nearly noon. We can dine together."

"I am not hungry, Maman. I still have not fully recovered from my journey." The truth is I have no appetite for food. Meats and cheeses and breads will not satisfy the hunger that gnaws at me.

"Suit yourself."

I shut myself away in the studio and stare at the blank sheet of paper for a long while. If I send a letter, there is the risk of it falling into hands other than his own. I cannot chance that risk. Besides, it will only delay matters.

After lunch, Maman will lie down for her afternoon nap. I will go to Édouard then. He will be at his studio, and we shall talk. Everything will be fine.

It is not a small canvas, and it is quite cumbersome to transport it in the carriage. But I must bring it to him. Until we can be together permanently, Édouard must have the painting to remind him of how much we need each other. How good we are together.

It makes perfect sense.

From the street below, I see his studio windows are open. It is a good sign. He is there. Although, never once did I doubt he would be anywhere else.

The air smells of springtime, of greenery and the faint scent of flowers from an open-air market down the street. I relish the aroma of brioche baking in the patisserie across the boulevard. No wonder Édouard's windows are open on such a fine day.

The horses whiney and the driver steadies them before offering to carry the painting upstairs, but I refuse his help opting to climb the four flights to his *atelier* alone. I have to go slowly, to take care not to lose my balance as I traverse the steep incline.

I pause outside his door in the dim, quiet hallway to catch my breath before I knock. I do not hear a sound coming from his studio. If I did not have such a strong belief in us, I might be concerned at how he would receive me, or worried about whether he was alone.

I draw in a deep, steadying breath before I rap lightly on the door. I stand there, my heart pounds beneath my bodice, and I fear I've knocked too softly and he did not hear me. I am about to knock again when the door flings open.

Never have I witnessed such a look of surprise on his expressive face. I think he will hug me, but instead, he places a hand on my shoulder and leans across me to look out into the hallway. "Are you alone?"

I nod, unable to speak for the sheer joy of seeing him. Pulling me inside, he shuts the door, and takes the canvas from me, placing it haphazardly against the wall. He draws me into a tight embrace and smothers my mouth with his, hard and urgent.

Oh, how I have craved his touch.

There is nothing gentle about his kiss, as when we were together beneath the willow tree in Lorient. But I encourage him to drink deeper. This kiss is fueled by pure, burning need—the rough desire of a parched man who is finally able to drink his fill. He holds me so tight, I feel him grow hard against me. An ache throbs in the vulnerable places he claimed when we were last together.

Any harbored doubts melt away with each caress, each muffled moan of satisfaction.

Finally, reluctantly, he pulls away slightly, still holding me against him. "Hello, my love. When did you get back? I thought you would be with your sister for some time."

"I returned two days ago. I could not stay in Lorient knowing you were here."

He pushes a piece of errant hair behind my ear, setting my hat slightly askew. He plucks it from my head, and the hatpin falls to the floor with a tiny *ping-ping*. We both bend to retrieve it and laugh at how we bump into each other. In our stooped position, he kisses me again, lighter this time; a peck of delight that welcomes me home. And I know I am right where I belong.

As he scoops the pin off the wooden floor, I am renewed—by the sound of his laughter, the bristle of his beard on my cheeks, the touch of his hands on my body.

It feels wonderful to be alive and I regret not coming to him the moment I arrived back in Paris.

There is something intimate in the way he sticks the pin in my hat—a task I had performed almost unconsciously hundreds of times before—yet something in the sight of his large hands performing such a mundane task thrills me.

"What did you bring?" He sets the hat on a stool and reaches for my painting. I realize it is facing the wall.

"A gift for you."

He looks at the canvas and his eyes brighten. "*Ahhhh, oui.* The masterpiece. But you should not give this to me. You should save it for the Salon."

"That is a long time off. I shall borrow it back when the time comes. But in the meantime, I want you to have it."

He inspects it at eye level and shakes his head, a look of appreciation washing over his handsome fame.

"It is much too good to be hidden away here. I shall take it home and hang it in a place of honor."

I like that. It feels satisfying, as if he is bringing me into his home.

As I glance around the familiar space of his studio, warmth fills me. Everything rests in its usual place—the books; the props; the collection of pigments and brushes stored in jars; the paint tubes—some covered in pigment powder and nearly spent; others brand-new; the dressing screen along the wall; the unmade bed in the far corner. It seems ages since I have been here. Is something different?

Of course it is. I am different

The last time I was here, Édouard and I were not lovers. I am seeing everything with new eyes, even his easel in the middle of the room.

"What are you working on?"

He gestures with his head. "Have a look."

I pull off my gloves, tugging one finger at a time and walk around to view the canvas.

I stop, stunned, to find Suzanne's likeness staring back at me. Clad in a delicate white dress and seated on a white divan set in front of frilly, sheer white draperies she looks almost . . . beautiful.

Shock knots into a dull ache in the pit of my stomach. I glance at Édouard for an explanation. He is busy cleaning his brushes, as if there is nothing extraordinary about him glamorizing his fat, homely . . . wife.

For a moment, I believe the smell of linseed oil will overpower me. Only then do I realize I have wadded my gloves into a tight little ball. I smooth them out—anything to divert my gaze from Suzanne's triumphant visage.

"What do you think?"

Édouard smiles—colleague conferring with colleague.

Why is he painting her? Olympia demands. *Why now?*

Because she is his wife, Propriety chides. *It is about time he painted her.*

But it doesn't even resemble her, says Olympia. *This is some idealized imposter.*

Perhaps this is how he sees her. Propriety reigns victorious.

"It's quite—white," is all I can muster.

He squints at the canvas, shrugs. "I began this painting years ago, but I never finished it. I guess I felt I owed it to her after the monstrosity Degas presented. It offended her . . ."

That's what was missing. My eyes dart to the vacant spot where Édouard had hung Degas' painting after he washed over Suzanne's image. It was gone. Now he was trying to make it up to her by portraying her in a falsely flattering manner.

"But Édouard, Degas' painting of Suzanne was *true.* It resembles her much more than this does." I can't believe I said it.

His eyes darken, and for a moment I fear he might defend her. I cannot bear it. I will not hear it.

"Édouard you have always painted what you see. Is this how you see her? Is this how you feel about her? If it is, then we have no business . . . *You* have no business—"

"Berthe, I care for you, but she is my wife."

His words bounce off my ears as a frantic tumult consumes me, blurring my vision and stripping away all semblance of steady ground.

"But in Lorient you said you loved me." I turn to leave so he will not see my vulnerability. Tears stream, and I dash the back of my hand across my face, but they fall too fast for me to conceal.

I manage but a few steps toward the door, and he is there. "Please don't go."

"Why did you come to Lorient?" I murmur.

"Because—" He looks anguished, as if he is searching for

the right words and reaches out and pulls me to him. He holds me, and I cry into his chest as if by expelling all my angst I can vanquish the demons that keep us apart.

But I know it will change nothing.

Not if he loves her.

I pull away from him, reach for the door handle. "Just let me go. You should have never come to Lorient."

He holds the door shut.

"Please, Berthe, do not leave. Lorient was not a mistake. We shall work this out. Somehow, we shall find a way."

Dearest Berthe,

Of course I forgive you. I only hope you can find it in your heart to excuse my outburst that drove you away. I am so frequently out of sorts, I scarcely recognize myself.

I try to remind myself of the miracle growing inside me—that is the reason my body feels swollen and tender. Sometimes it seems nothing consoles me.

I am ashamed of myself for misleading you during our walk along the quay. What I spouted was a romantic notion, and I believe I was caught up in the fantasy. Alas, as I have discovered, marriage is a sacred institution with which one should not trifle. I know you understand, my dear. Please forgive my foolishness.

I should be decidedly cheered if you would agree to come for another visit soon. Please, my dear, do.

Affectionately,
Your Sister Edma

Chapter Eighteen

Blow wind to where my loved one is,
Touch him and come and touch me soon,
I'll feel his gentle touch though you,
And meet his beauty in the moon.

—Ramayana

July 1870

I AM grateful for evening's darkness. It hides everything but the moon and stars that burn as if they are all that matter. At night, when I am alone, I look up and see the sliver of silver moon hanging crooked in the sky or pick out a pattern of diamond stars and know it is possible that Édouard is gazing at the same spectacle. It is as if I can draw a line directly from myself to the stars and down to him, wherever he may be. It connects us, and the night erases everything else in the world that does not matter.

I was naive to believe life would fall into place once we were lovers, that the extraneous would simply fall away to what mattered—our love. It is not so simple. If anything, life has become more complicated over the months since that day of new beginnings in Lorient.

Edma came home for her confinement. She has a beautiful baby girl. She named her Jeanne. With my sister here, I could hardly find time to steal away with Édouard. As much as I want to.

We do not see each other as often as I would choose. It is hard to sit idly by and accept that.

Alas, I am not trying to fool myself into false position. For I know that attraction climbs a steep grade to the crest of seduction. What follows is but a fall, hard and fast, with a most unforgiving landing.

I bide my time and resist the urge to push fate into action.

A star falls from the indigo sky.

I fear it is an omen and run my hand across my belly. I have no stomach for food, and I wish Edma were here so I could ask her about the signs of pregnancy. I cannot write and ask her such delicate questions.

Perhaps it is just nerves.

Everything is so uncertain. There is nothing left for me to do but wait, drawing lines in the nighttime sky, streaks of hope that connect my beloved and me.

After dinner, I join Maman and Papa in the sitting room. It is brightly lit with lamps, and I squint as I walk into the room. Papa is in one of his moods. "Do not call me unpatriotic. Anyone with common sense would support Adolphe Thiers."

Papa is ranting again. Something he has been prone to since his years as a prefect under Thiers. Papa was still as loyal as his first days, rallying around the former prime minister.

Poor Maman was bearing the brunt of my father's evening tirade. With my book, I turn to seek refuge in another room out of earshot.

"Garmont is an imbecile, I tell you. If he had left well enough alone we would not be on the verge of war."

War? I turn back. The subject had been on restless minds for the past two years, but it was just an idea—born of those who feared France being surrounded by hostile powers—not a reality. "Papa, what are you saying?"

"I'm saying that because of a grave diplomatic error, a war with Prussia is imminent." Papa wrings his hands. "France is ill prepared. It will be a disaster. But your Maman will not hear of it. She reproaches me, calls me a doomsayer. She calls me unpatriotic."

Papa can be difficult. This I knew, but something in his ashen face and knit brow tells me this is real.

JULY 14, 1870

Hundreds of Bonapartists march along the boulevards. I shutter the windows, but even that will not drown the shouts of *"Vive la guerre!"*

It seems all of Paris is starved for war. All too soon France erupts in a flurry of activity readying itself to fight the evil Prussian forces that have bullied our country for years.

All naval officers have been recalled. Edma's husband, Adolphe, ships out of Cherbourg, where Edma awaits his return. Alas, she writes that she knows in her heart it will be a long while before she sees him again, but she takes comfort in the fact that the navy is strong and well fortified.

I can only wonder where Édouard is, as I have not seen him since word of this crisis shifted everyone into hysteria. I ask my brother, Tiburce, what he has heard of our friends—I cannot ask for Édouard specifically—but he has no news. If Édouard has rejoined the navy, I hope I shall see him again before he ships out.

At least the navy is well fortified. I wish I could say as

much for the army. My brother, Tiburce, enlisted rather than waiting for the government to commit him. His youthful, fighting spirit landed him assignment in the Rhine.

Despite the army's weakened state, Maman is quite pleased. "This is my idea of how men should behave in a time of peril."

Is forgetting everyone not connected to the war the way a man should behave? I realize it is a time of national crisis, and I should not be selfish. But I should think Édouard would care enough to inform me of his plans or at least inquire about my well-being.

I am growing anxious with concern over my condition. I don't know the signs of pregnancy, but I certainly have not been feeling well. I contemplate taking the carriage to his studio, but with all the talk of fighting, Maman will not let me out of her sight. If I set foot outdoors she insists on accompanying me. I cannot talk to Édouard with her in tow.

So I wait, going mad with each moment that passes.

Maman and I try so hard to keep up our spirits. But it is difficult to be jovial when just after a few weeks into the fighting we learn that Tiburce's brigade, under the command of Marshal Bazine, was hemmed in at Metz. With this news, we cannot convince ourselves that this nightmare will soon end, that the sound of cannon fire in the distance is not as grave as it sounds. That the rain that falls from the sky is not Paris crying for its own.

SEPTEMBER 3, 1870

The Prussians have taken the emperor prisoner. We realize just how fast the situation is escalating toward crisis. Papa must stay in Paris because of his position with the new regime.

He implores Maman and me to go to Edma in Cherbourg, but Maman will not hear of it. "Where my husband is, I shall stay beside him. How can I leave when I have no idea what fates befall my son? He will not know where to find me when he is set free."

The look on Papa's face is such that I believe he wants us to go without him. All I can do is reassure my mother that everything will be fine.

I wish I truly believed it.

Dear Edma,

I received your letter yesterday. I have made up my mind to stay in Paris, because neither father nor mother told me firmly to leave; they want me to leave in the way anyone here wants anything—weakly and by fits and starts. For my own part, I would much rather not leave them, not because I truly believe there is any real danger, but because my place is with them, and if by ill luck anything did happen, I should have eternal remorse. I will not presume to say that they take great pleasure in my presence; I feel very sad, and am completely silent. I have heard so much about the perils ahead that I have had nightmares for several nights in which I have lived through all the horrors of war. To tell the truth, I do not believe all these things. I feel perfectly calm, and I have the firm conviction that everything will come out better than expected. The house is dreary, empty, stripped bare; and as a finishing touch, father makes inexplicable and interminable removals. He seems to be very much occupied with the preservation of some old pieces of furniture of the First Empire. On the other hand he smiles pityingly when

I tell him that the cabinet, the mirror and the console in the studio are not absolutely worthless. To avoid argument, I refrain from interfering in anything, and to tell the truth all this interests me very little. Since it is possible to work where you are, why don't you do so? I do not read the newspapers much anymore. The Prussian atrocities upset me, and I want to retain my composure.

I am stupefied by this silence. I certainly wish I had news of you—though I dare not hope for an answer to this letter—and of poor Tiburce, from whom we have not heard. Maybe you will hear from him before we do; there are moments when I think of him with a terrible tightening of my heart. I embrace you, my dear Edma . . . If you are cut off from Paris, do not worry on our account. Mother is better, and father is in as good health as can be expected.

Adieu.

SEPTEMBER 4, 1870

The rain has passed, giving way to heat and sunshine. It is much too bright outside for the state of our country. It seems at odds with national morale. We have received word that hoardes have stormed the Hôtel de Ville in support of a new republic. Looking out the window, I see mass chaos in the streets. The usually quiet boulevards of our beloved Passy are awash in a sea of red and blue uniforms, men rushing about. I do not know what will become of us in the face of such bedlam.

Papa maintains that this war is wrong. He fears for the safety of his children, Tiburce, Edma, baby Jeanne, and Yves.

Yet, I seem to irritate him by being constantly underfoot. He seems disgusted when I cannot eat. "Soon there may be no food, and I shall remind you of how you turned up your nose at the offerings today."

"Would you be happier, Papa, if I went to stay with Edma?"

"Of course not. Then I would have you to worry about, too."

Staying is the choice I have made. I will do my best to stay out of his way.

SEPTEMBER 6, 1870

Edma has finally agreed to take baby Jeanne and stay with Yves in Mirande.

In a letter informing us of her plans, she begs me to come, too. I wish she would come to the rue Franklin, but since Yves will not leave her home to be ransacked, as she puts it, there is no alternative but for Edma to go to Mirande to be with her.

I wander into the studio. Pick up a paintbrush and try to work. Instead, I end up staring at the canvases on the walls. The ones I had intended to send to Edma when it seemed we had all the time in the world.

I console myself that it is a good thing I did not send the paintings to her in Lorient. She cares nothing for her house, especially now that she has a bébé on whom to shower all her affections. The paintings would have only made it difficult to pack up and leave for Yves'.

My sisters are alone. Their husbands are off fighting. It makes sense for them to be together. I serve my duty here looking after Maman and Papa. I set down the brush without as much as having touched it to the paint. It rolls off the table onto the floor. I do not have the energy to bend down to retrieve it.

SEPTEMBER 8, 1870

Nearly two months have passed and still no word from Édouard. I do not know where he is or what has become of him. I scarcely know what to think, except that I am devastated. I do not know of his plans or if he is even alive. I shift between hopeless grief, sure of his death, to icy anger, certain he has forgotten me in the face of this national tragedy.

To add to my anguish, after two cycles' absence, Monday I received the sign that confirms I am not with child. Having learned the truth, I shut myself in my room and cried.

After weeks of being so sure, it feels as if our child has been taken away.

Not knowing Édouard's fate, the thought of having his child held vast importance. For if the worst were to befall us, at least I would have had a piece of him to carry forward once the tragedy of war is behind us.

Although I continue to pray for his safety, I cannot help but lose faith that Édouard is alive after so long an absence.

SEPTEMBER 12, 1870

Like a ghost standing in the foyer, Édouard has finally come to call, dressed in the smart red and navy blue uniform of the National Guard. He cuts a striking figure.

Emotion clouds my logic. Common sense should have me ecstatic to find Édouard alive, safe, calling on me. For an instant, I want to run to him and throw my arms around him and rejoice in his safety, but the sight of him standing there so nonchalantly, as if he has not abandoned me for the past two months, angers me, and I have to swallow against the urge to shout at him.

I do not want his reasons or his excuses or even to know how he has spent his time while I have been sitting here like a captive, missing him terribly, fearing I was carrying his child. As the edges of my vision start to crumble around me, I turn away and walk out of the room. I want to be as far away from him as possible.

I shut myself inside the studio and sit down in front of my easel, although I really do not feel like working. A few moments later the door swings open. Maman pauses, arms crossed on the threshold.

"Berthe? What is the matter with you?"

"Nothing, Maman." I pick up a brush and pin my eyes on my canvas, a painting of Edma at baby Jeanne's cradle.

"Come out and be civil to our guest. Manet has taken precious time away from his duty to call on us. The least you can do is receive him graciously."

"I do not feel like company right now. I want to work. The light is right, and I must take advantage of it."

She stands silent in the doorway for a moment—just long enough to make me hopeful that she will leave me alone. "Very well then, I shall invite him here. I should think he would like to see what you are accomplishing while he is out fighting for you."

Fighting for *me*? Édouard is not exerting himself in anyway for me. I suppress a snort, but by that time Maman is gone.

I hear her voice in the garden, "Berthe would love for you to come to her studio to see what she is working on."

Oh, Maman. No! I stand too fast and knock over my chair.

Hearing their footfalls, I quickly right my seat and sit down. Best to look calm and busy.

In my peripheral vision I see Maman usher him in. I squeeze a tube of azure onto my palette and realize I did not really need the color. Too late. They linger in the threshold.

"Come in," says Maman. "Look around. Please make yourself at home."

"Let me see what keeps you so busy," Édouard says, and moves behind me. "Eugène sends his regards to both of you."

"How is the dear boy adjusting to war?"

"Not very well, I fear," says Édouard. "He is not political by nature and even less of a fighter."

Maman clucks at this comment. Édouard shrugs and smiles at me.

"Four days ago, I sent Suzanne and the family to the safety of Oloron-Sainte-Marie in the Basses-Pyrenees."

So that is what has been keeping him. Worry over Suzanne. I do not want to know the nice things he does for her, the ways he demonstrates he cares. A reminder that she is his wife.

I cannot stand his hovering behind me—his not commenting on the painting. I stand up and walk to the divan leaving him at the chair.

"You are very quiet, Mademoiselle," he says.

"I am simply thinking about how relieved you must be to know that your loved ones are safe."

He perches coolly on the edge of the chair.

"I should like to see every person who is dear to me safe, Mademoiselle. Do you plan to evacuate?"

"Don't be ridiculous. Of course not."

He strokes his beard and closes his eyes. "Please get out while it is still possible. Pissarro, Sisley, and Monet have escaped to London. Degas has transferred from the infantry to the artillery. Renoir has been posted to Bordeaux. I do not believe you are aware of the gravity of this situation."

"Papa has determined it is safe for us to stay. That is what we shall do until he advises otherwise."

"I have hidden many of my unsold canvases in the cellar of my studio. Special canvases, such as *Le Balcon* and your painting of Edma in Lorient, I have given to Théodore Duret to store in his vault. I would not want anything to happen to them."

"What is taking Amélie so long with the tea?" Maman stands. "If you will excuse me, Monsieur Manet, I shall go hurry her along. I know you do not have all day."

She bustles out in a flurry of copper-colored skirt, leaving the door open behind her.

"I have missed you *mon amour*," he says.

I fear Maman is still within earshot, but I do not hear gasps of astonishment or footsteps hurrying back in regret of leaving us alone.

"How can you tell such falsehoods? If you missed me, you would not have stayed away."

"I am sorry, but in case you have not noticed, France is at war."

I glare at him.

"Your presence has been too scarce for you to notice, but since I saw you last, I feared I was carrying your child."

The color drains from his face, and I take perverse pleasure in watching him struggle with the thought. I stand and walk to the window.

"Do not worry," I say over my shoulder as I toy with the drape. "It is solved. You are free. We are not . . . I am not . . . The sign that proves I am not pregnant presented itself. There is nothing to bind us."

"Berthe, how can you say that?" He is standing now. "The heart is what binds us."

I laugh at him. A cold, humorless sound that makes me want to cry.

"We could not bring a bastard child into such an ugly world. And now I know it is all for the best."

He stands behind me now. The words that he does not know how to deliver hang between us unspoken. He simply lays a hand on my belly. I think I see moisture in his eyes, but he blinks. I am sure it is just relief.

"I have contemplated the logistics of freeing myself from Suzanne, but do you realize the scandal that would mire our relationship, Berthe? I am not sure you are strong enough to endure it."

"I am not strong enough? That is just an excuse—"

Footsteps sound in the garden. I hear the wheels of the tea cart. Édouard pulls away from me and walks back to the divan.

I stay by the window wishing for rain and dark gray skies, spouting emotion I cannot express.

Papa has a new fixation: our home is safe as long as the Forts of Issy and Vanves stay in French hands. He is so convinced that the worst will befall us, he is now preoccupied with what will become of our precious furniture in what he sees as the inevitable event that we are forced to move. Ever the doomsayer, he has already started making arrangements to have our possessions stored in a safe place in the center of Paris.

He is obsessed. When I mention it, we fight. So I avoid talking to him. What I find interesting is how he has not seemed to notice the lack of communication.

"How can you spend every spare moment fretting over possessions?" says Maman. "If the situation is as grave as Monsieur Manet declares, you should be more concerned over the safety of your family; do not worry over the furniture."

He bristles.

"If you wish to leave, you and Berthe should go to Mirande with Yves and Edma. But I will go nowhere. I have worked too hard for the treasures that you enjoy in this home, and I will not see them destroyed.

"You are so busy nagging, you did not give me a chance to tell you that I have made arrangements with a friend, Monsieur Millet, for us to move into an apartment in the rue Argensen should the fighting worsen."

"Both of you stop it," I say. "Stop yelling this minute."

But Maman, with that determined look in her eye, does not hear me.

"Manet has gotten you overly excited," she says. "You should not listen to him and you know it. He is always prone to exaggerate."

"You will thank me should the bombs fall on the rue Franklin." With that, Papa storms out the door and Maman collapses in a fit of tears, pushing me away when I try to console her.

I used to dream of going abroad. I had formed quite an attachment to the idea of visiting New York City in the summer. Of venturing out into the countryside and setting up my easel alongside a stream shaded by tall sugar maples with the broad green leaves the size of a man's hand. I imagined taking off my shoes and wading up to my knees into the cool water. It would be like a baptism for the start of a new life.

The world on the other side of the Atlantic was magical to me, like the secret life on the opposite side of a mirror. You could see it and press your hand up against it. When I was a child, I used to believe if you wished hard enough you would awaken one glorious day to find yourself there.

New York is where I dreamed Édouard and I would start over. There, we could be anyone we chose to be—newlyweds, the happy young couple embarking on a life together—pioneers exploring a brave new world. There would be no scandal—no Suzanne. No disapproving looks. No wagging tongues sharp with criticism.

Just Édouard and I and the life we painted—falling asleep in each other's arms and making love every morning as the sun rose. There we would be successful in conceiving a child.

As all able-bodied men defend Paris and I shut myself away from the outside world, I cling to that dream to keep myself alive. Édouard vowed to call again within the next week and that is when I would tell him. We could make plans, and he would see I am not so weak as to forfeit our life together.

The more I think about it, the more perfect it seems. The war is the perfect cover. Suzanne is away. My presence seems to irritate Maman and Papa more and more each day—so much so that I have come to believe they will be better off without me. I can tell them I am going to stay with Edma. Édouard and I would simply take a train to the coast, board a ship, and sail away.

SEPTEMBER 19, 1870

True to his word, Édouard calls at the rue Franklin with his brother, Eugène.

Maman and I entertain them in my studio, since it is the only place in the house with enough furniture to offer our guests a place to sit.

"The Prussians are so brutal. The atrocities they perpetrate defy logic." Édouard shakes his head, leans in, and lowers his voice. "Word is they desecrated a convent and raped a young novice. Mademoiselle, promise me you will not venture out alone."

I have no stomach for horror stories. Eugène must read as much in my expression. He scoots forward on his chair. His teacup clatters against his saucer.

"Édouard, stop such morbid talk." I have never heard Eugène speak so boldly. "Can't you see how you are scaring the poor woman?"

"I am fine, Monsieur. Thank you for your concern. Even so, I shall not venture out of doors. I do not think I could bear to see my beloved city in such turmoil. I have been distracting myself by reading and working. In fact, that reminds me. Édouard, could you assist me with something? There is a book on the shelves in the sitting room that is on a ledge much too high for my reach. Could I trouble you to get it for me?"

"Certainly, Mademoiselle."

As we stand, I hold my breath waiting for Maman to question my request or Eugène to offer his assistance, but the two commence talking about the strength of the National Guard.

Édouard and I walk to the sitting room, listening to the faint murmur of conversation streaming from the studio. I hear Eugène say, "With the speed in which the Prussian army advances, sometimes I fear I will not survive this terrible ordeal."

Once inside, he follows me to the bookcases. I turn to him.

"I am so happy to see you today. I wanted to believe you would come, yet the last time it had been almost—"

"*Shhhh.*" He slips his arms around me and covers my mouth with his. "Do not waste our time together on unhappiness," he says, pulling me closer.

"I was thinking about what you said. We would not have to endure scandal if we were not here to face it."

"Hmmmm. . .," he answers, his lips on my neck. My head tilts in automatic response, allowing him room to possess me.

"Édouard, listen to me." I plant my hands on his shoulders and make room between us, but he tries to close the gap, tries to reclaim my body. "I want us to go away. Tomorrow. I have it all planned."

He looks at me through hooded eyes, and I cannot tell what he is thinking. So I continue before he has the chance to stop me or before I changed my mind.

"Meet me at the Gare Saint-Lazare at ten o'clock. We can catch the eleven o'clock train for the coast. By the day after, we can be on a boat sailing for America."

Édouard blinks. He runs his hand through his beard. Sighs. "Berthe, we are at war. I—"

"*We* are not. We can be together if you will only give me your word."

He does not answer me. He only looks at me with sorrowful eyes that send a mournful shudder through me.

"Édouard, please—"

"Berthe? Monsieur Manet?" Maman's voice grew closer. "While you're in there will you please fetch me a book, too?"

"Tomorrow at ten?"

He nods and sweeps a kiss on my lips with his finger. "The Gare Saint-Lazare."

Chapter Nineteen

If all the world were mine to plunder
I'd be content with just one town,
And in that town, one house alone,
And in that house one single room,
And in that room, one cot only,
For there, asleep, is the one I love.
—ancient Sanskrit poem

AFTER Édouard and Eugène leave, I have much to do before the morning without making Maman the wiser. I've not even thought about how I will get out of the house alone without her noticing. I am contemplating how I will get to the station when Amélie brings me a letter from Puvis.

Dear Mademoiselle,

I am not able to pay you a call in person. So I write with high hopes that this letter finds you and your family well during this very sad time for our glorious country.

I am serving in the National Guard, in and around Versailles. Leaders assure us the fight will worsen before it gets better. For many, we will soon see our last hours.

At times like this, dear Mademoiselle, one is inclined to take stock of one's life and what is important. I decided if I were to die today, I shall pass in peace only if you know how fond I am of you. Your friendship has always been a bright spot in my life, and my only regret is that I did not pursue you more diligently in more carefree days.

As I fight, I want you to know I am defending you. Please do not hesitate to call on me if I may serve you in anyway.

Your devoted servant,
Pierre Puvis de Chavannes

I am quite astounded by Puvis's letter.

Flattered.

Touched by such a tender declaration. Quite frankly, I had no idea of the depth of his feelings. He has been a friend, appearing now and again in my life, but never has he given me any indication that his feelings run so deep. I am relieved he chose to express his feelings in a letter rather than conveying them in person. When one is so candid, so forthright they do not deserve to have their hopes dashed with the tender words still hanging in the air.

Oh, Puvis. Such a dear, sweet man. My heart is heavy as I utter a silent prayer that he will see the end of this terrible war.

I take the letter to my bedroom, tuck it beneath the mattress, and remove my valise from the closet to start packing for my new life.

* * *

The only way I am able to leave unnoticed is to time my departure between Papa's leaving for work and Maman's coming down for breakfast.

It is good that I am getting an early start because I must walk to the train station—a good five kilometers.

I wait for ten minutes after Papa closes the front door, then I quietly let myself out, hoping that Amélie will not hear the creaking floorboards and come out to investigate. Or that my heartbeat is not echoing as loudly in the foyer as it is thumping in my ears.

I do not want to explain—or lie about where I am going—as I stand here in my travel clothes with my valise in hand.

My heart weighs heavy as I pull the door closed for what I realize will be the last time. It clicks shut, and I step onto the sun-dappled walk bathed in early morning's gentle light. I shall miss my Passy. Although it is not my birthplace, it is where my heart will always reside.

Doubt seeps in around the edges of my tightly constructed plan. But Édouard will be there. There is no other option.

He will be there. We will board the train and be at the coast by midafternoon.

This is the only possible scenario.

The streets of Passy proper are a quiet contrast to the sound of cannon fire in the distance. A few people pass—businessmen in carriages on their way to work; mounted national guardsmen patrolling the area; a boy delivering newspapers. Strolling along the cobblestone street, I keep my head down for fear I might happen upon a neighbor or a friend of my parents.

I have packed only a change of clothes, as I knew it would be a long walk. Already the valise grows heavy. I switch the case to my left hand and adjust the strings of my handbag to assure it is closed securely. I am carrying only enough francs to pay for our train fare. Since Édouard and I did not have the time to discuss logistics, I have brought enough to pay for both of us. With his duties, I don't know if he will have the opportunity to get money. The rest of my francs are tucked away in a pouch I have sewn inside the bodice of my dress.

The breeze blows the faint smell of smoke from a faraway fire, but it smells like freedom to me. I focus on the fact that by this time tomorrow, Édouard and I will be on a ship sailing for New York.

All is going well until I travel about one kilometer down the Avenue Kléber and hit a roadblock.

"Mademoiselle, where are you going?" The armed soldier is young but talks as if he is a father reprimanding a child. "Why are you out this morning by yourself?"

I tilt my chin. "I am going to the Gare Saint-Lazare to catch a train."

"I am sorry, Mademoiselle, no trains running today. The station is closed until further notice. I cannot allow you to pass."

I step closer and he lifts his gun. The gesture startles me. Thought he is not pointing it at me, it is in the ready position. I am offended by the brash gesture.

"I beg your pardon, Monsieur, but I must get through I am meeting my fiancé."

"He is an idiot to let a woman walk alone in the streets. It is not safe after last night's tragedy."

The word causes gooseflesh to erupt on my arms. "What are you talking about?"

"Versailles has fallen to the Prussians. Paris is surrounded. I have strict orders that no one is to pass."

"But I must—" I contemplate turning away as if I am complying with his orders and then trying to find another way to the station.

"Bodier, escort the mademoiselle home and see that she gets safely inside."

The man called Bodier indicates for me to follow. I realize all is lost.

Mere words cannot describe this paralyzing dread expanding inside me. All that exists within me is bitter cold and utter helplessness. It is as if I have let go of Édouard's hand and he has drifted off into the heavens and there is nothing I can do to stop him.

Dearest Edma,

I am writing you because I do not know whether in another few days we shall still be able to correspond. Paris has changed still more. I think of life before this war, and it seems to me it is not the same city. I received a note from Puvis de Chavannes, who writes as if our last hour has come. Moreover, I see that the National Guard is very restive. Manet's brother told me very calmly that he does not expect to come out of this alive.

Papa pins all his hopes on the success of Monsieur Thiers's mission. Father continues to be in good health and is driving us all crazy.

Kisses for bébé.

Adieu, dear. Do enjoy the peace of Mirande. It is better than the agitation here.

Berthe

Dear Berthe,

We feel just as indignant as Mother does when Gambetta is unjustly attacked. It was he who did most for the defense, and it is he who is mostly denounced today. He is unanimously attacked in the provinces and held responsible for France's defeat. In this world success is everything.

This reactionary Chamber does not inspire me with great confidence. Those who advocate caution and moderation do not seem to be the men of the hour. However that may be, the task is grave and difficult. We must wait to judge them.

There is talk in the newspaper of the German army entering Paris. Perhaps you are now witnessing that spectacle. Nothing is to be spared us.

Affectionately,
Edma

You are right, my dear Edma, in believing that nothing will be spared us. The Prussians are to enter our arrondissement on Wednesday. Our area is explicitly mentioned among those to be occupied by them. This news was circulated in the afternoon; it was expected that they would arrive tonight; then the report was denied in the evening, but this only meant that the entry was being delayed. Our rue Franklin, usually so quiet, was animated, the Place de la Marie and the main streets are filled with noisy crowds. The National Guard was against surrendering its arms, and protested loudly. All this is very sad, and the terms are so severe that one cannot bear to think about them.

Each day brings us some new sorrow, some new humiliation. The French people are so frivolous that they will promptly forget these sad events, but I am brokenhearted.

If I happen to voice this opinion at home, father throws up his hands and says that I am a madwoman.

There was a great commotion yesterday. The National Guard contingent at Belleville declared that they intended to fire their guns when the Prussians enter. I think we are at the beginning of an emotional period.

Do you know all of our acquaintances have come out of the war without a scratch, except for that poor Bazille, who was killed at Orléans. The brilliant painter Régnault was killed at Bezenval. The others have made a great fuss about nothing.

Affectionately,
Berthe

The air is filled with so much acrid smoke I can barely breathe. The boom of cannon fire sounds so often I wonder why each explosion continues to startle me.

We feel the presence of the Prussian troops all around us. All I want to do is stay in my bed with the shutters drawn. I doze between cannon blasts, and in my fitful dreams, sometimes Édouard is there. We are boarding the train at the Gare Saint-Lazare or he is kissing me as we stand on the deck of a great ocean liner bound for New York. But then the cannon sounds, and I awaken in my dark room, remembering that two weeks have passed since Édouard and I were supposed to meet at the train station.

He did not respond to the note I sent him asking him to call. But I realize it is impossible with the Prussians closing in on us outside.

For two weeks I have taken to my bed, and as the cannons sound outside, I am waging a private war with the demons that have invaded my peace of mind. Maman called in the doctor, Monsieur Dally. But all he does is leer at me. I fear he will insist on examining me for his own pleasure rather than trying to help me feel well again. Although, I don't think it is possible to recover under these circumstances.

"Berthe, wake up." Maman comes into the room and throws open the shutters. "Get up. Get dressed. You have a visitor."

Squinting into the brightness, I sit up. My mind skitters from hope that it is Édouard, to fear that it is Monsieur Dally.

Maman goes to the wardrobe and selects a dress.

"Monsieur Puvis de Chavannes has come to call."

I scoot to the side of the bed and try to stand. But I sway from the effort. "Tell him I am not up to company."

"Nonsense. It will serve you well. You have been brooding far too long. Get dressed. I shall tell him you will be down momentarily."

Puvis. Maman must be truly worried about me to urge me on to receive Puvis. Her attitude toward him has cooled considerably. Although, I do not know why. It seems like one minute she was singing his praises, encouraging me that he would be such a good match. Then suddenly the very mention of his name sets her in a decidedly bad humor.

Today he is back in her good graces—for what reason I cannot discern. Probably simply to get me out of bed and dressed.

I throw an arm over my eyes attempting to block out the light. I should have known it would not be Édouard. Bitter disappointment builds in my throat until I feel I will gag on the repulsive taste.

I pull up the covers and try to go back to sleep, but moments later Maman is in my room again.

"Get up this instant. Monsieur Puvis has something remarkable to show you, but if you do not come down within the next five minutes you will miss it. Come on, I shall help you into your dress. Now, Berthe."

"All right! Stop shouting at me."

The thought of listening to Maman nag for the next two months about how lazy I have become is incentive enough to get to my feet.

It seems I have barely stood when she has me encased in a corset that has become almost too big for me.

"You have lost more weight," Maman murmurs as she throws the dress over my head. A swipe of the brush. A few well-placed pins in my hair. And Maman smiles and deems me presentable for company.

She accompanies me to the drawing room—probably afraid that if she leaves me to go on my own, I will go back to bed.

"Here she is." Maman sings my arrival as if I were a late guest to a party. Puvis stands.

"Mademoiselle, how wonderful to see you. I came as soon as I could, considering the circumstances that befall out beloved country. If you will forgive me for being so bold after having just arrived, I have something to show you. Will you and your Maman come over to the window?"

Maman herds me to where Puvis has thrown back the sash. High up in the sky is a giant red balloon. The bright light hurts my eyes and I blink at the spectacle.

Maman gasps. "What in heaven's name?"

"That is our good friend Nadar. He is the head of the balloon corps. Thanks to him we shall be able to resume communication with the outside world. I saw him floating in the clouds as I made my way here today and could not wait to share it with you."

We stand at the window in revenant silence.

"Everyone used to laugh at Nadar and his fixation with balloons," says Puvis. "Now he laughs at the world as he floats high above the ranks. 'Tis like a sign of hope, is it not?"

I blink. It more resembles a strange dream—this vision high in the smoky sky, like a child's toy left out in the rain. This sight coupled with Maman receiving Puvis so warmly, when I know how much she dislikes him. It is all very strange.

Am I still asleep and this is another nonsensical dream?

I glance up to the sky at the red balloon, my eyes adjusting to the daylight. I try to see Puvis's glimmer of hope. Is it a sign that the world will soon be right again?

Then I notice Puvis is gazing at me intently and remember his written declaration of love. I back away and sit on the sofa.

I do not want to hurt his feelings, especially after he has come so far. He is a good man, a steadfast friend. Alas, I do not have a single romantic feeling for him.

"Mademoiselle, you look exhausted. Are you all right?"

I nod. "By showing me this you have given me new hope that I might communicate with my loved ones who are so very far away."

Oh, why did I say that? I hope and pray the mention of writing letters will not inspire him to broach the subject of his letter. Surely not in front of Maman?

"Will you stay for lunch?" Maman offers. "It will be simple fare—bread and soup."

I can hear the frost forming around the edges of Maman's words. As the polite hostess, of course she would ask him to stay for a bite—especially in this time of war. But now that

Puvis has served his purpose, gotten me up and back among the living, Maman's invitation is as much a notice that the visit should wrap up as it is an offer to dine with us.

"*Merci, non.* I cannot stay. I simply wanted to stop by and check on you."

Maman and I sit, but Puvis remains by the window.

"How is everything?" I ask.

He shrugs. Shakes his head. "It is hard to say, Mademoiselle. Every day we hold off the Prussians is another day that prolongs the war." He shrugs again.

"And what of our friends? Several of them serve in the National Guard with you—Alfred Stevens and Édouard Manet? What do you hear of them?"

"I'm sorry, I have heard nothing. You received news of Bazille, of course. And Régnault. Both dead. It is so sad."

I nod.

"I have heard nothing else. But I am sure no news means the rest are fine. I have not seen their names on fatality lists, and I check it daily."

I breathe a silent sigh of relief and glance out the window again, but the balloon is gone. But that is all right. In fact, I believe it is a good thing.

NOVEMBER 1870

Dear Edma,

I write to you every day, hoping that out of all these letters some will reach you. The victory of Friday has raised the morale of many. We have heard the cannon all morning, but so far it is impossible to know the outcome. We are very well situated for hearing the cannon, but badly for obtaining news.

Would you believe that I am becoming accustomed to its boom? It seems to me that I am now absolutely inured to war and can endure anything.

We saw Monsieur Millet, yesterday; he very insistently offered us an apartment in the center of the city. We have resolved to move into the little *garde-meuble* in the rue Argensen. We shall put what remains of our furniture there. We would be very safe—and protected by the National Guard.

I think often of your Adolphe. I wonder what is happening to his squadron. The total ignorance in which we live is very distressing.

I embrace all of you.
Berthe

JANUARY 7, 1871

"Berthe! Berthe!" Maman shrieks from the opposite end of the apartment. My heart drops to the pit of my stomach, which in turn feels as if it has fallen to my feet. A thousand horrors flood my mind as I rush to her. When I reach her, she is sobbing and clutching a piece of paper to her breast.

"Maman? Maman, what is it?"

"It is a letter. It is Edma. Oh—" Her words give way to wails. Icy fear grips me. This is the first letter we have received since the post resumed service. I do not want to know the news that has caused her to weep. I want to place my hands over my ears and stay that way, shutting out all that is loud and ugly and hurtful, but my arms will not move, and I stand there staring at her dumbly.

"Here." She holds the white paper out to me with one hand and swipes at her falling tears with the other.

"Here, take it. Read it aloud." She waves the paper at me. The slack skin of her flabby arm jiggles with the effort. I shake my head and pull my hand away. As long as I do not read the words, no harm has come to Edma. This may well be my last moment of sanity.

She sighs—actually more of a huff than a sigh. "Oh, what is wrong with you? Do not stand there like such a ninny, Berthe. Everyone is fine. I just wanted you to read the good news."

What? I do not understand. The way she was sobbing and carrying on—

Maman sniffs and waves the letter. "That's what she says. Fine. Everyone, big and small, is well and accounted for."

She laughs through her sobs. Relief rushes over me in waves, yet I cannot cry. My legs, still numb with aborted shock, are weak. I must sit down. I back into the divan just in time and land with a soft thud.

Maman peers at the letter through her lorgnette. "Edma says everyone is in good health, that Adolphe is at sea, and that Tiburce—Oh!" She gasps, then closes her eyes, crosses herself and tilts her head to the heavens, as if reciting a prayer.

"What, Maman, please?"

"She says Tiburce has *escaped* from Metz—and is now a lieutenant! Such joy!"

Her words push me to the edge of the cushion.

"He is fine, Berthe, and a lieutenant to boot."

"Maman, I cannot get beyond the fact that my brother was a captive to share your joy in his promotion. He was a prisoner of war."

"Really, Berthe, if one is to be a hero, one must suffer a few close calls. But my Tiburce, he is wily and will pull through unscathed. I shall never doubt that for one minute. Don't you doubt him, either. After all, he has the brains to outsmart the enemy and that is how he will rise to the top."

A cannon explodes outside in the distance. The Prussians were encamped along the Faubourg Saint-Honoré to the Place de la Concorde. All the French militias clear out, taking up station on the opposite side of the Seine, with a line of sentries guarding the bridges. And Maman is celebrating Tiburce's promotion as if he worked in a bank?

I wonder if she has a true grasp of what is happening beyond these walls?

January 14, 1871

Today is my thirtieth birthday. I do not know who has dreaded this day more—Maman or me. None of us feel a reason to celebrate because the day holds only two realities: there is no end in sight for the war, and I am old—a disappointment to my parents.

Provisions are scarce. We have been living on biscuits for nearly a fortnight. They are stale and unappetizing. Sometimes I feel my stomach is better off without food.

This morning, since it is my birthday, Maman makes a fresh batch, and I feel obliged to at least try to eat. So I sit with her at the tiny breakfast table and pick at the crumbling pieces.

"You are getting too thin, Berthe," says Maman. "You have hollows in your cheeks. You are no longer young. So you must make the most of what you have. No man will find a malnourished waif attractive."

"Puvis has certainly been attentive these past few months," I say, to spite her.

He gathered a bouquet of wildflowers and brought them to me yesterday because he was not sure he would be able to call today for my birthday.

"Pierre Puvis de Chavannes is a strange old man," says Maman. "I do not like him, despite his wealth and his art. I have decided he would not make a suitable husband for you."

"Why, Maman? Because he dotes on me? Because Puvis and I have much in common, unlike the fat, boring Monsieur Dally who would probably rather eat me for dinner than have a pleasant conversation. I seem to remember a time not too long ago when you encouraged me to pursue a relationship with Monsieur Puvis de Chavannes."

She tries to interject, but I am too furious to let her berate me anymore. "What really galls me, Maman, is that even in the midst of a war you still pin the worth of my existence on how attractive men find me. I would laugh at you. Only today I do not feel any humor."

She sits, head bowed, staring silently at the half-eaten biscuit on her plate. I leave the table and retire to my room.

She is right. I am old. That is why Édouard has forsaken me. Why, when he could have his choice of beautiful young models, would he want me—tired, sad, old, and broken?

JANUARY 30, 1871

Maman comes to my room with a cup of tea. She has given up trying to cajole me into eating. But I do appreciate the tea. Now that Paris has surrendered and agreed upon an armistice with Germany, perhaps life would resume. This above all is the easiest to swallow.

As she hands me the cup and saucer she wears a strange smile, an expression I have not seen in months.

"I have a wonderful news, Bijou. Edma has received word that Adolphe is at home in Cherbourg. She has decided to join him as soon as the trains are running again. When she does, she says she will stop in Paris to visit us for a few days. You can accompany her to Cherbourg."

I sip the hot tea and long to spend time with my sister. Yet, staying in Paris is my only chance to see Édouard. The thought leaps into my mind unbidden and makes me angry at myself. That I could even think of forsaking my sister after Édouard has deserted me is unfathomable. I realize he has been fighting a war, but if Puvis has found the wherewithal to make regular trips from Versailles, couldn't Édouard at least send me a note to reassure me of his safety? Unless that means—

No!

He is fine.

Tea splashes over the rim of my cup as I return it to the saucer. Propriety sits next to Olympia, trying to talk sense into the brazen whore. *What a pitiful creature you have become, willing to put your life on hold for a man who obviously does not care. You cannot continue to rip out your heart and offer it to a man who does not want it.*

"That is wonderful news, Maman. A trip to Cherbourg would be lovely."

FEBRUARY 10, 1871

Dear Edma,

If you knew how sad this poor Paris is! And how sad everything is! I have come out of this siege absolutely disgusted with my fellow men, even with close friends. Selfishness, indifference, prejudice—that is what one finds in nearly everyone.

I am eager to see you; it seems to me that we have so much to tell one another, so much to grieve about together. Father says he has written you a long letter. He is far from sharing Yves' opinions; I do not share them either, nevertheless I still manage to disagree with Father. We talk so little to each other that this does not make much difference. We are awaiting the results of the elections with the same impatience as you.

Adieu.

Chapter Twenty

I love you
The more in that I believe
You have liked me for my
Own sake and for nothing else.
—John Keats

MARCH 1871

FINALLY, the trains are running again. Edma sent us a letter saying we could expect her within the week.

"I wish I could be more specific, as to an arrival time, but it will depend when I can secure passage. So many people are moving about after being confined for so long. Please do not worry about me. When I get to the station, I shall hire a carriage to bring me directly to you on the rue Argensen."

We want to believe the worst is over, but by the time we receive her letter, we are in the midst of a new situation which makes us fear for Edma's safety.

The Prussians are preparing for their ceremonial victory march through Paris toward the Champs Elysées. When that fated day arrives, all we can do is pray Edma does not arrive in the midst of it.

The Prussians march in the deserted streets, while Parisians sequester themselves inside, bolting their doors and shuttering their windows against the ceremony. Those monsters have caused enough misery. We refuse to acknowledge how they have brought our nation—and every French citizen—to its knees.

It's all over within two days.

We hold our breath until our dear Edma and little Jeanne arrive with Tiburce two weeks later.

Our parents are elated by the family reunion.

"Too bad Yves could not be here," says Papa. "But it gives me comfort that she is safe at home with Théodore."

I believe once Maman picks up baby Jeanne she does not set her down again. That gives Edma a much-needed break and time for us to talk.

"What do you hear from our friend Manet these days?" There is a sparkle in her eye that encourages me to tell her everything.

"Which Manet? We have seen Eugène more than his brother."

Tiburce, Edma, and I decide to go for a stroll along the quay. But once we arrive, we discover hordes of people milling about. Some are shrieking, others are shouting, still more are weeping. They seem to be overcome by some sort of madness. Then we notice that the quay and the two main streets leading up to the Hotel de Ville are barricaded and lined by rows of armed National Guard, *chasseurs,* and soldiers of the line. A red flag flies on the hotel tower. The military has cordoned off an area, making room for the unceremonious rolling out of three cannons.

The sight makes the hair on my arms stand on end. Edma links her arm through mine and scoots closer.

"Tiburce, what is happening?" she asks.

"I don't know."

He tucks us in a relatively quiet spot and says, "Stay here. I'll try to find out, but please do not move from here or I will not be able to find you again."

As Tiburce disappears into the crowd, I scan the faces of the guards dressed in the red and blue uniforms, reflexively looking for Édouard, but I do not see him. In the midst of this frenzied scene, a familiar pang tugs at my heart. No matter what has passed between us, I hope he is safe and unscathed.

Tiburce is only gone a few minutes when I see Eugène Manet elbowing his way through the throngs.

"Monsieur Manet!" I call.

His eyes brighten when he sees us and he pushes his way to us. I look around to see if Édouard is with him.

"Madam, Mademoiselle, I am happy to see you, but what are you doing here? This is no place for the ladies."

"We were out for a stroll with Tiburce," I say. "He has gone to inquire of the situation."

"I shall stay with you until he returns. It is not safe. I fear the worst is not yet over. There is unrest over the new government. Thiers has ordered the National Guard disarmed. Many are unhappy that the siege ended in an armistice and not victory. I don't know if the discontent that is brewing will come to a peaceable end without more bloodshed."

Edma gasps.

"Please tell me this is not true. I am on my way home to Adolphe, whom I have not seen in eight months. Will this madness never end?"

Eugène places a gentle hand on her back.

"I wish I could assure you it would."

I can see Edma growing anxious. She stands on tiptoes and scans the crowd—for Tiburce, I assume. She steps a few feet away looking.

Eugène and I stand in awkward silence.

"How is your brother?" My heart pounds so loudly, each beat recalls a cannon blast.

A noisy bunch, push between us, laughing and shouting and reeking of drink and unwashed bodies.

"He was released from duty a week ago and has joined his family in the southwest. I am set to follow tomorrow."

With those words, my heart stops. So that is the situation. If any lingering hope of Édouard returning to me simmered within my heart, Eugène had supplied the water to douse the remaining embers.

"I see." I feel as if my insides have been hollowed out. I could not cry if I wanted to, which is a good thing, standing here with his brother. I cannot feel anything except a numb dread that is slowly spreading throughout my body. "Please give Monsieur Manet and his family my regards. Tell him I am much relieved to hear he has escaped unscathed."

Eugène nods and strokes his beard.

"With trouble brewing, I wonder how long he will stay away. He harbors strong opinions about this regime, and I am sure he will want to help the cause."

The *cause.* Papa detests the *cause.* As far as he is concerned, they are a band of revolutionary zealots looking to reinvent trouble. How ironic that Édouard should be among them. I had determined to take a wait-and-see attitude before I branded myself for or against them, but I am beginning to believe I detest them as much as Papa does.

"And you, Monsieur?" I ask. "Will you change your plans with this shift in political climate?"

"I am not inclined to fight, Mademoiselle. If I were to

change my plans, it would take the promise of something much more alluring to entice me to stay."

A man with an empty wine bottle in one hand and his arm around a woman wearing a dirty, low-cut dress push their way between us.

"You speak as if you have already met this—alluring enticement, as you say."

He looks thoughtful for a moment. I am surprised by how focused he remains despite the hullabaloo unfolding around us.

"Yes, he says. "I have long known said *enticement*."

The way he looks at me makes me uncomfortable. Not quite a smile, not quite a—I do not know what, nor do I know how to respond.

I am doing my best to hold my hollow self together in the wake of his news about Édouard's departure, but each new turn weakens the glue that keeps me intact. For lack of knowing what to do, I turn to my sister who is no longer there. I turn in a circle looking for her, bumping into people who are trying to pass.

"Where is Edma?" Nearby, a cannon blasts and I cover my ears. "Where is my sister?" I feel as if the crowd is closing in on me, and suddenly it's hard to breathe.

A burly man shoves past me. I fall backward. An arm catches me. Rights me. Encircles my waist to steady me. It is Eugène.

"I see her," he says. "She is over there with Tiburce." Through the crowd, I catch a glimpse of her. She is wringing her hands talking to my brother and I know the situation must be grave.

"I want to get them so we can go home."

Eugène takes hold of my hand and pulls me through the crowd. Someone gropes me and we bump from one dirty drunk to the next, inhaling vile, fetid odors the likes of which

I have never in my life experienced, but Eugène does not let go of my hand. In a matter of moments, he deposits me next to Tiburce and Edma.

"We must get the ladies away from this madness," Eugène says. "May I accompany you to the rue Argensen? I should very much like to pay my respects to your parents."

We take a different way home, thinking it will be safer to keep to the wide boulevards rather than the winding back streets.

But about halfway home, we encounter an odor the likes of which I hope never to experience again. It is so strong that even covering our mouths and noses gives us no relief.

We see a rotting corpse propped in an open doorway holding a sign that says "Death to Thiers." Edma screams and faints into Tiburce's arms.

I close my eyes and bury my face in Eugène's shoulder.

He puts an arm around me and holds me close the rest of the way home.

My Dearest Edma,

The day of your departure, after that sad walk on the boulevard that upset us so greatly, we had a visit from the fat Monsieur Dally. I was still disturbed. The doctor had been returning from the Place Vendome, where he had been attending the wounded and helping to collect the dead. He told me their names, at least the names of those he knew; I was greatly worried, nervous, being troubled for fear of hearing bad news. This sad evening that the four of us spent together brought back the siege to me as if I had never come out of it. Life has been a terrible nightmare for six months, and I am surprised that I am strong enough to bear it.

May 1871

The courts are closed. Papa is free to go. He insists on moving us from the rue Argensen to Saint-Germain.

"How can we leave our son in the thick of battle?" Maman insists.

"Your staying in harm's way does nothing to keep him, safe," Papa yells. "If you wish to support him, you will go to a safe place so he may remove you from his list of worries."

Maman looks as if she has been slapped into reality. She says nothing, only starts packing what is left of her belongings to take to Saint-Germain.

Because of the new outbreak of fighting, I decide against accompanying Edma to Cherbourg. It is a good thing, too, now that we must move once again.

The day before we leave, I receive a letter from Puvis:

Mademoiselle,

Please be so kind as to send me news of you and your family to Versailles, *poste restante*. I have been here for several days with my sister and brother-in-law, who is a member of the Assembly.

No other place is more unlike Paris than this. That is why I should have chosen it in any case, in order to escape certain sights and certain contacts. I was happy to leave my awful quarter, where informing against one's neighbor is becoming a daily occurrence, and where one may at any moment be forced to join the rabble under penalty of being shot by the first escaped convict who wants the fun of doing it.

I hope that your parents will not think that the place can hold out forever, and that they will leave Paris to await the denouncement elsewhere. If Versailles were not overflowing with refuges, it would be the best place for you, but short of Versailles, there are Cernay, Saint-Cyr, Marly, and many other places.

One is truly bathed in a feeling of grandeur in this admirable and magnificent setting, the sight of which is reassuring, since it recalls a beautiful and noble France, and one can forget for a moment how false and corrupt she is today. Once again, I repeat my prayers to you: please let me know what is happening to you. I assure you all my respectful devotion.

Pierre Puvis de Chavannes

Saint-Germain is a haven compared to the ugly, dirty Paris we leave behind. But it doesn't shelter us from news of the further tragedy that befalls our beloved city.

"The rue Royal is deserted. The entire quarter is dismal and dreary," says Papa, who has just come in from his afternoon stroll. "All the shops are closed; people stand at the window watching the marchers move toward the Place Vendôme to seize the post of the National Guard."

Papa shakes his head. Maman and I can do little but stare at his drawn face. "It is a bloody massacre. They were marching without arms. Twenty-five men killed."

He sinks into a chair at the table in our new accommodations and buries his face in his hands. None of us need utter a word to know what each is thinking.

Tiburce leading the unarmed front. My brother, who thrives on being in the thick of the fight, believes he is invincible.

All we can do is wait and pray he is unscathed.

★ ★ ★

A few days later Tiburce drops in for a moment to assure everyone of his well-being. He looks handsome in his uniform adorned with a party ribbon in the buttonhole. Maman makes such a fuss one would think Thiers himself had paid a call. But I, too, am relieved to see Tiburce looking so well.

"I am on Admiral Saisset's staff. We have taken over the Grand Hôtel. The greater part of the place is barricaded. The windows are covered with mattresses, and we have plenty of cannons and guns." He pauses to sip his tea, and he makes me think of a little boy who has come in for refreshment after spending the morning playing war with his friends. "During the first negotiations, I volunteered to relay communications to Generals Chiseret and Lullier. I am acquainted with them, so I was the natural choice to deliver the *communiqué*."

Maman sighs, "Ah, so brave, my boy."

Tiburce puffs. "I have known some tense moments." His eyes shift to Papa, who looks very old as he slumps in his chair, the vacant expression of worry creasing his forehead.

"It is all in the posturing. For example, we publicize that our forces are two thousand strong. In reality, five hundred is a more accurate count." He laughs. "Never fear, reinforcements are on the way."

Papa frowns. The clock ticking in the background seems overly loud. "This is an atrocity. You cannot fight with so few men. Please stay here and forget this foolishness. They will get by without you."

Maman snorts and throws her head back. "He has a commitment to Admiral Saisset. He cannot simply *forget* to follow through on his word, as *you* would have him do."

Papa looks dejected and Maman indignant. Tiburce's expression does not waver. Ever the diplomat, he tries to mend the peace between the two. "Father, I have men who rely on me for their orders. I am no longer on the front line. When we rally tomorrow at the Grand Hôtel it shall go quickly. We shall be covered. Since they have used force, we shall pick up our arms."

He stands to leave. Maman rises to hug her hero. Papa turns his face to the window.

"You have done your duty," she says, holding his face in her hands. "Take good care, my son.

I watch Tiburce walk out the door. I am proud of his zest. I envy his sense of purpose. It has been a hard time for everyone, but he has not stood by passively subjecting himself to the whims of fate. I have wasted the last year of my life fretting over situations rather than fighting to change them.

Actually, my discontent has been growing longer than a year, beyond the disruption of war. It started with Édouard. I placed my happiness in his hands, gave him permission to mold my emotional well-being as he deemed fit, and look where it has landed me. I am to blame for my own unhappiness.

I received another letter from Puvis. He asked me to call him Pierre. He is sweet, showering me with attention where Édouard has removed himself from my life.

Pierre wants to see me. Wants to win Maman's and Papa's approval. I admit it overwhelms me sometimes, but in him, I have found the affection of a fine man who understands my soul belongs to my work.

Tiburce has found his purpose in his work. I should follow his example. I may not be equipped to go to battle on a national scale, but seeing Tiburce march off so proudly, I realize I can take possession of my life and trump the demons I have battled for so long and win my own war.

My Dearest Edma,

The more I think about your life, the more favored it appears to be. I wish you would tell me whether it is really possible to work in Cherbourg. This may seem an unfeeling question, but I hope you can put yourself in my position and understand that work is the sole purpose of my existence, and that infinitely prolonged idleness would be fatal to me from every point of view.

The countryside here is the prettiest in the world; there would be a lot of subject matter for someone who liked bare landscapes and had the necessary equipment for work. Neither of these conditions exists in my case, and I no longer want to work just for the sake of working.

I do not know whether I am indulging in illusions, but it seems that a painting like the one I gave Manet could sell, and that is all I care about.

Since you understand perfectly well what I mean, answer me on this point and now let us talk about more interesting things. Everyone is engrossed in this wretched business of politics. We can hear the cannon throughout the day; we can see the smoke on Mount Valérien from the terrace. From time to time we meet people who have got out of Paris. Their accounts are contradictory: according to some, people there are dying of starvation; according to others, the city is perfectly peaceful. The only thing certain is that everyone is fleeing from it, and this is sufficient proof that life there is not pleasant.

We are almost reassured about the fate of our house on the rue Franklin, but I see this morning that they tried to destroy the batteries of the Trocadéro from Mount Valérien; such an operation cannot be carried out without splattering the neighborhood, and we are philosophically awaiting the outcome.

Affectionately,
Berthe

There is nothing for me in Saint-Germain. Nothing to paint. Nothing to anticipate.

If I am to quit dwelling in the past and move forward, I must move myself to a place where I am able to move on. With a valise filled with enough painting supplies for Edma and myself, I board the train to my sister's home in Cherbourg. Maman and Papa are quite safe in their little Saint-Germain sanctuary. I can go to my sister with a light heart.

As the engine pulls out of the station, I do not even glance back at the old life I leave behind. The war has torn down more than walls and monuments. I am a different person than I was a year ago, although I do not see how anyone could suffer through the terrible atrocities we have lived through this year and emerge the same. It is not possible. I am broken, yet not irreparably damaged. It is as if I have been taken apart and reconstructed anew. The old ways were certainly less complicated, but now . . . Now I know I shall steer my ship wisely, as Maman is so fond of telling me.

I do not know if it is just that I am happy to be in Edma's company again or if it is merely a relief to be out from under the web of tension Maman and Papa have spun. Even the air here is lighter in Cherbourg. I find many pleasing vignettes to paint outside so I can enjoy the charming spring days. I have begun a new life in this charming place, leaving behind my old unhappiness.

"Edma, turn your head to the left and look down at little Jeanne. This will make a beautiful painting."

My sister's morale seems remarkably improved from when I visited her in Lorient, where she led such a bleak existence. She has a baby now. She has discovered purpose in life. Although she shows no more interest in picking up a paintbrush—she showers all her attention on Jeanne and is content to sit for me.

Dear Mademoiselle,

Your letter brings me much pleasure, and I should like to prove this to you by my promptness in answering it. I wish, however, that it had been more detailed about several things, such as the welcome you received from your sister, who must have been happy to see you again, and also about the outcome of your journey. You know how much such things interest me, whether they pertain to your art or directly to your personal life—which I presume to be the case at the present, for one hardly paints while traveling in a railway carriage. You are enjoying fresh air in the company of your family who love you, you are seeing a place that is new to you, and you are no longer hearing the stupid cannon. Meanwhile, you are as well informed as we are of every important event, and, finally, you are always in your own company. Why then should one be sorry for you? You ask me what is being talked about and what is happening in Versailles. Well, it's always the same things. The rue des Reservoirs has not become easier for Parisians to climb, and they mark time in their souls even more than on the street. As for me, I produce as much as I can, but these things remain in a latent state, so to speak—formless sketches or spots of color that I expect nevertheless to turn to account some day. It is cold, sharp, unpleasant. The shade frigid and the sun pitiless. Add to that some great dust squalls that blind you from time to time and an absolutely artificial existence and you will know as much about Versailles as if you were living here.

Thiers upbraided the Chamber in very severe terms at yesterday's meeting, to the acute displeasure of the great majority, despite appearances to the contrary, and despite the vote of absolute confidence that followed his lashing.

Above all, please write and tell me everything you are doing and thinking. It is more than likely that we shall soon return to Paris. You must come and see what is left of my poor studio.

Ah, those cannon balls—brutal things, aren't they? I often think of those very pleasant hours I spent last year in that big bazaar that has become a dressing station, filled today with every sort of disease. Not so long ago, it was full of strollers, paintings, sculptures, pastries, etc. The point is that time passed quickly there. All this is now strangely gone with the wind, and no sooner will the ruins be more or less restored than one will be oneself a ruin. If only ivy would grow around old me the way it grows around the statues of Versailles.

And so you see you must tell me in great detail what is happening to you, whether you are working, whether you are succeeding—in other words, everything.

Adieu, dear Mademoiselle.

I remain forever your faithful servant,
Pierre Puvis de Chavannes

June 1871

Maman wrote that Tiburce came home yesterday. He gave additional details, of the horrors, but did not confirm everything the newspapers are saying. Montmartre is taken, but the Place de la Concorde put up such a resistance that the shells rained all about our house. We have not much hope that the rue Franklin will soon be cleared. There was a rumor that a neighbor's home was gone, but only part of the wall of our home was damaged and the furniture is still intact.

The Communards have stolen the linen, some pictures, a clock—all the things they can carry, and of course, they emptied the wine cellar, then scrawled disgusting epithets on every available surface.

What is going to happen? I tremble to think. Maman says that once Paris is taken, Monsieur Thiers will resign, and without him there will be nothing to restrain the reactionaries. We shall advance to full-fledged monarchy. New struggles, open or hidden, with no respite. I am afraid that such will be our lot.

MAY 25, 1871

My Dear Bijou,

Paris is on fire! This is beyond description. Throughout the day the wind kept blowing in charred papers; some of them were still legible. A vast column of smoke covers Paris, and at night a luminous red cloud, horrible to behold, made it all look like a volcanic eruption. There were continual explosions and detonations; we were spared nothing. They say the insurrection is crushed; but the shooting has not yet stopped. Hence, their claim is not true. By ten o'clock, when we left the terrace, the fire seemed to have been put out, so that I hoped very much that everything had been grossly exaggerated, but the accounts in the newspapers this morning left no room for doubt. Latest official dispatch: the insurrection is now driven back to a very small part of Paris, the Tuilleries is reduced to ashes, the Louvre survives, the part of the Finance Ministry building up from the rue de Rivoli is on fire, the Cour des Comptes is burned down, twelve thousand prisoners, Paris strewn with dead.

JUNE 1871

Maman writes that she saw the Hôtel de Ville the day after she returned to Paris. What she saw was frightful—the substantial building has been ripped open from one end to the other!

It was smoking in several places, and the firemen were still pouring water on it. It is a complete ruin. Your father would like all this debris to be preserved as a perpetual reminder of the horrors of popular revolution.

It's unbelievable, a nation thus destroying itself! Going down by boat, I saw the remains of the Cour des Comptes, of the Hôtel de la Legion d'Honneur, of the Orsaybarracks, of a part of the Tuilleries. The poor Louvre has been nicked by projectiles, and there are few streets that do not bear traces of the struggle. I also noticed that half the rue Royale is demolished, and there are so many ruined houses, it is unbelievable—one rubs one's eyes wondering whether one is really awake.

Tiburce has met Manet and Degas. Even at this stage they are condemning the drastic measures to repress them. I think they are insane, don't you?

Maman

JUNE 10, 1871

Dear Mademoiselle,

We returned to Paris several days ago, and the ladies asked me to send their regards to you and to Madame Pontillon.

What terrible events have befallen us this year. How shall we ever get back to normal? Each of us blames another, but we're all responsible for what has happened. We're all ruined; we shall have to work hard to glimpse life as it was before.

I happened upon your brother a few days ago. Yet I have not been able to visit your mother as I had hoped. Eugène went to see you at Saint-Germain, but you were out that day. I was pleased to hear your beautiful home in Passy escaped damage. I hope, Mademoiselle, you will not prolong your stay in Cherbourg, as I would like very much to see you.

Ed. Manet

Chapter Twenty-One

Many Waters cannot quench love,
Nor can the floods drown it.
—Song of Solomon 8:7

JULY 1871

IF we begin again, it will end. It has become a pattern with Édouard and me. He senses my pulling away, and courts me vigorously to close the distance. His charm will whitewash the gray distance between us, over which he will paint a new scene of budding possibilities that in the end will never blossom.

Only this time I shall not allow those seeds to take root. I leave his letters unanswered, which makes him all the more attentive, makes him write more frequently, nearly every day, as a matter of fact.

As I sit at the breakfast table, I see another of his attempts at correspondence lying beside my plate.

He has sent twenty-eight letters since I have been at Edma's. I pick up this latest one and hold it for a moment, unopened. Seeing my name scrawled in his bold, familiar script a dreaded sense of compression grips my chest.

Why is it that he does not want me when he can have me, yet tries so desperately to win me the moment I resolve I am finished with him.

And I am.

I am *finished* with him. It is as simple as that.

"What does Manet have to say today?" Edma asks, then bites into her brioche. Her gaze lingers on the letter.

I place it on the table and sip my coffee. "I don't know. I have not opened it."

She looks up at me expectantly. "He has written you nearly every day for the past month."

"He has."

She bites into her bread again. Chews. I stare out the window at Marie, Edma's maid, who is hanging bed linens out to dry on a clothesline that runs parallel to the house.

"Is it about business? Perhaps he wants to introduce you to his dealer?"

"Perhaps." I take another sip of coffee. My stomach is too upset to consider a bite of food. "When Jeanne awakens, shall we go back to the meadow so I can work on the painting?"

"That is fine." She nudges the note with her finger. "But aren't you going to open it?"

The truth is I cannot. Not sitting here with Edma. She would expect me to read it to her and how would I explain? If this letter is anything like the others he has sent . . . declarations of love, remorse for having fallen out of my favor. The content is so familiar it would surely raise Edma's eyebrow.

Possibly even both of them.

"You're still involved with him."

She states the words matter-of-factly, as one would say "the coffee is cold" or "it is raining outside." Still, they catch me off guard. I stare into my cup.

"He is my friend, yes. If that is what you imply?"

The words feel like a lie and raise my ire to a burning level. What kind of friend deserts another in such a dire time?

I am not good at deception. And I know I will do myself a disservice to say too much.

"Then if he is just a friend, why does he write to you every day? Even Puvis, who has announced his plans to discuss his intentions with Maman and Papa, does not write you on a daily basis."

"I do not write to Édouard." My words are a sharp knife slicing through the thick air.

"Exactly."

It is warm in the house. The table is next to a window with an eastern exposure that intensifies the heat. As does Edma's grilling me. I pick up Édouard's letter and fan myself.

"If he were your friend, as you claim," she says, "you would feel compelled to write to him on occasion. And you have not written him a single note." She reaches out and touches my hand. "Oh, Berthe, what are you doing? Puvis is in love with you. Do not ruin this chance."

I pull my hand away and tuck the letter into the folds of my skirt, out of her line of vision.

"Ruin what?"

"Your chance at marriage."

I pick up my cup again, resisting the urge to let my sister anger me.

"I have had no proposals. Even if he does speak to Maman and Papa, they will never accept him. You know their feelings."

"Yes, but he is so obviously smitten with you."

I set down the cup with a thud. "Edma, since you have married, you have become as bad as Maman when it comes to selling me to the highest bidder. The part that angers me the most is that you have never once asked me if I am in love with him."

She dabs at the corners of her mouth with a *serviette.* "Which one gentleman should I inquire after, Berthe? Manet or Puvis?"

I glare at her. At least she has the decency to look away, down at her half-eaten roll.

"Oh never mind," she finally says. "It is obvious."

I spend the morning in my room. We do not go out to the meadow, but it is just as well. The time alone working on the canvas from memory softens my mood. Even in my rage, I have mind enough to realize I do not want this visit to end poorly. I do not want to run home in a fit of temper as I did in Lorient. I do not want to say things to Edma I'll later regret. After all, her concern holds a grain of truth—that Manet himself has proven to be an unworthy candidate for my devotion.

Maybe *unworthy* is too harsh a word. I would like to think he would have behaved much more reliably had circumstances been different. Alas, he is married, and whether he married Suzanne out of love or pity, the woman obviously has a hold on him that runs deeper than his feelings for me. That is the point I will hold firmly in the forefront of my mind.

I slip my brush into a jar of linseed oil. The red paint disperses in the oil like blood in water. I pick up his unopened letter and deposit it in the trash. Édouard and his scattered whims are not part of my new plan for my life.

I shall make a name for myself as an artist. That name will be my own, not that of a man I do not love; not that of a man I marry for the sake of becoming someone's wife.

By noon Edma and I make amends, but it is too hot to paint in the meadow. We sit outside in the shade of the willow tree, fanning ourselves while little Jeanne toddles about in the tall, wispy grass.

"Are you in love with Puvis?" Edma asks.

I sigh, but am not put off by the question. It has been hanging between us like a curtain begging to be pulled back.

"I admire him and appreciate his steadfast friendship, but if Monsieur Puvis wants to ask for my hand in marriage, I'm afraid I have given him the wrong impression. You are the one who has helped me realize this."

We sit for a few moments in companionable silence, but I can feel my sister's disappointment although she does not voice it.

The white sheets hung to dry that morning by Marie, flutter in the faint breeze. Edma and I tilt our chins up to catch the gentle wind.

"Give it time," Edma says. "Emotions are still running high after the terrible year we have just spent. The world is upside down."

I nod. "But when it is right again, I do not expect my feelings to have changed. Don't you suppose Puvis is so anxious to marry because he feels the need to attach himself to something stable, something normal and familiar after the events of this year? Every letter he's written talks about the war causing him to take stock of his life.

"I hesitate not so much because I fear he will change his mind after life resumes, but because . . . because I do not possess the feelings for him a woman should possess when contemplating marriage."

Edma nods and traces a seam in the quilt we are sitting on.

"Maman and Papa would be glad to hear that." My sister seems a bit deflated, but acts as if she is trying to come to terms with my revelation. "You know how they disapprove of him. So you see Maman is not willing to marry you off to just anyone." She smiles and imitates Maman's voice: "I will not settle on just anyone for you. He must be respectable, a man of means—preferably a businessman or politician."

I make a face at Edma, and she laughs.

"Oh, Berthe, it is not that I am trying to marry you off." Jeanne toddles over and plops down on the blanket next to her mother. "I simply want you to know the happiness I have found."

I squeeze her hand.

"But Edma, you are making a life with the man you love. It is not an arrangement born out of middle-aged necessity."

She gazes at me, and I can see the wheels of her mind turning. For a moment I fear she will bring up Édouard again. "So it is not necessarily marriage that you are against?"

"Of course not."

She nods as if she has just fit another piece into a complicated puzzle. She starts to speak again, but the rattle of a carriage off in the distance distracts her. We both shade our eyes against the glare of the unrelenting sun to watch a driver coax horses to a stop in front of Edma's house.

Two handsomely dressed men disembark.

"Messieurs Manet!" Edma calls as she gets to her feet.

My breath lodges in my throat. I want to run—far, far away—but instead, I sit there, rooted to the earth like the giant willow I am sitting beneath.

"Bonjour!" Édouard calls. He throws his arms wide and laughs as if he has just delivered a magnificent joke.

Eugène doffs his hat and waves. It will be nice to visit with Eugène. I have grown quite fond of him. His brother, however, is another matter entirely.

My sister meets them halfway, but I stay with Jeanne, who holds out her little arms for me to pick her up. I do, grateful for the diversion.

As they draw closer, shock courses through my body at

how thin Édouard has become. His cheeks are hollow and his once robust frame is but a spit of what it was.

I draw baby Jeanne to me and bury my face in the downy softness of her hair to avoid looking at him.

I hear Edma say, "What a lovely coincidence. Berthe and I were just talking about you."

"Berthe, why didn't you tell me the Messieurs Manet were coming today?" I detect a certain glint in Edma's eyes that warns of mischief. Pure mischief.

I pick up the painted fan Degas had given me and fan myself. "*Moi?* How was I supposed to know any better than you? The Messieurs Manet are popular gentlemen. I cannot keep up with their social schedules."

Édouard shifts, and I sense a bit of discomfort beneath his affable exterior. He clears his throat. "Did you not receive my letters, Mademoiselle? I sent word of our plans, but it is possible the correspondence has not yet arrived. The mail is still unpredictable. I do beg your pardon for barging in seemingly unannounced. I hope we are not intruding."

Surprisingly, he makes no attempt to leave.

Something about his presumptuousness galls me, or maybe what bothers me is the part of me that I have taken care to bury deep inside is singing at his presence. Realizing this, I am the one who fidgets.

No. No, this will not do at all.

"Come to think of it," I say, "a letter did arrive this morning. I have been so busy with my work that I have not had the opportunity to read it."

It gives me great pleasure to let Édouard know I am not hanging on his every word.

He raises a brow. "Does work keep you from answering my letters?"

A beat of baited silence paints the room with nervous tension. I silently vow not to be the one who breaks the quiet.

"Work certainly occupies her thoughts, as does a certain Monsieur Puvis de Chavannes," says Edma, with a dreamy look on her face.

I dart a narrowed glance at her. What is she doing?

Édouard stiffens and Eugène's head snaps in my direction. All eyes are on me, and Edma's dreaminess has changed to a wicked smile. I am stunned for the first few seconds my sister commences leading Édouard down the false path, but seeing how mention of Puvis's name visibly gets under Édouard's skin, tingles of excitement skitter through me.

"I shall hint at a piece of news I am sure my sister won't mind me sharing."

Eugène's gaze shifts to Edma, but Édouard stares at me.

"There could very well be an *announcement* soon. All I will say is that it has to do with there being a certain addition to the family." She giggles impishly and covers her mouth. "Oh, but it is much too soon to talk, and I have already said far too much."

Edma gets up and walks over to the window. The Messieurs Manet slump dumbfounded in their chairs. I want to laugh out loud. I want to leap up and hug my sister for telling such impious tales—even if I have absolutely no intention to make them true.

Oh, Edma, Edma, Edma. You wicked girl!

It serves Édouard right. And to think Edma does not even know the half of it.

Édouard's upper lip curls back. "What, you and Puvis? How? When? When did this happen?"

I want to say, "It happened while you were away, Édouard." Instead, I cover my tracks. "Monsieur, nothing has happened. Edma should not have said what she did, since there has not been a proposal."

There is dead silence in the room.

"Berthe, dear, may I prevail upon you for a favor?" Edma turns back to me from the window. "I know you wish to visit with our guests, but would you be so good as to go outside and take the wash off the line. It is starting to cloud, and I am afraid we will get a shower. If you will be so kind, I shall make arrangements with Marie to start preparing dinner. Messieurs, you will stay to dinner with us, will you not? We shall not hear of sending you back to Paris with empty stomachs."

Édouard does not answer. As I pass him on my way to the door, I notice he looks positively green as he stares at the wooden floor. I wonder if he has even heard Edma's invitation.

"*Merci,* we would love to say," Eugène finally says. "In fact, I shall help Mademoiselle Berthe gather the wash."

My hand on the knob, I glance back at him.

"No, Eugène." Édouard's voice is a growl. "I shall help the Mademoiselle outside. You stay here and assist Madame Pontillon."

Eugène does not protest. Why does he not stand up to his brother? I stifle the reminder that I do not like weak men who cannot stand up for themselves. But it should not apply to Eugène. In the same vein that my soft spot for strong men who tirelessly pursue me should not apply to Édouard.

They are the exceptions to those rules.

I do not wait for Édouard. I go outside and retrieve the basket on the grass near the clothesline and start yanking down the fresh linens.

"Your sister is right." He is standing behind me now. I do not turn to him. "See those clouds? It looks as if a storm is brewing."

A warm wind, a few degrees cooler than when Edma and I were sitting outside, catches the sheet. It billows up around me. A strong arm reaches over my head. I look up and see his arm silhouetted against the stormy sky. His hand toys with the pin that holds the sheet to the line, but he does not pluck it loose. "Are you going to marry Puvis?"

My shoulders sag, and I want to turn around and scream at him. It is not Puvis whom I love.

Is Édouard so blind that he cannot see it? But then again he has not been around for the past year to gauge my feelings for Pierre.

How can this be happening? How can I be so misguided and lacking in self-respect that I allow my walls to crumble with a single question?

As much as I hate myself for it, at that moment I know all it would take was for Édouard to say the word and I would leave with him, never look back. But I won't suggest it. I did once and it did not come to fruition. He did not even bother to contact me.

No, I shall never suggest it again.

How can I be so weak as to even contemplate it?

I yank a pin from the line, grab the corner of the sheet, and move down the line and repeat the yanking and tugging process. I toss the sheet in the basket.

Discontent is a curse. I feel nothing for Puvis, the good man who tries in vain to woo me. Yet I suffer as if my soul will die without Édouard, the one man I cannot have.

"Do you love Puvis?" He voice is a coarse, rumbling growl, a low shout that bores into me, but I do not answer him.

With one strong tug, he turns me to face him. I stumble and fall flat against him. We stand chest to chest as the breeze carries the scent of rain and the white linens billow around us.

His arms slide around me, and I can feel his hot breath on my cheek.

Reflexively, I lay my head on his chest. "You deserted me," I whisper.

He kisses the top of my head. "Berthe, there was a war between us. I could not very well have gone off with you."

His words mock me. I push away from him. Stumble back a few steps. I need room, because standing so close to him clouds my senses. Now I want to curse Edma for starting this. Why did she do it? If not, we most likely would have had a polite visit, he would have gone back to Fat Suzanne and I would have carried on with my new life. But now too many words have been spoken, too many wounds reopened. What was one more—"Then you had no intention of going away with me that day?"

He closes his eyes and takes a deep breath. "My feelings for you remain unchanged."

He reaches for my hand. I pull away.

"I don't know what you want from me Édouard. When I try to forget you, you reappear. When we get close, you push me away. I refuse to play this charade."

I remember that first day in the Louvre and my mind skips back to an even earlier time when that unbidden attraction first lit the darkness. For a moment I long to go back to that time. But it is hopeless. I wish I did not know all I know now, that so much had not passed between us.

"Édouard, we have been tormenting each other for three years. I cannot bear it another moment. Go away. Please let me be."

A raindrop falls onto my arm. I try to move away from him to save the rest of the linen from the coming storm, but he grabs my arm. The wind blows even stronger now, and I jerk out of his grasp. A gust pulls a corner of one sheet loose from the line and the soft cotton whips around my legs.

"Please, Berthe. Come back to Paris with me."

I grab the sheet—a fistful—to keep it from falling to the ground.

"Why, Édouard? What are you asking me?"

My pulse races, and I tighten my grip on the fabric.

"I want to . . ."

His eyes are tender and frantic as he searches my face. I hold my breath against his unspoken words.

"I want to paint you. I haven't been able to work since you've been away."

"What?"

So that's it? That's what it comes down to. I yank the other corner from the line and toss the sheet into the basket.

"It is the aftermath of the war, Édouard. Find another model. Any beautiful tramp will do. You do not need me."

"Yes I do."

His voice cracks. I turn and face him, my hands on my hips.

"I do need you." I see his courage waver. He looks away. "*Le Balcon* was so well received. Not like *Olympia;* not like the others."

"The others." I laugh. "There are the others and then there's me. Is that all I am to you? Instant respectability? Is that the face you're putting forth to the world now? Édouard Manet, painter of chaste decency?"

He gapes at me as if he cannot comprehend what I am saying.

"What happened to the rebel who would risk anything if it was true?"

He does not answer me, and I find this weakness unattractive. "I do not have the time or patience to play this game of chase anymore." I turn away and snatch down another sheet.

He walks around and stands in front of me, blocking me from finishing my task.

The rain falls harder.

"Get out of my way."

I try to push past him, but he grabs me and pulls me to him, covering my mouth with his. There is nothing soft about his kiss. It's hard and hungry and desperate. The sheet, our erratic screen, flies up around us then back down again. All Edma and Eugène need do is look out the window, and they will see us. But I don't care. I can't help myself, I kiss him back as angrily and punishingly as he's taking me. Leaning into him, I grab handfuls of his jacket, pulling him to me. Then my hands fist into his hair. I anchor myself to him, every centimeter of my body melting into his this one last time, because I know when I let go it will be the end of us.

"Do not marry Puvis."

He pulls back just enough to let the desperate words take flight on his husky, breathless voice.

"Don't," is all I can manage.

"Do not marry him," he says again, his forehead pressed to mine his lips a whisper away, "because I love you. I cannot bear to think of you with him."

Chapter Twenty-Two

Is the day better than the night?
Or is the night better than the day?
How can I tell?
But this I know is right:
Both are worth nothing
When my love's away.

—Amaru

DAYS later, Édouard's words still reverberate in my heart. I have come to the conclusion that if he would have spit in my face, it would have been easier to accept than his mocking declaration of love. For uttering those sacred words of love only because he *cannot bear to think of me with another* is not love. He does not love me, but simply wants to place me on a shelf, safe and away from the hands of other men, taking me down at his whim, and storing me away when I become an inconvenience.

He goes back to Fat Suzanne.

I stay in Mirande with Edma.

It is better this way.

The relationship with Édouard is over. Why had I not realized it would come to this before my love for him slipped in through the cracks of my character, deepening them so that they will never fully close again? Now I am paying the exorbitant price for my lack of self-control.

It's sad how relationships end. One person inevitably finds the other lacking and love ceases. That's why I will not prolong the inevitable.

I hear Edma and Marie bustling around downstairs and feel guilty for holing up in my room for the past few days. Edma has been gentle with me, not asking too many questions.

On that day, she knew what had happened without even asking. I'm sure it was perfectly obvious when Édouard returned alone with the clothes basket. That is, if they didn't see our final good-bye through the window.

I didn't ask.

She didn't mention it when I returned that night, long after he and Eugène had gone. I'm grateful for her prudence.

As I dress, I hear footsteps outside my bedroom door. Then comes a faint knock. It's Edma, holding a breakfast tray.

She looks very pretty standing there smiling in the dim hallway. Like a patch of sunshine lighting the darkness. I can't help but smile, too.

"Oh, Edma, you needn't bother to bring food to me. I was just dressing to come downstairs and help you."

"Really, it was no trouble." She sets it on the small writing desk and turns back to me positively beaming.

"What?"

"I received a letter from Adolphe this morning. He's coming home in three days."

"That's wonderful. I know how much you've missed him."

She perches on the edge of the bed, and I can tell by the look on her face she has more to say.

"I'm sure you remember what I said to the Messieurs Manet about there likely being an addition to the family?"

I groan inwardly because I am not at all prepared to discuss the events of that day.

"What I said was true," she continues. "I can't believe I'm telling you even before Adolphe gets home—again—but the doctor just confirmed it, and if I don't tell you, I think I will simply burst—"

"You mean?"

Edma nods. "We are going to have another baby. A gift from Adolphe's last leave."

I hug my sister, enjoying the rush of joy surging through me. "So then, you did not lie to the Manet brothers."

She shrugs and shakes her head. "*Moi*, lie? Never!"

"Well that's good. I was beginning to worry at how convincing you are in your falsehoods."

I wink at her, and we laugh together.

"Speaking of that, there is a letter on your tray from Puvis." She walks over to the desk, retrieves the letter, and hands it to me.

I open it.

My Dear Mademoiselle,

Today I went to your home in Passy with the purpose of conveying a certain intention to your parents. A challenging feat, no doubt, given their feelings for me.

Alas, my future with you, my dear, is much too important to allow the matter of their feelings for me to inhibit me. Make no mistake, I shall win them over in due time.

I would have pursued this quest at once had I found them at home when I called. Alas, your brother,

Tiburce, was the only one in residence. He assured me they would be gone for the better part of the day.

Upon hearing that news, I set out walking—all the way to the Bois de Boulogne. Where I stayed until the sky turned gray, finally opening and raining down upon me. I took the bad weather as a sign that the time was not right to speak to your parents. As I certainly could not prevail upon them to receive me soaking wet. I went home, since I was right there, instead of walking back. Another day, my love. Another day.

Until then, I remain yours faithfully,
Pierre Puvis de Chavannes.

Coward.

It is as if a strong wind has blown out a sputtering flame. He is nothing but a frightened little boy, and this confirms my instincts that a life with Pierre Puvis de Chavannes, even if he is my only viable marriage prospect, would be a huge mistake.

I want to laugh the kind of humorless laugh one can't help emit when something they've known all along is proven a fact, but I feel Edma's hand on my shoulder, and it stifles the urge like a cork in a bottle.

"Is everything all right?"

"Yes. It's fine. Everything is absolutely fine." I fold the letter and stare at it for a moment, not sure what to do with it. After Edma leaves, I tear it to shreds and throw it in the garbage.

Edma does not want me to leave Mirande, but I can't stay with Adolphe coming home. They need their privacy, their time together after all this time apart. So much good to celebrate, what with France finally settling back into peace, and a new baby on the way for them. No, I will just be in the way. As much as I love Cherbourg, I am quite homesick for Paris.

I am ready to go home.

Maman is up to her old tricks again. Only this time she has recruited an accomplice in Madame Manet. It seems the two of them have put their heads together and decided that Eugène and I are like the remainders of two pair of socks, each with a missing mate.

Alone we serve no purpose, but together this mismatched pair can function nicely—even if we aren't a perfect complement. With that in mind, they have set their sights on bringing the two of us together.

Only because he is a nice man, who has become a good friend since that terrible walk home during the Commune, have I decided to attend tonight's dinner party that Maman is hosting under the guise of a welcome home soirée.

It is simply an excuse to throw Eugène and me together. He must be as confounded by the idea as I am. Tonight we will have a good laugh at the preposterous notion.

I sit at my dressing table and dab Parma Violet perfume on my neck. As I glance in the mirror, I think of how it will be good to see Degas. I've missed him and his wry humor.

Of course, Édouard will also be in attendance. That is a matter with which I am not entirely prepared to deal. I have not heard from him since that visit in Mirande. Alas, since Maman and Madame Manet have grown so close, I must learn to come to terms with this change in our relationship.

If he is angry, there is always the chance that he will be otherwise engaged this evening. I try to ignore the thud of disappointment that grips my chest at the thought and instead count my blessings. We are all well and able to come together after such a horrendous year.

Smoothing the low-cut emerald *moiré* silk, I try to focus on the positive. The dress has always been one of my favorites. It is the first occasion I have had to wear it since the war, and it hangs on my frame quite a bit looser than I would like, but it still makes me feel good.

Yes, we are alive. Tonight I shall celebrate the fact that my family and friends have lived through hell to gather together again.

As my foot hits the last step, the door knocker sounds. Amélie bobs a curtsy as she whisks in front of me to greet the guests.

I hear Édouard's voice among that of several others, and it annoys me the way my heart beats a little faster in my chest. As Amélie takes hats and wraps, I scoot into the empty drawing room and arrange myself on the divan, trying to look unconcerned.

His words in Mirande taunt me. They eat my confidence as gangrene devours a body. I know cutting him from my life, as a surgeon's knife cuts away a rotting limb, is the only measure by which my heart will heal.

If only it were easy.

I hear the party moving toward the drawing room, and I wonder how it will look when they find me in here waiting.

Too anxious? Would it have been better to make an entrance? Too late for that. I move to the window, and that is where I am standing when I hear Édouard's robust, *"Bonjour, Mademoiselle."*

I turn.

He smiles. Walks to me, takes my hand in his, and lifts it to his lips, raising his eyes to meet mine the moment before his breath whispers over my hand.

For all appearances, one would never dream that our last exchange had been so volatile. I am flooded by a sense of relief—he is here. It is as if I have fallen backward into the plush safety of a big cottony cloud, but I catch myself before I allow my good sense to slip through and seep away into the stratosphere of his eyes.

The reality touchstone is Suzanne, who glares at us from across the room. She is a contrast in size to the others, for it seems as if everyone else has wasted away during the war, but somehow she has managed to increase in girth. I am astounded that Fat Suzanne is fatter than ever.

Édouard straightens and follows my gaze to his wife. He lets loose my hand, and I step away from him to greet her, Madame Manet, and Eugène. Much to my relief, Maman floats into the room and takes charge.

"*Bonjour!* Do come in. Make yourselves at home. I am so very happy you could come."

I feel Édouard's gaze on me, and I feel myself tempted to slip back into places I swore I would never find myself again.

"Come, Berthe." Maman's voice trills. "Sit next to Eugène."

She motions him to sit on the dark blue flowered chintz divan. He obeys. She motions me next to him.

So it begins. If I protest, I will only embarrass the poor gentleman. So I do as Maman bids, giving Eugène a smile of resignation. In return, he looks a bit sheepish, but not at all disagreeable to my proximity.

Maman directs Édouard and Suzanne to sit across from Eugène and me. As they walk over, Maman gasps and stares at Suzanne as if seeing her for the first time this evening. "Oh, my, Suzanne! Don't you look . . ." Maman raises her quizzing glass and rakes her gaze down Suzanne's rotund figure. "Well, from the looks of you, you've certainly come out of the siege with the weight we have all shed. You're quite healthy, aren't you?"

Pink washes over Suzanne's chubby face. Her lips bunch into a thin pucker, but she does not respond verbally.

"We were in the good fortune to have plenty during the war," says Édouard, wearily. He looks thin, drawn. Half the size of his wife. "If we had been near, we would have shared with you."

It's a pathetic attempt to justify her overindulgence during a time of crisis. I wonder if she ate his share of the food. I have this absurd image of Suzanne being Édouard's overstuffed pet, sitting up and begging as he feeds her prime morsels from his plate. I certainly don't understand what she possesses that holds him captive. They are so opposite. She is so contrary to everything he stands for.

Since I learned the truth about Léon's paternity, I've often wondered what tale their lack of conceiving a child tells of the intimacy of their relationship. But how could he desire such a body? Even as seldom as Adolphe is at home, he and Edma have managed to conceive twice. I realize not every woman is quite so fertile as Edma. But after being married for as many years as Suzanne and Édouard . . .

"Superb weather we are having tonight," says Eugène. He has angled his body toward me expectantly—one leg crossed over the other, his hands stiffly laced over his kneecap. Although, he is not sitting inappropriately close, I have the urge to scoot away from him.

"It's cooling off nicely," he adds.

I nod, not really in the mood to discuss the weather. Suzanne and Édouard look on in awkward silence.

Finally, Édouard says, "Mademoiselle, pray tell me what you are working on. Your mother says you have redoubled your efforts to make a name for yourself as a painter."

I feel a pang for Eugène, who is so obviously outmatched by his older brother. So I direct my words to Eugène hoping to draw him into the conversation.

"In Mirande, I completed several small landscapes of Edma and Jeanne. I'm talking to several dealers about representing me."

"Would an introduction to my representatives be in order?"

Reflexively, may gaze shifts to Édouard.

"If that would help you?" Because of his smile, I wonder if he is sincere or if it is a power play to get my attention.

"If you are sincere, an introduction would be very much appreciated."

"Well then, I shall set it up."

Degas arrives and the party shifts into higher gear. I can tell he is in rare form the minute he walks into the room and wedges himself squarely in between Eugène and me.

"I'm sure you don't mind, do you, Manet? It's just that I have not had the pleasure of this fine woman's company for far too long and we have much to catch up on."

If Eugène minds, he does not voice his opinion. I smile at the sheer gall of Degas, the way he slides right into the space he desires for himself. For a moment I let my imagination take flight and consider how it would be as his wife—until he opens his mouth, and I realize the two of us could be great friends, but as lovers we would certainly tear each other apart.

Lovers . . .

Édouard's presence tugs at me. My gaze drifts to him. Maman has perched herself on the other side of him and he intently listens to one of her tirades. Before I look away, his eyes snare mine and the faintest smile tugs at the corners of his lips. He has grown so thin over this hard year. He looks utterly human sitting there all gaunt and hollow. An angel fallen to earth.

"So what is this I hear about Puvis courting you?" Degas' words pull me back. His arched brows and curled upper lip leave no margin to ponder his opinion of the matter. "What exactly is the nature of your relationship?"

He drums his fingers on the back of the divan while I try to formulate words for that which I cannot explain. Finally I shrug and throw up my hands. "He has been a good friend to me during a very difficult time. Unlike others whom I shall not name."

I pointedly avoid looking at Édouard.

Degas strokes his thin mustache and makes a satisfied grunt. "Yes, and didn't I warn you that you could not count on Manet when it mattered? You didn't believe me. Perhaps you will listen to me now when I warn you away from Puvis."

I roll my eyes. "I beg you watch what you say. He's my good friend—"

"No, Mademoiselle, I beg you listen to me. It is my duty to make you aware of the rather scandalous relationship your *good friend,* Puvis, has been carrying on with Princess Marie Cantacuzène. Are you aware of his relations with her? It has been going on for the past fifteen years."

The pit of my stomach feels as if it has dropped to my knees, and I shift in my seat to glance around to see who might have heard his rubbish. But everyone, including Eugène, who still sits next to Degas, seems to be engrossed in anecdotes all their own.

"You know nothing of the kind, do you?" His nostrils flare as if he smells something foul. "*Um-hmm.* I figured as much. Allow me to enlighten you. She's the estranged wife of the Rumanian prince, but they are still very married. What makes it even more interesting is that she is your mother's age if she's a day old." Degas examines his nails in that bored manner he has perfected, and I want to slap him.

"Do not look at me like that," he says. "I haven't manufactured this for my own entertainment."

I run a hand over the dark blue flowered-chintz upholstery, knowing full well he hasn't made it up. That makes it worse. Suddenly everything makes perfect sense. Puvis's hesitation to talk to Maman and Papa. Their irrational distaste for him. They *knew*. Yet they didn't bother to tell me. I wonder what might have transpired had Puvis found them at home when he called? Were they at home and thought it best to not receive him? Oh, how ridiculous. I could speculate for days and it wouldn't change a thing.

The air in the room is stale and close with so many chattering people. It is hard to breathe. If I sit here for another moment, I think I shall scream. "Please excuse me for a moment."

Degas nods. *"Naturellement."*

My shoes sound too loud on the parquet floor; I can hear the tread over the din of conversation as I walk to the window at the other end of the large room.

I twist the knob until my knuckles turn white and wonder if there is anything in this world that is real, that turns out as it seems.

My hand slips off the knob and smacks against the wooden casement. My reflection stares back at me and I try to process the odd emotions brewing inside. The ache that pulses inside me in the chasm that should contain my heart; the melancholy discontent bubbling up from the depths of me. The calm finality that it is over with Puvis.

Click. Just like that.

It is almost a relief and that in itself worries me more than the discovery of his unattainable lady love.

I lean my forehead against the cool glass. A white moth performs loops outside the window. I hear the hopeless *thud* as it futilely throws itself against the pane. The little creature does not know that it is not always better on the other side.

If I loved Puvis, I should ask him for the truth.

I would if it mattered.

I reach up and give the knob one last grinding crank. It turns. The bar latch gives. I stumble backward, into someone standing behind me.

It is Édouard. His hands fall to my waist. I pull away.

"I came to assist you with the window. You were struggling."

It is not much what he says, but how he looks at me as he speaks. He so thin, so intense, a shadow of the carefree dandy who used to own the city. My heart aches because the man I loved is still very much intact.

"Thank you, but I have managed quite well on my own."

"*Oui*, I can see that."

I turn back to the window. The cool night air washes over me. The moth has flown in and rests on the windowsill. Now that it is in, I wonder if it is damaged from banging so fiercely against the glass.

"I couldn't help but overhear what Degas was saying to you. He has no manners. I'm sorry he revealed Puvis's secret to you in that manner."

I wonder who else might have overheard.

"I suppose I'm a bad judge of character," I say, not quite sure why. Not quite sure how I expect him to respond. I can't see his face because he stands squarely behind me, but I can imagine his expression, see him crossing his arms and stroking his beard as he frowns.

"*Au contraire, Mademoiselle.* You're quite astute. Save for the misconception that you believe I do not care for you."

He shifts behind me. I can see his face reflected in the angled glass. It's a gentle face, and my heart softens.

"Do you care, Édouard?" I whisper.

"I love you. I wish you would stop punishing me long enough to believe me."

A chestnut dances in the breeze and a slip of pale moonlight peeks through. Édouard steps closer. Runs a finger along my arm. I cannot speak as each caress stitches closed the chasm around my heart.

"Berthe," he whispers. "I have not been able to eat or sleep or paint without you. I need you. Come to me tomorrow."

A bell rings in the background. As if from another dimension, Maman's voice announces dinner is served.

Édouard joins the others on their pilgrimage to the dining room. I linger a moment, as solitary as *Victorie de Samothrace,* and stare at the sliver of moon that lights the black abyss of night.

High above the Aegean Sea, *Victorie* unfurls her wings in celebration. Zephyr's warm wind blows in from the west, and the white moth takes flight.

Chapter Twenty-Three

Love does not consist
in gazing at each other,
but in looking outward
in the same direction.
—Antoine de Saint-Exupéry

MAY 1873

ÉDOUARD is as bold as the blue violets he sends early the next morning. An unsigned note accompanies the flowers. It simply says: *I care.*

The truth in Édouard's voice last night steals my breath.

Blue violets. I try not to think about the symbolic meaning—love. I know it is not coincidence. What man but Édouard would be schooled on the significance of flowers?

I take them to my chamber and set them on the dressing table, where I can see them as I attend to my toilette.

I take my low-cut black dress from the *armoire*—the pretty one with the lace around the neckline and the black ribbon that ties at the waist. I hang it on the door and sit down at my vanity to brush my hair.

It is by sheer luck that Maman is still sleeping. Papa has already gone to work. Amélie received them, brought them to me with a knowing sparkle in her eyes.

I pick up the small nosegay, twirl it in my fingers, and sniff it. The petals tickle my nose, but it's his audacity that makes me smile.

I will go to him.

I can no more stay away than the Seine can keep from flowing down stream.

Perhaps it is my destiny to be the *other woman*. It seems my lot. Should I have married Puvis, I would have been the respectable wife. Yet the Rumanian princess would always possess his heart.

Suzanne is Édouard's wife. Yet she is most certainly not the woman of his heart. Either way, I am the other woman.

Is it such a terrible position?

He is not at all surprised to see me.

Édouard's new studio takes up the entire second floor of number four rue de Saint-Pétersbourg, two blocks from his home at number forty-nine. Suzanne could walk down if she dared. Or cared. Somehow, I find it hard to believe she would expend that much energy.

Édouard moved his studio after his *atelier* on the rue Guyot was destroyed during the Commune. A total loss.

My eye is drawn to *Le Balcon*. It is hung, not merely propped haphazardly against the wall. Next to it hangs my painting of Edma at the Lorient harbor. My hand flutters to my lips, and I swallow against the emotion bubbling in my throat. Maybe I haven't been so absent from his life for all that we have been apart. *Merci Dieu* he had the foresight to entrust his paintings to Théodore Duret, or all would be lost.

It's a beautiful place. Spacious and elegant with high ceilings and walls of tall windows.

Rubbing the stem of the nosegay between my thumb and fingers, I stand near the door and look around the cavernous space in wonder. Not quite as much natural light as the rue Guyot with its windowed roof, but the light here is quite nice. It will be cooler in the summer.

I walk to the center of the room, turn in a slow circle, memorizing every detail, picking out the old familiar pieces, learning their place in the new environment. The big red buttoned divan. His easel. The stool. The table with paint tubes and brushes. Jars of pigment in jeweled colors. The books. The props. The rolls of fabric and paper.

The dressing screen.

The bed.

It's all here, like old friends welcoming me home. But somehow everything is different.

The studio must be twice the size of the other. Everything has its place. Nothing is haphazardly tossed or strewn. Even the bed is made. Guyot had the air of a rogue artist's *atelier.* But this place—this place has the feel of a master.

"It used to be an old fencing school," he says.

The floor trembles like the hand of God is shaking the building. I brace a hand against his easel and fear for a moment that the earth will open and swallow us whole.

"The Gare Saint-Lazare," he says over the rumble. "The trains coming and going—makes the place shake all day long." He smiles. "Keeps me awake."

My gaze darts to the bed. The blanket is pulled taut. The pillows are fluffed. It looks as if it has never been slept in. A sharp contrast to the rumpled mess that stood in the corner of the *atelier* on rue Guyot. As often as I have been to his studio I have never been in that bed.

I release my grip on the easel, and only then does it dawn on me that it is empty of canvas. That his pallet is hanging on a hook and the brushes look almost dusty.

"The place is lovely, Édouard. Please show me what you have been working on."

His face goes blank. He crosses his arms over his chest, tucking his fingers in his armpits.

"I have not yet begun to work."

"Surely, you're joking? It's been several months now. You should see the canvases I have completed. I should have taken you out to the studio last night . . ." As I speak, I am looking for hints of new work and realize the only canvases I see are old ones.

White-hot sparks of concern pop in my belly and I look at him askance. He shakes his head. Shifts from one foot to the other. Extracts a hand to rub his eyes, and mutters, "I told you, I have done nothing since we returned to Paris."

"Édouard?"

He is looking at me, his eyes dark and forlorn. A helpless child of a man.

I don't know who moved first, him or me, but we stand together now, inches apart. He cups my face in his hands and holds me like that, rubbing a thumb over my lips, then two over my cheekbones. He slides his hands back and laces his fingers in my hair. A pin falls to the floor and the back of my hair falls free. He runs his fingers through the curls, slides them down my shoulders, over my breasts.

He pulls me to him, and I can feel his hardness as we stand together, like two parched travelers preparing to drink from the well of life.

I lean into him, aching for the feel of his body against mine, and kiss him. Softly. Tentatively. Reminding myself this is the fork in the road. If I embark in the direction my body burns to travel, there is no turning back.

I know where I must go. It has been a long journey to this point, but every step I have taken has led me to this very spot.

"I will make what is between us right." His whispered promise is rough as gravel. "I will make you happy. You'll see—"

"Shhhhh." I drown his words with a deep kiss. At that moment, I love him so much it is painful.

There is only one way to ease my ache.

I take his hand and lead him to the bed.

"Let's go away." He punctuates the words with a kiss on the top of my head.

I snuggle into his chest, molding my body to his side. He pulls me closer.

"I want to stay here. With you. Just like this." I snuggle into him, relishing the scent of our union. *Mon Dieu*, I love the smell of him. I duck my head under the blanket and plant a kiss on his belly.

He sighs. "This is nice, but I want to go somewhere we can be like this every day, every night." With one finger, he tilts my chin up to him. His eyes are bright. I am glad to see the energy shining in him again.

"Let's go," he urges. "Right now. I'm serious."

He pushes himself up. The blanket slides down my naked back.

I run my fingers through the hair on his chest. "Édouard we can't. Not right now. Not like this."

"Of course not. We'll put our clothes on first."

He arches a brow at me, grins, and pushes himself to a sitting position.

He is serious.

I fall onto my back.

A funnel swirls in my stomach as I contemplate the logistics of what he suggests. All the work I have started, the dealers I have interested . . . I rest my arm across my forehead. My other hand grasps the covers to my breast. If we leave we must start over professionally, too.

You're afraid to go because he hasn't exactly proved to be reliable in the past, has he? says Propriety. *What do you expect, falling in love with a married man? If you run away with him, he will only end up leaving you for someone else.*

Be reasonable, says Olympia. *It's not as if the relationship has had a chance to grow under normal circumstances. You've been through a war. Give the man a chance to prove his worth.*

"Papa has not been well. I can't go off and leave him now."

I hear him rustling around and sit up to watch him dress. Wrapped in the blanket, I draw my knees to my chest.

"I thought it was what you wanted?" he says.

"I did. I do. But everything is so different now."

He finishes buckling his trousers and stands there—shirtless, his hair rumpled and his eyes looking deeply into me. I desire him all over again. I want to cry for the astonishing depth of my love for him.

"Édouard." I motion for him to sit on the bed. He does, and I lace my fingers through his, and bring his hand to my lips and kiss them. "There is nothing I want more than this. But we can't go now. We need to be here. For Papa. For our futures. Together. We must both draw on the resources we have built in Paris to build a new life for ourselves. A life together."

He shakes his head. "It will never work here, Berthe." He draws his hand away and braces stiff arms on the bed. "We will both be ruined."

"Since when have you been concerned about that?" I caress his bare back. "Édouard, I am not afraid to face the music here. You can withstand it, too. You have before, and you've come out stronger on the other side. Stand tall. Let us be who we are in the place where we belong."

A train rumbles past and shakes the room. I get out of bed, aware of his eyes on me, quiet, contemplative. I pull my black dress over my head. Not bothering with my corset, I tie the black ribbon at the waist, then pin my hair away from my face, leaving the back to fall free about my shoulders.

I sit down next to him on the bed again, leaning back on my elbows.

"You look like an angel sitting there like that," he says.

He goes to the chest of drawers and pulls out a slip of black velvet ribbon and ties it around my neck, forming a little bow, then picks up the bouquet of violets and tucks it in the bodice of my dress. He backs away until he reaches his easel, where he touches his brush to the paint, touches paint to canvas.

With each brushstroke, we talk, and a picture of our new life together emerges.

La Figaro—by Ansel Racine—May 25, 1873

Manet's New Olympia?

Speculation on the exact nature of the relationship between Mademoiselle Berthe Morisot and Monsieur Édouard Manet is the talk of Paris. Given his Salon entry, Repose, *his sensual portrait of her sprawled, seductively and inviting, on the red divan, one cannot help but wonder. The black shoe is a sharp contrast peeking out from beneath the virginal white froth of dress. Alas, it is the way she holds her red fan in her right hand, while her elegant left hand is placed so boldly on the seat next to her. That coupled with that come-hither expression, she seems to beckon the viewer to sit next to her for an intimate tête-à-tête.*

Given Monsieur Manet's well-known propensity to paint what he sees, one cannot help but speculate that Mademoiselle Morisot's smoldering glance is meant for him and him alone. I wonder what his wife has to say about that.

I suggested to Édouard it might not be prudent to enter *Repose* in the Salon. Not until he was ready to reveal our relationship. But he would not hear of it. He insisted it would show in good contrast to his painting *Le Bon Bock*. He painted that portrait of me before the war, and while I am quite fond of it, it's an extremely intimate portrait, so telling. He certainly captured everything I was feeling that day, as Racine pointed out.

Édouard borrowed it back from Durand Ruel, who bought it just after the war for twenty-five hundred francs. Édouard didn't want to part with it, but after living through such a grave year, one does what one must to survive.

I don't mind the furor, but we've been seeing each other steadily for more than six months now. Frankly, I am surprised no one has caught on.

I almost wish they had. Édouard is still reticent about starting a new life in Paris. I will not leave. We have come to a standoff, and do not talk about it. I shall not push him, but I won't leave.

"You should have seen Maman this morning," I say to Édouard as he paints. "She was furious over the *La Figaro* article."

He makes a soft sound of amusement.

"She said, 'I hope you're happy! It seems you are intent on ruining not only yourself, but your entire family as well.' She slammed her quizzing glass onto the table on top of the newspaper. I am surprised the glass did not shatter."

I glance over Édouard's shoulder at the canvas. It is the portrait of me in the black dress reclining on the bed. I remember the tender way he tucked the blue violets into the bodice of my gown, and it makes me desire him all over again.

"I wonder what Racine will make of this one?" I ask. "This is far more seductive than *Repose,* don't you think?"

Édouard grunts, and I get the feeling he is not completely present.

"It's been awhile since I've seen Maman in such a temper, but this will seem a picnic once we announce our plans."

This time he says nothing.

"Édouard?"

"Yes, my love. Your mother was upset?"

He is lost in his own world, and I know better than to expect much from him when he gets like this. It will just end in an argument.

I walk to the window and look out. Really, I should go home to my own work. God knows I have plenty to do. I am not happy with my showing in the Salon. Quite disappointed, in fact.

Once it was a thrill merely to be selected. Alas, with only one small painting in the show, the one of Edma and Jeanne in the field, no, it was not a good showing, as it has garnered no attention. It hangs on the wall unnoticed, like rainwater collected in an abandoned pot. I think it is worse to go unnoticed than receive a negative review.

I envy Édouard the attention, and try not to begrudge the fact that once again it is my image that is the subject of speculation.

Oh, let them talk. Let them speculate.

I walk over to the wall where I notice a lone canvas on an easel turned toward the wall. It was not here yesterday. Gently, I scoot it back. It's a woman and a child against a backdrop of a wrought-iron fence. Steam seems to billow in the background. It must be the train yard—the Gare Saint-Lazare. The child, captured from the back, is smartly dressed with a big blue sash tied into a bow at the back of her crisp white dress. The woman sits with a sleeping puppy in her lap, reading a book. It is kind to say she looks slightly bedraggled in her unfashionable bonnet and plain blue dress.

Her face is familiar, yet out of context. I cannot place her, although I'm certain I know this woman, with her penetrating stare and long red hair hanging loosely around her shoulders.

"Édouard, who is this?"

He throws a distracted glance over his shoulder. I see him tense as he turns around to face me.

"Be careful. The paint's not yet dry."

Irritation burns in the pit of my stomach. "I can see that. Who is she? She looks familiar."

He stands there for a moment staring first at the canvas, then at me. He turns back to his easel.

"It's Victorine Meurent."

Victorine? Victorine Meur— I gasp. *Mon Dieu.* My heart squeezes with terror. Olympia.

"She is back?"

"Ummm-hmmm . . ."

I don't like this. I don't like it at all, especially when I notice the red fan nestled in her lap behind the puppy. The fan I have held in so many of the portraits Édouard has painted of me. My fan. Tears sting my eyes. I get my cloak and walk toward the door.

I am out in the hall when Édouard throws open the door and calls after me.

"Berthe, where are you going?"

"Home." My foot hits the first landing, and I do not even look back. Édouard married Suzanne after Victorine left. I do not have to be a scholar to understand what his Olympia meant to him. Now she is back, and he is painting her with my fan—

"Stop, will you? What is the matter? One minute I am painting, and the next minute you are storming out. Come back inside and talk to me."

His voice is more irritated than tender. I have to hold my breath to keep from sobbing. But I let him take my hand and lead me back upstairs, all the while I hear Propriety's voice in my head: *Do you know what this will do to your father?*

My heart squeezes at the thought. For if I have one regret, one reason for not pushing Édouard into action, it is Papa.

His health has been steadily declining over the past year. I fear he will not live to see the new year.

But with this, with Victorine back in Paris, Édouard and I cannot go on like this indefinitely.

He closes the door and picks up a rag to wipe his hands. Victorine's haggard face stares out at me. Propriety's voice screams in my head. *He has no intention of marrying you. I must insist you distance yourself from Édouard Manet once and for all. For your own good.*

He follows my gaze to Victorine's portrait. "Is that what's upset you so?"

"She's holding my fan."

"What?" He seems genuinely surprised. I feel foolish.

"Never mind. Édouard, I have thought long and hard about our situation. It is time. You must either move out with me now or this is the end. We will stay in Paris, for you know as well as I do I cannot leave right now with Papa's condition as it is."

"Do you believe staying here and dragging both of our good names through the Parisian mud will heal him?"

"This is where we belong. This is who we are."

He opens his mouth to speak, but no sound comes out.

Then he continues to wipe his fingers with the rag. He knows as well as I know that we cannot go another day living like this.

A train rumbles by. I think of the cloud of smoke in the portrait of Victorine. My heart squeezes. She has been here.

Olympia who lay bare for the love of a man. We are not so dissimilar, she and I.

The train passes and the room is so still Édouard's sigh seems to echo.

"I shall tell Suzanne tonight."

Chapter Twenty-Four

Love is strong as death
Jealousy is cruel as the grave
—Song of Solomon 8:6

JANUARY 1874

I LOVE to paint in the garden beneath the chestnut tree. I awake early and drag my easel out of the studio so that I might distract myself while I wait for Édouard to call. We did not make definite arrangements, but I am sure he will come after he tells Suzanne. *Oui,* he will come so we might tell Maman together.

I want to tell Maman first to give her a chance to get used to the notion before we tell Papa. She will take it hard at first, but she is strong. She will get used to the idea once she sees she has no choice.

"*Madame, non! S'il vous plaît,* you may not go into the garden unannounced!" Amélie's cries shatter the quiet a spilt second before the gate slams open, banging against the stone wall.

I turn and see Suzanne Manet standing with her hands on

her considerable hips. She is dressed in a plain gray frock with a black hat that looks too small for her considerable head. Amélie skids to a stop alongside of her.

"Mademoiselle, I beg your pardon, I tried to tell her to wait—"

"It is all right, Amélie. That will be all."

Suzanne at least has the good grace to wait until the girl disappears inside before she tears into me.

"I will not give up Édouard without a fight. He is the only thing Léon and I have. If we lose him, we are destitute."

I twirl my paintbrush in my fingers, notice the way the yellow paint contrasts with the dark brown bristles.

"Léon is Édouard's brother. We will see that you and the boy are well provided for."

She takes a step toward me. I set down my brush, put my hands on my hips to match her stance.

"You don't seem to understand, Mademoiselle. I love him. He loves me."

Her voice is a low growl, and it's incongruent with the mealy-mouthed blind wife I've come to know as her. I liked her better when she was silent because it made me think she knew her place.

"He married you out of pity, not love. He told me so."

"Did he tell you he enjoys making love to me? Did he tell you about the others? There are others, you understand. Don't think you are special. Victorine Meurent is back. She was special to him." She laughs a dry, brittle sound.

"Get out of my garden."

She closes the distance between us. At this close range, I can see her gelatinous chin quiver with anger. Her eyes are narrow slits and she shakes a finger in my face. I push it aside and I fear for an instant she will strike me.

"I will leave, but only after I say what I have come to say."

She is screaming at me, and I wonder if Maman will come out to see what all the commotion is about. "If you do not leave my husband alone, I will ruin you. If you think Racine's insidious article in *La Figaro* was bad—"

"I do not think it bad at all." I match her pitch, but then lower my tone. "All those things he said about the painting are true. Édouard painted it after he made love to me."

Suzanne bristles like a cat arching her back. "Leave him alone!" She grits her yellow teeth. "Leave him alone or I shall make you so miserable you will wish you never met me."

She shoves over my easel. I sidestep it so it does not hit me. I shake my head and give her a pitying smile.

"Your threats do not scare me, Suzanne. You cannot ruin me. You are nothing and even less without Édouard."

"Heed my warning, Mademoiselle."

She turns and walks out, leaving the gate open behind her.

I set out on foot for Édouard's studio. I am shaking uncontrollably. Halfway there the wind blows my hat off my head. I scarcely remember going inside to get it and my coat. Now a man hops off a carriage, catches it, and presents it to me with a flourish.

"Are you all right, Mademoiselle?" he asks. "You're crying. May I assist you?"

"Merci, non, Monsieur." I take my hat and hurry on my way.

I have no idea how long it takes me to walk the distance from Passy to Édouard's studio. Time seems to stand still. When I arrive, the sun is high in the October sky, so I know it is midday. Hours have passed.

I do not knock, but throw open the door, half expecting, half dreading I will find him with Victorine or Suzanne. Or both.

Édouard is alone. He turns to me wide-eyed.

"Berthe, what's—"

"Do you still make love to her, Édouard?"

He rubs his hand over his beard in a gesture that covers his mouth.

"Answer me! Do you still make love to her? Do you do all the things to her that you do to me?"

My screams scald my throat, and my body is shaking so hard I feel as if I have no control over myself.

"What are you talking about? You're not making sense."

"Suzanne! I am talking about Suzanne. She came to me this morning and said—"

He takes me in his arms, and I melt into him, sobbing against his chest.

"Of course she would say that." He kisses the top of my head. "She is upset. I told her I was leaving her. It stands to reason she'd brandish anything to hurt you."

"Answer my question." My words float out between sobs. "Do you still make love to her?"

"*Shhhh* . . . What kind of question is that?"

"An important question, Édouard. She said there were others, too. Is it true?"

I can hear his heart beat through his white shirt as I lay my head upon his chest.

"Berthe, don't do this."

I push away from him so I can see his face.

"Answer me!"

The way he looks at me, I do not need a reply.

I know.

I clench my fists and start flailing, hitting him. My vision is blurred by tears. I knock into his paint table. It crashes to the floor. His palette skids. Paint tubes and brushes scatter at my feet.

Finally, he grabs me with both hands and holds me tight against him, until I collapse, crying hysterically.

He holds me until I have calmed down, then he walks me to the red divan, helps settle me down. He hands me his handkerchief and sits next to me, one arm draped over my shoulder.

I dab my eyes. “You might have at least warned me she was coming.”

He shrugs. “I did not know. She locked herself in her room after we talked.”

“Have you told your mother yet?” I ask.

He shakes his head.

“Suzanne will ruin us.”

“She can only cause damage if we afford her that power. I do not care what she does or who she tells.”

“We are courting scandal. We will face dire social consequences. I cannot do this to you. I will not be the cause of your ruin.”

“I do not care.”

“You will. You will grow to hate me—”

“Édouard, this is the same speech you have given me over and over again. I am tired of it. I should have called your bluff and gone with you that day you wanted me to go away. Either we make a new start, here in Paris, today, or it is over. For good.”

His elbows are propped on his knees and he bows his head so his face falls into his hands.

“Berthe, be kind.” His voice is muffled, but I can still hear the choke of emotion. “Consider my position. I have a responsibility to protect my family name.”

“Is that more important to you than I am? Than us being together?”

“It is equally important.”

My breath escapes in a heavy gasp. I start to stand up, but he holds my arm, and I fall back onto the divan.

"Please listen to me. I have something very important for you to consider."

His throat works and a muscle in his jaw twitches. I can tell by his expression that I will not like what he has to say. A knot of dread tightens in my stomach.

I want to stay there, silent, just as we are, because somehow I know after his next words nothing will be the same.

My stomach seizes, and I fear I will vomit, but I cannot move. I cannot breathe. I wish at that moment Hermes, the god of people who live by their wits, would swoop down in his golden, winged sandals, and carry me off . . . somewhere, anywhere but here.

"Please, Berthe, please understand. The only reason I would ask this of you is because I love you too much to lose you. If we open Pandora's box, it will be the end of us. You will never show at the Salon again—"

"I do not wish to show at the Salon."

I don't know where the voice comes from. It does not even sound like my own.

"My love . . ." He reaches out, traces a finger down my cheek. "We have been clinging to fantasies. You will grow discontent with me all too soon and end up hating me for ruining your life."

"It is Victorine, isn't it?"

He groans. "*Mon Dieu, non.* There is no one else."

"You are just looking for a way out."

I am shaking again. I stand. Tears stream from my eyes, blur my vision. An hysterical scream creeps up the back of my throat. I clasp my hand over my mouth, and walk out the door.

This time he does not stop me.

* * *

The seasons have changed since I last saw him. It grows cold outside. Today, I go strictly for professional purposes. On a quest far more important than the personal worries or reservations I harbor about seeing him.

I sent a note to advise him of my intent to call. As I did not want to surprise him. He answered the note quite hastily, saying he would be happy to receive me. I will go alone. I thought about asking Maman to accompany me. Yet I decided against it, realizing if she went, Madame Manet would feel obliged to greet her and possibly Eugène and Suzanne would be in attendance. Suzanne would gloat, no doubt. I can't bear to see Eugène after Édouard's suggestion. We wouldn't be able to talk business. There would be far too much commotion with everyone chatting, catching up.

We have had no soirées. Nor have the Manets. A cooling-off period, as Maman calls it. Distance designed to quell the speculation over the debut of *Repose.*

No one talks about it now. We're quite civilized despite reverberations that linger like a bad aftertaste on the palates of those too decent to make a face. In fact, everyone puts on a pretty face, smiling cordially, going about their business as if all is right in the world.

It rather reminds me of the story *The Emperor's New Clothes.* If everyone looks the other way and pretends Berthe and Édouard are not in love, then surely they will not be. My situation is hopeless from every angle.

Actually, as I think about it, I believe it more closely resembles a sore thumb. Painful when inadvertently bumped and so often in the way I scarcely think of much else.

So I slip out, murmuring excuses about art business, to which Maman rolls her eyes before returning her attention to the morning edition of *Le Fiagro.* The carriage ride gives me time to gather myself, to coax free the knot drawn tight in my belly.

I have come with a purpose. This is my mantra, and I repeat it over and over as the carriage rolls to a stop at number four rue de Saint-Pétersbourg.

When the door swings open, Édouard stands on the other side. The knot in my stomach tightens. He smiles, steps back. *"Bonjour, Mademoiselle."*

Mademoiselle. It is a cordial greeting. The brand he would bestow upon any of his colleagues or Maman, perhaps. An icy draft extinguishes a fire kindled at the thought of seeing him this morning. A fire I hadn't even realized burned until snuffed out. I stand cold and awkward, not quite sure what to do, inwardly cursing Degas for having put me up to this task. But this is not personal. I would be wise not to forget.

I step inside, dwarfed by the immensity of the place, although the studio looks the same as the last time. Neat. Almost too tidy, in fact. The capped jars of pigment lined up in a perfect row on the table in front of the window. The light shining through makes them look like great cylindrical jewels—ruby red, emerald green, sapphire blue. They seem untouched. No signs of dust or stray color. Everything is in its place. The bedcovers pulled taut as if never used.

The only sign that Édouard works here is the canvas on the easel. But I do not see any new work lining the walls. It has been nearly three months. If he is not working, he will not be happy.

I look at him standing a safe distance away, neither of us seem to know where to begin.

I am tempted to peek at the canvas. It's a different size than the painting of Victorine at the train station. I wonder if he has done more work of her. Where is that one? My gaze skims the room, but I do not locate it. Of course he would have given it to his dealers. Of course.

"Would you like to see?" He points at the canvas.

"Oui, s'il vous plaît."

He turns the easel around. It is me, or at least a woman who looks like me. I look dumfounded at the black-clad image with heartbroken eyes starting back at me.

"It is not right." Édouard's voice cracks. "And I cannot seem to fix it."

I cannot speak. I don't know how to respond to a remark that seems so full of innuendo. Or perhaps it isn't. Maybe from the start, I read too much into Édouard's intentions.

"I understand you came to talk to me about business, Mademoiselle." His voice penetrates my thoughts. "But could I trouble you for an hour of your time to work on the face? To . . . get it right?"

My stomach spirals, and I hate myself for it. Because I shall not put myself through it again. *I came with a purpose.*

"Of course, Édouard, as long as you dispense with the formalities. I would be most unhappy if I thought we were no longer friends after all we've shared."

He exhales a heavy breath that seems to relieve a great weight from his brow.

"Certainly, Berthe. While I paint, you can tell me what you have come to say."

"No, I think I shall wait until I have your undivided attention."

He nods. "You make me curious. I shall work in haste."

"No, take your time. It will keep."

His brows lift, and he smiles. "Quite curious, indeed."

He drags a high stool over for me to sit on, and I feel better because he seems more himself now. The atmospheric pressure in the room has diminished dramatically. I can breathe again.

So he paints, and we talk—about everything and nothing.

Talking and laughing and it is so obvious we belong together it is painful. It feels so good to have broken through the awkward standoff. I know that even if we cannot be together in the true sense of the word, I cannot be without him.

Nor he without me, whether he knows it or not.

He looks up. His gaze lingers. There is a moment of baited silence. I can tell he wants to say something.

"What, Édouard?"

He starts to speak, then stops. Shakes his head.

"What is it?"

"I have figured out a way for us to always be together." He closes his eyes and blows out an unsteady breath. "It is a compromise, but one that could be the best solution for all involved."

My heart beats against my ribcage like a trapped dove. "A compromise, Édouard?"

"If you were to marry Eugène—"

I gasp. "Are you joking?"

He holds up a hand. His throat works. "Please, let me finish."

"Do not make a joke of it."

"This is an unbearably painful sacrifice to ask of you. But it's the only way. If you married my brother, you would become a member of the family. We would be united forever by respectable bonds."

I sit for what seems an eternity in stunned silence. I cannot believe he would ask this of me. That he is willing to give me away to his brother as Édouard himself took on Suzanne, his father's mistress.

A vision clouds my thoughts—it is of Édouard that day in Mirande when he learned of my possible engagement to Puvis. He could not tolerate the thought of me with another, yet he would send me to his own brother's bed. My insides twist.

"Please, my love." He closes his eyes against the words. "Please, consider what I have asked of you.

It is our only option. Think about it—the very constraints that kept us apart will actually preserve us. If you marry Eugène, you will sign your name Madame E. Manet. We will see each other daily."

"And I will spend my nights in your brother's bed. Could you live with that Édouard? Could you be content knowing you had bequeathed possession of my body to Eugène?"

He doesn't answer me. Simply focuses on the area of the canvas he is painting and lets the subject drop. While I sit, trying to sort out what just happened.

What did just happen? His trying to pawn me off on Eugène? Could Édouard really, truly have me marry his *brother* merely for the right to keep me in his life? I shudder at the thought. Why not just let me go? Fade into the horizon like the last light of a sunset. He has watched his share of fading sunsets. The thought sends an uncomfortable rush of ire pumping through my veins.

"How is your friend Victorine?" I ask.

He glances up absently. "Victorine? I suppose she is fine. I haven't seen her in several months."

What constitutes several? Actually, I believe what I really want to ask is how long she was in his life before she departed. I want to know if he offered his Olympia the consolation option of being his brother's wife. But I say nothing. If I bring it up, he might misconstrue it to mean I cared.

I came today for professional purposes. I shall act as if nothing has happened because I must talk to him about a far more important matter.

"All right," he says, finally, his gaze on the canvas. "I think I have accomplished something." He gives me a stiff smile. Look at this and tell me what you think."

I stand, walk around the easel. It's the same black hat and dress. Only now the sad green eyes have been transformed into great sensuous brown pools. "Oh, Édouard. It's lovely."

"You are lovely."

His compliment makes me tingle, but I brace myself against it. "But my eyes—my eyes are green. You have painted them brown."

I notice he has also added a nice touch—he has painted in a small bouquet of blue violets into the bodice of my dress.

I look stronger. Somehow more sure of myself. He has transformed the despondent, green-eyed girl from the earlier version, into a confident—one might almost say *sultry*—brown-eyed woman. With violets.

What is art if not a revelation of what lives inside us?

"You like it?" he asks.

"*Oui,* very much."

We stand side by side, silently regarding the canvas. We are so close all one would need do is list slightly to touch the other. The moment is ripe to lose ourselves. To allow the beat of a heart to push us into each other's arms, into bed, headfirst into the vicious cycle of love and obsession will begin again only to end in the same way it always does.

I can't. I am no longer the despondent green-eyed girl. I step back to regard the painting from a safe distance.

Édouard shifts, too, away from me. "I have a gift for you."

"A gift?"

He opens a draw in the chest and removes a small canvas. With a sad smile he hands it to me.

It takes a moment for me to understand, but slowly, the charming and bittersweet pieces collide.

A hand flutters to my mouth. I need to sit down, but somehow, my legs hold me upright.

The painting is a still life. It contains just three simple objects, mementoes of the portraits he's painted of me: a bouquet of blue violets, the red fan, and a note inscribed to Mlle. Berthe from E. Manet.

For a moment I believe my heart will break into tiny pieces. Until his words ring in my mind . . . *If you marry Eugène you will be able to sign your name Madame E. Manet.*

That knocks the wind right out of me.

The name would not make me Édouard's wife any more than the marriage would bind my heart to Eugène. It would not be the same. How can he think that twisted web would ensnare happiness—for any of us? It is almost too much to bear.

"It is lovely, Édouard. *Merci.*"

The look on his face seems to implore, *Have you considered my suggestion? Marry Eugène.* I cannot, will not discuss it with him and decide to change the subject before he voices it.

I lay the painting on my coat and prepare to get down to business.

"Édouard, I wanted to see you today about an important matter. The painters who gathered at Degas' table that day—do you remember?"

He nods, motions to the divan, and sits down.

I choose a chair across from him.

"What are the scoundrels up to now? No good I presume."

"I wouldn't say that. In fact, they—*err*—we have been quite productive as of late. We have joined forces against the Salon."

Édouard frowns and pulls at his beard but does not comment.

"We are finished with the Academy and are planning an independent showing to coincide with next year's Salon. I have come today with an invitation. We would like it very much if you would join us."

He stares at me, blinks several times, as if he cannot comprehend what I am talking about.

I scoot forward on my chair.

"Édouard, don't you get tired of being bound by the Academy's strings? Dancing when they tug and left to dangle lifelessly when they leave you hanging? I have endured my last Salon rebuff."

"The Salon did not reject you last time. You showed a wonderful little piece."

"A wonderful little piece that all but went unnoticed. It garnered me nothing."

"You're being overly dramatic."

"No, Édouard, you are the one who cultivates the drama with your larger-than-life paintings. I have simply been Victorine's successor in fulfilling your needs."

He throws his head back but does not laugh, then slaps his lap with his palms. "Is that what this is all about, Victorine?"

"What?"

I have the strange jolting sensation that we are two trains traveling different tracks.

"I am talking about my career, for a change. Not my private relationship with you. Édouard, I cannot wait for you. I have decided to move on and carve out a life for myself, and that life revolves around my career. Pissarro, Renoir, Monet and Degas, and I will exhibit together. Right now we're calling ourselves the Independents. Will you please join us?"

"And make a public stand against the Salon?"

I nod. Vigorously.

"You must be out of your mind. You are making a grave mistake. Do you want to be branded subversive?"

Heat spreads to my cheeks. "You of all people are afraid of being different? Who am I talking to? I came to see Édouard Manet, the rebel, the revolutionary. Did I happen upon somebody's grandfather, instead?"

He challenges, "Why don't you stay with me?"

"Merci, non. I am quite disillusioned with the official system and would be quite happy to concede the privilege of conventionality to Eva Gonzalés or whomever you choose as your next protégée."

"Degas has put you up to this, *non?*"

"Degas has been instrumental in orchestrating this group, but no one has put me up to inviting a great talent to join us. Why are you behaving like this, Édouard?"

"After all we have meant to each other, how can you be so disloyal as to abandon me for a doddering old fool like Degas?"

I stand and glare down at him. His words are a swift blow, a carpet yanked out from under my feet. For a moment I feel as if I might fall. But I do not.

"You just can't seem to accept that this is not about love or sex or anything other than art. But while you are on that subject, there is nothing more that I would rather do than be with you, Édouard, but you are the one who has dictated our fate by staying with Suzanne."

"You knew from the start that I was not a free man. No, I cannot leave Suzanne and Léon. They need me. They would have nothing without me."

"I am a free woman. Free to do as I please. Free to make a life for myself as you have so securely made one for yourself. My life will include Degas and the Independents."

Standing there in the middle of his immaculate studio, I carefully lay aside the small canvas—I will not accept it—and pick up my coat. I have an epiphany—Édouard is so used to having everything his own way and on his own terms that there will never be hope for us.

I have always prided myself on being open-minded. Yet my own modernity has been severely tested since meeting Édouard. I have pushed myself to bounds I thought certain I was not prepared to tread. Yet, as I stretched, I touched the outer realms of possibilities and pushed my limits far beyond what I fathomed possible. Doing so, I have become the person I am today: a person far more forward-thinking than even the great Édouard Manet.

As I leave his studio, the two halves of myself—Propriety and Olympia—finally meld into one whole person. For the first time, they both agree I can no more back away from participating in this show than I can cease breathing.

Chapter Twenty-Five

I am in love with you. I have been thus since the first day I called on you.

—Alfred de Musset

"I HAVE received a nasty note from your friend Manet," says Degas to me at the next meeting of the Independents. "He says it is one thing for me to ruin myself. But says it's quite another when my self-destruction spills out and taints the careers of others. He seems to believe I am corrupting you. Am I corrupting you, Mademoiselle?"

I roll my eyes at him. "I can assure you, Monsieur, if you were and I objected, I would see to it that you ceased and desisted."

Degas' brows peak into little umbrellas over his eyes. Yet he manages to maintain an expression that borders somewhere between annoyance and boredom. "Yes, that's what I thought. Manet will likely live to regret his decision. There must be a realist's alternative to the Salon, and that's what he does not seem to understand."

Renoir, Degas, Pissarro, and Monet frown and nod.

"I definitely think him to be more vain than intelligent. So, what else do we have? Any new business?"

Monet signals the floor. "I'm talking to Nadar about the use of his space on Boulevard des Capucines for the show. It's on the second floor. Large. A nice space. I don't think we could do better. I know we have time, but try to stop by and see it when you get the chance."

"That's a good idea," I say. "Once we have secured the space, we will have a better idea how many artists we can recruit for the show."

"Which brings up a good point," says Pissarro. "What does a name like the Independents say about us? It says nothing. I suggest that we adopt something less radical and a bit more businesslike. Something more inclusive."

"Why do I have the feeling you have already come up with a suggestion?" says Degas.

"Now that you mention it, how about the *Societe Anonyme des Artistes*?"

"It's awfully long," says Monet.

"But it says exactly what we are," offers Renoir.

I nod.

"Think about it," says Pissarro. "We have time."

Dear Mademoiselle,

> I hope this note finds you well and working.
>
> As your friend, I feel it my duty to express my concerns about your potential alignment with the artist group calling themselves the Societe Anonyme des Artistes.
>
> You possess such talent. I beg you consider what involvement with such a radical group will do to your fine reputation and subsequently to your career. I know at times you experience frustration with the official system. We all do, Mademoiselle. Please believe me

when I say, it will be far worse for you should you trod the less traveled road.

You faithful servant,
Pierre Puvis de Chavannes

FEBRUARY 1874

My beloved Papa is dead.

I don't know how we shall ever be the same. What will become of our family now that he is gone?

Financially, he left us quite well off. It is more a dearth of spirit that concerns me. This loss has shaken the very foundation of our lives.

Tiburce is off chasing rainbows. Edma and Yves have families of their own. It is just Maman and me now. Sometimes I believe Papa was the glue that held us together. Now I fear we will come apart at the seams, scattering each in our own direction.

Maman has sold our beloved home on the rue Franklin. All my memories are here. My studio. My flowers and trees. I cannot fathom someone else living in our home, but she has already found an apartment—on the rue Guichard. There is no turning back.

Poor Papa had such a hard time of it. Three days before Christmas his declining health forced him to retire. Nearly one month to the day later, he was dead.

Now Maman leans on me for strength. Over the years, I have caused her more than her share of heartache. Now I shall stand strong for her, putting forth a countenance resilient enough for the both of us, keeping my woes to myself.

"Berthe, dear," she says from across the breakfast table. "I have learned the hard way I cannot tell you what to do. You are much too headstrong to listen to me. I respect that you have your own way of doing things. But my Bijou, I fear I am not capable of weathering this storm on my own."

I reach across the table and take her hand.

"Maman, please do not worry. I am here for you."

She squeezes my fingers, releases me, and wipes a tear from her eye.

"I must ask something of you. I know it will not be easy, nonetheless I must prevail upon you."

"Anything, Maman."

"The Manets are coming for a visit today."

This news gives me a jolt. Édouard and I have not spoken in months. My lack of communication with him has spilled over to the rest of the family. I am sure Suzanne is no worse for my absence. She got her way. In fact, I'm sure she is quite happy. However, Eugène and Madame Manet, they did nothing to deserve my silence.

"I beg you to mend your differences with the family. Make peace with them before we lose their friendship forever."

I think about the ups and downs Édouard and I have experienced over the past six years. It gives me pause to consider where we can go on from here. Where do you go when you've tested a relationship to its limits and blown a few holes in it while trying. Do all further attempts simply leak out through the wounds and abrasions never mended? Or is this our chance to heal?

Although a tiny voice inside warns me against hoping for too much.

"Of course, Maman. I should be happy to help you entertain them."

They arrive less than an hour later. Édouard, Suzanne, Eugène, and Madame Manet.

Édouard carries a small package. He hands it to me and says, "Please open this later."

He does not smile. His gaze does not linger about my face as it used to. He simply hands me the package, takes Suzanne's elbow, and helps her to the sofa. I notice now that she is limping and wonder what she has done to herself.

Maman gives the package a curious glance, but does not belabor the matter. I excuse myself and take it to my room.

I set it on the foot of the bed and turn to go, but my curiosity gets the better of me and I tear off the plain brown paper.

It is the small still life Édouard had presented to me that last day. The fan, the bouquet of blue violets, the note with that inscription. In the air directly above the letters I trace the words to Mlle. Berthe from E. Manet.

My heart fills with a hollow longing the likes of which I believe will never be quenched.

All this emotion brewing inside me like a storm rolling in over the sea. *Merci Dieu*, it does not slip past the iron barrier I have erected.

I rejoin our guests in the drawing room. As I enter, I see them all sitting there as they have so often during visits and our weekly soirées. I am overcome by a sense of loss that runs deeper than Papa's death. I have the feeling that long after Maman and I vacate the house, our laughter and tears will be imprinted on these walls.

I cannot imagine the memories of so many good times just fading away.

"Berthe, dear, the brothers Manet have expressed an interest in visiting your studio. Would you be so kind as to take them?"

Out of courtesy more than genuine interest in her joining us, I cast Suzanne a glance.

"Would you like to come?"

"Merci, non. I have twisted my ankle and the doctor has advised me to stay off of it as much as possible. But thank you for asking."

A vibration passes between Suzanne and me. It is hard to explain—she is not completely smug, not entirely warm. It is somewhere in the middle. I might call it a certain understanding.

I don my cloak and lead Eugène and Édouard to the snow-covered garden, with its leafless trees and frozen ground, toward my sad little studio that sits all alone.

The naked trees stand dark and barren, silhouetted against the gray sky. I have always wondered at winter's light. The sky looks a seamless quilt of clouds that hang so low it seems possible to reach up and touch them. I've been trying my entire life, yet they've always managed to remain just beyond my reach.

The men's footsteps crunch the frozen ground as they walk behind me, and I sink deeper into my cloak. Something in the air reminds me of my childhood, makes me wistful. This garden contains so many memories of our family, when we were whole. The sound of children laughing somewhere on the other side of the garden wall. The smell of hot brioche drifting from a nearby home. The steady puff of gray smoke escaping from the surrounding chimneys. Households so alive, and so unaware that time is a bandit that prowls in the night, stealing lives and beauty and purpose.

I open the studio door to admit the brothers Manet, and snowflakes begin to fall from the sky.

The men shake them off as they enter.

"Please excuse the mess." I rub my hands together to warm

them. "I have already started packing. Everything is in a bit of disarray."

"No need to worry, Mademoiselle," says Eugène.

I am surprised to hear him speak up like this. While Édouard, a bit sullen, hangs back, for once allowing his brother to take the lead.

"If you require assistance with the move," Eugène says, "I should be more than happy to lend my services."

"*Merci, Monsieur.* I might accept your generous offer closer to the date of the actual relocation."

"And when will that be?" Édouard asks. His back is to us as he looks out the window.

"A fortnight yet."

"And what will you do for a studio?" he asks, still gazing out onto the frost-covered lawn.

"There is an extra bedroom that will work nicely. Not as spacious as what I am used to." I sigh. "But as I said, it will do."

Édouard turns around as if I have uttered something that has grabbed his interest.

"How is your collection of work for the Anonymous Cooperative Society shaping up? I should very much like to see it."

He holds out his hands palms up in an arrogant gesture. A small bolt of ire zags through my veins. He is being proud. Calling me to task because I dared defy him.

"Monsieur, I have recently lost my father. I have not been in the position to produce much work as my mother has required all my devotion."

Édouard looks as if he has swallowed a frog. He bows his head. "Of course, how thoughtless of me. I beg your pardon, Mademoiselle."

"But will you show?" asks Eugène.

"At this point it is unlikely that I will have a large enough body of work."

"What a shame," says Eugène. "From what I hear, the organization sounds like a dynamic outfit."

Édouard's glance is a poison dart. Yet it seems to bounce off Eugène without effect. I am intrigued. Surely Eugène was aware of his brother's stance on the Societe. Yet he was bold enough to have an opinion to the contrary.

"I quite possibly might get involved with them myself," he says.

Édouard snorts. "What, pray tell, would you show?"

Eugène turns to face his brother square. "I would not *show* anything. You are well aware that I am not the artist of the family. What I can do is offer help on the business end. Promotion, tickets, hanging the show.

"I suppose there is always next time," Eugène says to me.

"Perhaps."

Hmmmm . . . perhaps.

Since I had all but decided not to show with the Societe, I submitted two of my finest pieces to the Salon.

Both were rejected.

This is the last straw.

Now I have no choice but to forge ahead with my original plan. Maman will be none too thrilled, but I shall break the news to her gently. She is resilient even in her fragile state of mind. She might surprise me as she was as disgusted with the Salon jury's rejection of my work as I was.

The tricky part will be prevailing upon Édouard to lend me the canvas of Edma at the Lorient Harbor. But it is time he and I settled our differences once and for all.

Chapter Twenty-Six

My queen, my slave, whose love is fear
When you awaken shuddering,
Until that awful hour be here,
You cannot say at midnight dear:
I am your equal.

—Baudelaire, *Les Fleurs du Mal*

Le Charivari—by Louis Leroy—April 25, 1874

Exhibition of the Impressionists

Oh, it was indeed a strenuous day, when I ventured into the first exhibition on the boulevard des Capucines in the company of M. Joseph Vincent, landscape painter, pupil of the academic master Bertin, recipient of medals and decorations under several governments! The rash man had come there without suspecting anything; he thought that he would see the kind of painting one sees everywhere, good and bad, rather bad than good, but not hostile to good artistic manners, to devotion to form, and respect for the masters. Oh, form! Oh, the masters! We don't want them anymore, my poor fellow! We've changed all that.

Upon entering the first room, Joseph Vincent received an initial shock in front of the Dancer by M. Renoir. "What a pity," he said to me, "that the painter, who has a certain understanding of color, doesn't draw better; his dancer's legs are as cottony as the gauze of her skirts."

"I find you hard on him," I replied. "On the contrary, the drawing is very tight."

Berlin's pupil, believing that I was being ironical, contented himself with shrugging his shoulders, not taking the trouble to answer. Then, very quietly, with my most naive air, I led him before the Ploughed Field *of M. Pissarro. At the sight of this astounding landscape, the good man thought that the lenses of his spectacles were dirty. He wiped them carefully and replaced them on his nose.*

"By Michalon!" he cried. "What on earth is that?"

"You see . . . a hoarfrost on deeply ploughed furrows."

"Those furrows? That frost? But they are palette-scrapings placed uniformly on a dirty canvas. It has neither head nor tail, top nor bottom, front nor back."

"Perhaps . . . but the impression is there."

"Well, it's a funny impression! Oh . . . and this?"

*"*An Orchard *by M. Sisley. I'd like to point out the small tree on the right; it's gay, but the impression . . ."*

"Leave me alone, now, with your impression . . . it's neither here nor there. But here we have a View of Melun *by M. Rouart, in which there's something to the water. The shadow in the foreground, for instance, is really peculiar."*

"It's the vibration of tone which astonishes you."

"Call it the sloppiness of tone and I'd understand you better—Oh, Corot, Corot, what crimes are committed in your name! It was you who brought into fashion this messy composition, these thin washes, these mud splashes against which the art lover has been rebelling for thirty years and which he has accepted only because constrained and forced to it by your tranquil stubbornness. Once again, a drop of water has worn away the stone!"

The poor man rambled on this way quite peacefully, and nothing led me to anticipate the unfortunate accident which was to be the result of his visit to this hair-raising exhibition. He even sustained, without major injury, viewing the Fishing Boats Leaving the Harbor *by M. Claude Monet, perhaps because I tore him away from dangerous contemplation of this work before the small, noxious figures in the foreground could produce their effect.*

Unfortunately, I was imprudent enough to leave him too long in front of the Boulevard des Capucines, *by the same painter.*

"Ah-ha!" he sneered in Mephistophelean manner. "Is that brilliant enough, now! There's impression, or I don't know what it means. Only, be so good as to tell me what those innumerable black tongue-lickings in the lower part of the picture represent?"

"Why, those are people walking along," I replied.

"Then do I look like that when I'm walking along the Boulevard des Capucines? Blood and thunder! So you're making fun of me at last?"

"I assure you, M. Vincent—"

"But those spots were obtained by the same method as that used to imitate marble: a bit here, a bit there, slapdash, any old way. It's unheard of, appalling! I'll get a stroke from it, for sure."

I attempted to calm him by showing him the St.-Denis Canal *by M. Lepine and the* Butte Montmartre *by M. Ottin, both quite delicate in tone; but fate was strongest of all: the* Cabbages *of M. Pissarro stopped him as he was passing by and from red he became scarlet.*

"Those are cabbages," I told him in a gently persuasive voice.

"Oh, the poor wretches, aren't they caricatured! I swear not to eat any more as long as I live!"

"Yet it's not their fault if the painter—"

"Be quiet, or I'll do something terrible."

Suddenly he gave a loud cry upon catching sight of the Maison du Pendu *by M. Paul Cézanne. The stupendous impasto of this little jewel accomplished the work begun by the* Boulevard des Capucines—*Pere Vincent became delirious.*

At first his madness was fairly mild. Taking the point of view of the impressionists, he let himself go along their lines:

"Boudin has some talent," he remarked to me before a beach scene by that artist; "but why does he fiddle so with his marines?"

"Oh, you consider his painting too finished?"

"Unquestionably. Now take Mlle. Morisot! That young lady is not interested in reproducing trifling details. When she has a hand to paint, she makes exactly as many brushstrokes lengthwise as there are fingers, and the business is done. Stupid people who are finicky about the drawing of a hand don't understand a thing about impressionism, and great Manet would chase them out of his republic."

"Then M. Renoir is following the proper path; there is nothing superfluous in his Harvesters. *I might almost say that his figures . . ."*

". . . are even too finished."

"Oh, M. Vincent! But do look at those three strips of color, which are supposed to represent a man in the midst of the wheat!"

"There are two too many; one would be enough."

I glanced at Bertin's pupil; his countenance was turning a deep red. A catastrophe seemed to me imminent, and it was reserved for M. Monet to contribute the last straw.

"Ah, there he is, there he is!" he cried, in front of number ninety-eight. "I recognize him, Papa Vincent's favorite! What does that canvas depict? Look at the catalogue."

"Impression: Sunrise."

"Impression—*I was certain of it. I was just telling myself that, since I was impressed, there had to be some impression in it . . . and what freedom, what ease of workmanship! Wallpaper in its embryonic state is more finished than that seascape."*

*In vain I sought to revive his expiring reason . . . but the horrible fascinated him. "*The Laundress, *so badly laundered, of M. Degas drove him to cries of admiration. Sisley himself appeared to him affected and precious. To indulge his insanity and out of fear of irritating him,*

I looked for what was tolerable among the impressionist pictures, and I acknowledged without too much difficulty that the bread, grapes, and chair of Breakfast, *by M. Monet, were good bits of painting. But he rejected these concessions.*

"No, no!" he cried. "Monet is weakening there. He is sacrificing to the false gods of Meissonier. Too finished, too finished! Talk to me of the Modern Olympia*! That's something well done.*

"Alas, go and look at it! A woman folded in two, from whom a Negro girl is removing the last veil in order to offer her in all her ugliness to the charmed gaze of a brown puppet. Do you remember the Olympia *of M. Manet? Well, that was a masterpiece of drawing, accuracy, finish, compared with the one by M. Cézanne."*

Finally the pitcher ran over. The classic skull of Pere Vincent, assailed from too many sides, went completely to pieces. He paused before the municipal guard who watches over all these treasures and, taking him to a portrait, began, for my benefit, a very emphatic criticism:

"Is he ugly enough?" He shrugged his shoulders. "From the front, he has two eyes . . . and a nose . . . and a mouth! Impressionists wouldn't have thus sacrificed to detail. With what the painter has expended in the way of useless things, Monet would have done twenty municipal guards!

"'Keep moving, will you!' said the portrait.

"You hear him—he even talks! The poor fool who daubed at him must have spent a lot of time at it!"

And in order to give the appropriate seriousness to his theory of esthetics, Pere Vincent began to dance the scalp dance in front of the bewildered guard, crying in a strangled voice: "Hi-ho! I am impression on the march, the avenging palette knife, the Boulevard des Capucines *of Monet, the* Maison du Pendu *and the* Modern Olympia *of Cézanne. Hi-ho! Hi-ho!"*

PARIS-JOURNAL—by ERNEST CHESNEAU—May 7, 1874

Le plein air, Exposition du Boulevard des Capucines

A young group of painters has opened an exhibition on the Boulevard des Capucines. If they had had the complete courage of their convictions or strong enough backs to run and bear the risks they might have managed to strike a considerable blow.

Their attempt, very deserving of sympathy, is in danger of being stillborn because it is not sufficiently emphatic. To have invited the participation of certain painters who are shuffling around the edges of the official Salon's latest batch of inanities, and even artists of unquestionable talent, but who are active in areas quite different from their own, such as MM. de Nittis, Boudin, Bracquemond, Brandon, Lepine, and Gustave Colin, was a major mistake in both logistics and tactics.

One must always reckon with the inertia of public judgment. The public has no initiative. Initiative has to be taken on its behalf. If it has to choose between two works presented to it simultaneously, one in conformity with accepted conventions, the other baffling all tradition, it is a foregone conclusion that the public will declare itself in favor of the conventional work at the expense of the work of innovation.

That is what is happening at the Boulevard des Capucines. The only really interesting part of the exhibition, the only part worthy of study, is also the only part whose curious implication eludes the great majority of visitors.

This rapprochement was premature, at the very least. It may work in a few years' time. So it is possible that it may offer a lesson and, in certain conditions, may provide the opportunity for a triumph for the "plein air school."

For this is what I would like to call this school—which has somewhat oddly been christened the group of the Intransigents—as that pursuit of reality in the plein air is its clearest objective.

The plein air school is represented at the second floor studio in the Boulevard des Capucines by MM. Monet, Pissarro, Sisley, Degas, Rouart, Renoir, and Mlle. Morisot.

Their leader, M. Manet, is absent. Did he fear the eccentricities of certain paintings? Did he disapprove of the compromise which allowed into so restricted an exhibition pictures conceived and painted in a spirit quite different from that of the school? I do not know. Was he right or wrong to hold back? I offer no answer. But there is no doubt at all that a selection of his paintings would have provided this exhibition with a more decisive, or at the very least more complete, statement of intent.

It is also possible that M. Manet, who has a fighting spirit, prefers to fight on common ground, that of the official Salon. Let us respect each man's ideal freedom to prefer one course of action to another.

It may be helpful to inform the visitor that none of the pictures exhibited here has been submitted to the scrutiny of the official jury. As the exhibition opened on 15 April, it is by no means an exhibition of Refuses. But those who have seen it do not need to be told that not one would have been accepted, had they indeed been subjected to that trial. Why? In my eyes, that is their merit, for they break openly with all the traditional conventions.

But let the Limited Company—since that is what it is, indeed it might even be described as a cooperative—take stock. Its current organization opens the door to all the inept painters, all the laggards of the official exhibitions upon application for a share. This is the kiss of death.

If the company does not alter its status, does not affirm a common principle, it will not survive as an artistic company. That it might survive as a commercial one does not interest me at all.

"Impressionist." Maman scoffs. "Is that how you want to be known?"

"Frankly, I can think of worse things to be called than an Impressionist."

"Is old maid among them?"

I sit perfectly still and weigh my words because I do not want to fight with my mother. I do not have the energy. The move, the exhibit. Nearly half the year is gone and so is my will to forge headlong into battle.

"What people think is very important to you, isn't it?"

She frowns at me as if I have just uttered a riddle or posed a trick question and is in no mood for games. But what I say is perfectly clear and true.

The showing of the Societe Anonyme des Artistes was a disappointment in many ways—not a single sale, mediocre attendance, mixed reviews tilting toward bad.

Maman is simply mortified and she's been spoiling for a fight since the first snide words appeared in print.

I can't even fight with her because I don't even know what I want anymore.

At least Maman has conviction.

What kind of existence is this—waiting to live, waiting to be happy, believing better days will befall tomorrow, when tomorrow never comes.

"I took the liberty of contacting your former teacher Monsieur Guichard and asked him to view the show and render his opinion of the horrors in which you were involving yourself."

She pulls a letter from her pocket and holds it up.

"I almost chose not to share it with you, but then thought better of it. My dear child, you are thirty-three years old. Well beyond marriageable age." Her voice cracks with the emotion I see swimming in her eyes. "My Bijou, I am not well—"

"Maman stop this nonsense, you are as fit as I am."

She waves the letter to silence me. I fall back against the cushions on the divan.

"I worry about you," she says. "I worry what will happen to you when I am no longer here. Who will care for you, what fate will befall?"

I bite the insides of my cheeks because I want to remind her that it is I who take care of her. That I am perfectly capable of existing on my own. As she is so fond of reminding me, I am thirty-three years old and have had quite a while to grow comfortable with my own company.

"It is with these reasons in mind that I have decided to share Monsieur Guichard's words. I hope you will take them to heart.

I sigh. I am so tired of this back and forth, push and pull. She's accepting when the reviews are favorable or the sales large, but the moment the sky clouds, she runs to escape the rain.

I realize as I sit there, that my own mother is more of a fair-weather source of support than even the critic Louis Leroy.

She unfolds the letter, and I brace myself for what I am sure is to be the evidence of my mortal failure.

> Madame, the kind welcome you gave me this morning touched me deeply. I felt younger by fifteen years, for this I was suddenly transported back to a time when I guided your girls in the arts, as teacher and as friend.
>
> I have seen the room at Nadar, and wish to tell you my frank opinion at once. When I entered, dear Madame, and saw your daughter's works in this pernicious milieu, my heart sank. I said to myself, "One does not associate with madmen except at some peril." Manet was right in trying to dissuade her from exhibiting.

Maman pauses to glance at me, to make sure the dart landed squarely where intended. Yet what baffles me is how Monsieur Guichard learned of Édouard's feelings toward my participation. I certainly did not tell Maman.

> To be sure, contemplating and consciously analyzing these paintings, one finds here and there some excellent things, but all of these people are more or less touched in the head. If Mademoiselle Berthe must do something violent, she should, rather than burn everything she has done so far, pour some petrol on the new tendencies. How could she exhibit a work of art as exquisitely delicate as hers side by side with *Le Rêve du Celibataire*? The two canvases actually touch each other!
>
> That a young girl should destroy letters reminding her of a painful disappointment, I can understand; such ashes are justifiable. But to negate all the efforts, all the aspirations, all the past dreams that have filled one's life is a madness. Worse, it is a sacrilege.
>
> As painter, friend, and physician, this is my prescription: she is to go to the Louvre twice a week, stand before Correggio for three hours, and ask for forgiveness for having attempted on oil what can only be said in watercolor. To be the first watercolorist of one's time is a pretty enviable position.

Maman glances up at me to see if I am still listening. I am not so happy at his deeming the members of the Societe—the Impressionists madmen. It does not sit well with me. But the moniker Impressionism is starting to grow on me. The more I consider it the more I like it. His letter surprises me in that it is not proving to be as harsh as I might have feared. It is actually quite complementary.

"Berthe, are you listening to me?"

"Yes I am, Maman."

"Good, this is the most important part."

> I hope, Madame, that you will be kind enough to answer this devoted communication, which comes straight from the heart. For I am greatly interested in this promising artist; she must absolutely break with this new school, this so-called school of the future.
>
> Please forgive my sincerity,
> Joseph-Benoît Guichard

Maman slaps her leg with the letter. "There, you see? If you will not listen to me, will you not heed the warning of your teacher? He sees it as a monstrous association."

I scratch my head and a piece of hair breaks free.

I appreciate Monsieur Guichard's flattering encouragement toward my talent, but I wonder how it is he can be so blind to the fabulous talent of the likes of Monet, Renoir, and Degas. If they are madmen, then brand me as demented as they, for I shall reside in good company.

"Berthe, will you give up this nonsense and settle down? I insist you get your life together."

It is suddenly clear to me that the beauty in his letter completely escapes Maman. "All you can read in his words is that he wants me to give it up?"

"You might as well if you insist on carrying on in such an unbecoming manner. You are too old for such antics."

I am stunned silent. Absolutely aghast at her narrowness. She would rather see me the idle spinster sitting at her side with needlework in hand rather than making a happy independent life for myself.

"Are you suggesting I should quit painting as to stop drawing attention to myself and the fact that I have chosen not to marry?"

Maman grunts. It's a sound that might as well be an affirmative, but she considers my question for a moment before making the verbal commitment. Then, as if sent by the heavens, Amélie enters the room.

"*Pardon, Madame et Mademoiselle.* Monsieur Eugène Manet calls. May I show him in?"

"Oui, merci." Maman seems relieved. Yet I know her answer. She already confirmed as much. "Bring us some tea, *s'il vous plaît.*

I am not at all disappointed to see Eugène. He has become a good friend in the six months since Papa died. Eugène was gentle in offering his condolences and quite indispensable assisting with the administration of the show. All this despite his brother's vocal stance against Societe.

My newfound friendship with Eugène has been quite refreshing. He has even painted alongside me on several occasions. While he does not possess the talent of his brother, or the sparkling personality, it is nice to not feel the burn of competition that simmered beneath the surface of my and Édouard's relationship.

What did I expect? With Édouard, I built the beast that nearly consumed me.

I tuck the piece of stray hair into my chignon just before Eugène enters the room.

"Bonjour, Madame et Mademoiselle." He bows to Maman and me, then takes a seat on the divan next to me as Maman suggests.

Maman makes the appropriate small talk before she excuses herself, leaving Eugène and me alone.

A beat of awkward silence hangs between us as we stare at each other at a loss for words.

I smile. He smiles back, and flushes, and looks away.

"Your brother received nearly as much press from our exhibit as the Societe members. It seems we shall forever be tied to him."

Eugène frowns and blinks.

"Yet he is dismayed at the lack of attention his paintings received in the Salon."

"At least he was accepted by the jury. I guess it is human nature to always want more despite one's accomplishments."

A rueful expression washes over Eugène. He's a handsome man. He doesn't wear it as comfortably as Édouard dons that self-possessed, determined suit of armor.

Eugène is a good man. There is sincerity in the set of his jaw, the gentle notes of his quiet voice, and honesty in his gray eyes. I have never noticed the color of his eyes until now. He holds my gaze for a moment, laces his fingers in his lap, and glances down at his large hands. I get the feeling he has something on his mind.

Amélie carries in the tea tray and sets it down on the table in front of the divan. Eugène shifts his knees out of the way and it dawns on me how much smaller this room is than the drawing room in the house in the Rue Franklin.

"May I get you anything else?" she asks.

"No, *merci,* this is lovely."

I lift the pot and pour two cups of tea.

Eugène has settled back against the cushions with his cup in his hands before he speaks.

"Mademoiselle, my family has secured a house in Fécamp next month, and we would be delighted if you and your mother would accompany us."

I want to ask him if Édouard will be in attendance, but I do not. The earnest note in his voice and the manner in which he presents the invitation won't permit me.

"Thank you for thinking of us. I shall talk to Maman."

Society has cast woman in a rather unfortunate role. We are daughter, wife, mother—beyond those perimeters our very person is diminished. We are born to find love. Yet finding love is possibly the most difficult challenge a woman faces.

Until now it has been much easier to funnel all my devotion into my career. It is the safe existence as Eros has not smiled kindly upon me.

I could blame the poets for creating an impossible standard—we are all Juliet, the devastated lover who would rather plunge a knife into her heart than live a moment without the love of a man.

I could blame Maman for bending me to the breaking point. Perhaps I should blame Édouard for making me love him; for loving me so intensely and letting me go. Even after all we've been through, in my heart I know the true depth of our feelings. Maybe that is all that matters. If it ever mattered. Perhaps it is time to let go.

On the Fécamp shoreline, I set a paper boat out to sea. Into that tiny vessel I have released all the blame I held inside. The tide pulls it out, pushes it back, finally to consume it in a frothy bite of azure wave.

The tidal dance is much like Édouard's on-again-off-again summer plans. In the end, he opted to travel to Argenteuil rather than joining his family and mine in Fécamp.

I accept Eugène's arm and his vow to make me the most cherished woman in the world. He is a good man, a strong man.

As we begin our journey down the beach, I glance back. Light glints off the floating remnant of the little paper boat. The pressure of its journey under the sea has flattened it back into its original shape and the tide swells and swallows it once and for all.

Chapter Twenty-Seven

The night has a thousand eyes,
And the day but one;
Yet the light of the bright world dies
With the dying sun.
The mind has a thousand eyes,
And the heart but one;
Yet the light of a whole life dies
When love is done.
—Francis William Bourdillon

JANUARY 1875

My dear Tiburce:

Eugène tells me this is the day the mail goes off and for fear of missing another opportunity of writing to you, I am scribbling a few words in haste. The thought of you has obsessed me for several weeks, *mon pauvre ami;* where are you? What are you doing? I should give a great deal to know these things and even more to be able to contribute in some small way to your happiness.

As for myself, I have been married a whole month now; it is strange, isn't it? I went through that great ceremony without the least pomp, in an ordinary dress and hat, like the old woman that I am, and without guests.

Since then, I have been waiting for events to take shape, but so far fate is not in our favor. The trip to Constantinople, so definite, so certain at first, is no longer certain at all. However, I shall not complain. For I have found a very nice garçon, whom I think genuinely loves me.

I have entered into the positive side of life after living for so long with foolish chimeras that did not make me very happy, and yet, thinking of my mother, I wonder if I really fulfilled my duty. These are all complicated questions, and it is not very easy, at least not for me, to distinguish clearly right from wrong.

Your loving sister,
Madame E. Manet

even more to be able to contribute in some small way to your happiness.

As for myself, I have been married a whole month now. It is strange, isn't it? I went through that great ceremony without the least pomp, in an ordinary dress and hat, like the old woman that I am, and without guests.

Since then, I have been waiting for events to take shape, but so far fate is not in our favor. The trip to Constantinople, so definite, so certain at first, is no longer certain at all. However, I shall not complain. For I have found a very nice garçon, whom I think genuinely loves me.

I have entered into the positive side of life after living for so long with foolish chimeras that did not make me very happy, and yet, thinking of my mother, I wonder if I really fulfilled my duty. These are all complicated questions, and it is not very easy, at least not for me, to distinguish clearly right from wrong.

Your loving sister,
Madame E. Mauer

FROM

ELIZABETH ROBARDS

AND

AVON A

When my husband and I set off for Paris in May 1999, little did I know the trip would change my life. I'd lived in France and longed to return to Paris. It was my husband's first trip to this magnificent country. Our main focus (besides food) was art. From the Louvre to the Musée d'Orsay to the Musée National de l'Orangerie, we immersed ourselves in the works of the great masters.

I was particularly interested in the French Impressionists. I'd always loved their work and was anticipating a day trip to Giverny, Claude Monet's home and famous gardens. Before we boarded a train at the Gare Saint-Lazare, to make our way to Giverny, we stopped at Paris's Musée Marmottan to gaze upon Monet's infamous Impression, *Sunrise* (Impression: *Soleil Levant*), the image that launched the French Impressionist movement.

On the second floor of the Musée Marmottan, I met Berthe Morisot for the first time. Not literally, of course, but her essence permeated her luminous paintings on display. Even though I'd been a fan of the Impressionists, I wasn't familiar with her work. I was immediately captivated by her style and drawn to a photograph of Berthe and her family. Something about the photo haunted me and urged me to research her life. In doing so, I discovered the tale of a deeply complex, richly talented woman who bucked nineteenth-century convention to become one of the world's greatest artists. It also became exceedingly clear she was likely very much in love with the great painter Édouard Manet, the brother of the man who would become her husband.

Very little is documented about the depth of Édouard and

Berthe's affinity for each other. Biographers recognize their intense friendship and acknowledge hints of romantic fancy in her correspondence. Also telling are reports of Berthe's extreme jealousy of Manet's wife, Suzanne, and his pupil, Eva Gonzalés. Most revealing, though, are the portraits Édouard painted of Berthe between 1872 and 1874. In the span of his career, Manet did not paint anyone as often, or as passionately, as he portrayed her.

It's well documented that the Manet brothers doted on Berthe. Some biographers have implied a bit of sibling rivalry ensued over her attention. Alas, Édouard was a married man. Eugène was not. For all intents and purposes, Eugène won when Berthe became his bride on December 22, 1874.

Upon the announcement of her engagement to his brother, Édouard painted Berthe one last time. The portrait prominently showed off her engagement/wedding ring. Once she married Eugène, Édouard never painted her again. According to documentation, Berthe took her marriage vows seriously, and settled into a close platonic relationship with Édouard, but it's unclear to whom Berthe's heart really belonged.

While I have attempted to portray the documented facts of Berthe Morisot and Édouard Manet's lives as accurately as possible, this book, *With Violets*, is most definitely a work of fiction. I have drawn on her correspondence—several letters are reproduced within the pages of this book. Although, some of the "letters" in the book are strictly fictional. I have attempted to "paint in" the missing pieces of Berthe and Édouard's relationship, exploring what might have happened between them during the years prior to Berthe's marriage to Eugène. It is with great awe and respect for Berthe and Édouard and their nonconforming, artistic spirits that I have asked the question "what if" and sketched a love story of what might have been. . . .

Elizabeth Robards

Courtesy of Phyllis Redman

Award-winning author **ELIZABETH ROBARDS** formerly lived in France and has studied art and writing. She earned a degree in journalism only to realize reporting "just the facts" bored her silly. Much more content to report to her muse, Elizabeth has found Nirvana doing what she loves most–writing contemporary and historical women's fiction full time. She loves to travel—and when she can't, her imagination transports her all over the world. For more information about her work, please visit her website at http://www.ElizabethRobards.com.